MURDER
at the
Castle

BOOKS BY LISA CUTTS

A BELINDA PENSHURST MYSTERY

Murder in the Village

MURDER
at the
Castle

LISA CUTTS

bookouture

Published by Bookouture in 2021

An imprint of Storyfire Ltd.
Carmelite House
50 Victoria Embankment
London EC4Y 0DZ

www.bookouture.com

Paperback ISBN: 978-1-80314-014-8
eBook ISBN: 978-1-80314-013-1

For my dear friend Liz Hubbard.
Here's to books, wine and friendship.

PROLOGUE

Under the cover of night, the dark figure approached the barn, their black clothing in keeping with the entire covert operation. After all, no one drew attention when planning a murder, not unless they wanted to get caught.

A gloved hand felt around the loosened wooden panel on the far side of the barn, away from any prying eyes. It still paid to leave nothing to chance by choosing the side partially obscured by some overgrown shrubs – useful for a culprit to hide in.

With one steady movement, the panel was pushed aside, leaving a gap big enough for a slim frame to fit through.

After some manoeuvring through the hole, the prize was in sight.

It only took the briefest of moments to unzip the shoulder bag, take out the bottle of wine and swap it for the one at the head of the tasting table.

As soon as the task was completed, it was as if nothing had ever been disturbed.

The planning had been time-consuming. The execution was a completely different matter.

ONE

Belinda Penshurst woke to the sounds of birds singing and sunlight streaming through the window.

One of her all-time pleasures was to open her eyes in the morning and look out across the gardens to the beautiful scenery beyond the castle grounds. The green rolling hills of her home county was a sight she loved more than anything. The patchwork quilt of the fields dotted with sheep, broken only by the glint of the river in the distance.

With a smile, Belinda stretched her arms out and stifled a yawn.

After a while, she propped herself on her elbows for a better view of the lush countryside, the panorama before her lifting her spirits. Then thoughts of the downs were pushed aside and replaced with images of her friend Harry Powell, and what he might be up to that morning.

They were only friends, although even in the short time they had known one another, she had come to rely on him for help and advice. It was too early to tell whether they would ever be more than friends. His heart was still bruised from a previous relationship and her own a little fragile. Different sets of circumstances, same feelings of hurt.

One thing at a time.

Today was a day Belinda had been looking forward to for some weeks. She had planted the idea in Harry's mind that a wine tasting society was desperately needed in their mostly peaceful village. The recent murderous tendencies of some of the inhabitants had briefly marred Little Challham's reputation, but it had bounced back. To begin with, Harry hadn't realised that he was the perfect person to assist Belinda with her latest venture. But it hadn't taken her very long at all to persuade him to help her.

She threw back the duvet, got out of bed and picked her dressing gown up from the chair beside the window. As she put on the silk gown and tied the belt around her waist, she thought how lucky she was to live where she did, in such a close-knit and thriving community.

So many people had taken up her offer of a free wine tasting, not that that surprised her. Belinda was well aware that she was giving away alcohol, and in a small village that supported two pubs and a microbrewery, it was little wonder that the take-up had been so good.

It felt nice to give something back to them. After all, she owned the tea room, one of the pubs, and the delicatessen. Belinda was thinking of the wine tasting as a customer appreciation day, and, of course, an opportunity to sell some of the nearby vineyard's wine.

It was all about the local people, and that was where Harry came in. He was a neighbour, a fairly recent newcomer to the village, and he would steer her in the right direction. If she were being completely honest, Harry could perhaps bridge any awkward gaps between her enthusiasm and any ignorance about wine she might encounter.

The last thing Belinda wanted to do was come across as preaching. Harry would probably hit the spot.

Suddenly aware that she was wrapping her arms around herself at the thought of Harry, she smoothed down her dressing gown, ran her fingers through her shoulder-length black hair, and wondered exactly what time he would arrive.

Belinda walked to her wardrobe and ran an eye over her outfits, keen to choose the right clothes for the day ahead. But never one to spend an inordinate amount of time getting herself ready, especially when it came to business, Belinda was showered and dressed in a knee-length red linen dress within half an hour.

She made sure she ate a decent breakfast washed down with a strong coffee, gave her Labrador Horatio a walk around the grounds while they were still empty, and ran through a few final checks with the staff who were busy getting ready for the event.

Some hours later, satisfied everything was in order, Belinda settled at the kitchen table with a freshly brewed cup of coffee in front of her. The gardeners' kitchen where she sat was to the side of the castle. The open door looked out on the gardens, a sight she never took for granted. Her view to the south was framed by a brick archway, leading her eye along the stone steps flanked on either side by lavender, alive with the hum of bees. In the distance, past the hedge that separated the terraces, lay a bank of trees, the last interruption before forest and perfect blue sky.

She could feel the warmth of the day and, closing her eyes, took a moment to savour it. Letting out a sigh, a smile spread across her pink glossed lips. She opened her eyes and there, standing in the doorway blocking out the light, was Harry Powell.

At a little over six foot, his generous frame all but filled the gap. With the sun behind him, she couldn't see his face, but saw him put his hand up to scratch at his stubble.

'Hello, Belinda,' he said, stepping inside the kitchen. 'Lovely day for it.'

'Hello to you, Harry,' she said. 'Fancy a coffee?'

They were wasted words as Harry had already walked over to the percolator. Belinda knew from the clink of china that Harry had helped himself to a mug and was in the process of pouring himself a drink.

It made her smile that Harry was comfortable enough to know he didn't need to stand on ceremony in her home. They had spent a fair bit of time together over the past few weeks, her being buoyed up by the thought of a wine tasting society in Little Challham and him pausing every step of the way to question her ideas and processes. It had given her time to get to know him better, understand what made him tick.

Still gazing out towards the gardens, Belinda heard Harry pull out a chair and sit beside her.

'Are you ready for this afternoon?' he said.

'Oh, I think so, yes,' she said, turning her head in his direction, momentarily blinded by the dimness of the kitchen in contrast to outside. 'But you don't look as if you've slept all that well,' she added, leaning closer to get a better look.

'In all honesty,' said Harry, 'I really didn't.'

'Something I can help with?' Belinda's voice was thick with concern.

'No, it's only a couple of things on my mind,' he said. 'I'll work them out.' He held his mug up towards her. 'Cheers. We'd better get on with the final preparations. I don't know a great deal about local wine celebrity Sadie Oppenshaw, but apparently, she doesn't like to be kept waiting.'

'I've dealt mostly with her PA, Peggy Abnett. Sadie herself was recommended through the owner of Challham Valley winery and vineyard,' said Belinda. 'I know she's somewhat overwhelming, yet she's a highly regarded expert, and both a food and wine critic. Rumour has it, Sadie can make or break a business. Just her agreeing to today's tasting is a phenomenal boost for the vineyard, and Little Challham itself. This is a big deal. I'm proud it's happening in my home.'

'You've talked me through the set-up: Sadie's going to start with the VIP tasting for the two of us and the lucky five special guests before the free for all starts.'

'It's hardly a free for all.' Her voice skirted laughter at Harry's words. 'The rest of the village will enjoy a tasting in the barn once we've had our small gathering, all overseen by Sadie. She knows her stuff, but can be quite – what's the word? – *passionate* about it. In the meantime, there'll be a barbecue for everyone to enjoy, and finally, hopefully, they'll be in the mood to place some serious orders with the vineyard.'

Harry indicated towards the grounds and said, 'All of the work you've put into the event, we don't want to leave things to chance.'

'Now, don't be modest, Harry,' she said. 'You've put some hours in too. It's only fair that you take half of the credit for everything, both good and bad.'

'It's wine tasting,' said Harry with a chuckle. 'What could possibly go wrong?'

TWO

The immaculate castle grounds looked welcoming: the lime trees that flanked the long driveway were festooned with lemon bows and matching ribbons. The team of gardeners had worked with pride in all that they did, from the beautiful rose gardens to the arboretum, the informal gardens to the pristine lawns.

The grounds stretched further than the eye could see. Since opening the castle and its grounds for guided tours, Belinda had managed to bring in much needed revenue. Tours were booked almost continually throughout May to September in the gardens and for most of the year inside the building itself.

The wine tasting, however, was a new venture for her.

Belinda was feeling a little more anxious than she was letting on. She hated to admit it, but she felt out of her league beside Sadie's experience. Harry stood next to her at the top tasting table, the heels on her shoes putting them almost shoulder to shoulder. Although the temperature in the barn was comfortable, she was still pleased she had chosen a lightweight dress that would allow her to keep as cool as possible.

'What time did you say Sadie was getting here?' said Harry, scanning the barn.

'Any minute now,' Belinda muttered, hiding her jangling

nerves at the idea of the formidable wine buff. She ran an eye over the space in front of them. They were at the far end of the large barn, surveying the flurry of caterers and waiting staff all busy making everything perfect.

'Madam,' said Cliff, one of the staff, as he paused in his task of laying out glasses on a side table. He stepped towards them. 'Could I respectfully ask you and Mr Powell not to disturb the air around the tasting table too much?'

Harry's laugh caught in his throat when Belinda nudged him in the ribs.

'Sorry, Cliff,' she said, 'we were waiting for Sadie. Moving and breathing wasn't something we'd factored in as being an issue.'

'Of course,' said Cliff, with a slight bow. 'It is a mistake that some make, although not twice around Ms Oppenshaw. She has been known to storm out of a tasting for a lesser insult to her senses.'

Cliff peered at Belinda, then turned his attention to the bottles of wine set out on the tasting table behind her. He said, his voice gluey with concern, 'This is something of a way of life for her. In fact, it probably means more to her than life itself.'

He gave the smile of a fraudster and returned to the very serious task of positioning the glasses beside the tasting notes.

Harry leaned over to Belinda and whispered out of the corner of his mouth, 'Not sure what you've got me into here. Some sort of wine cult. And what's wrong with him?'

He nodded towards Cliff, who was bending down and squinting at the line of glasses on the table to ensure they were in a perfect line.

'They look spot on to me,' said Harry, waving a hand at the trestle table sat at ninety degrees to the head tasting table. Another trestle table directly opposite mirrored it: crisp white tablecloth, name cards and all.

Cliff raised an eyebrow in Harry's direction and mumbled something which sounded to Belinda's ears like 'amateur'.

She smothered a laugh and said, 'I expect that Sadie will be here soon if you're laying things out for the public?'

The word 'public' seemed to cause Cliff's back to straighten like a ramrod, and perhaps there was even the start of a tic on his face as he turned and said, 'I think she's just arrived.'

Both Belinda and Harry looked towards the barn entrance, open wide to let the fresh air and sunshine in.

It also allowed Sadie Oppenshaw in, not that she looked particularly pleased about it.

'You said she was a tad whingy?' said Harry in a low voice.

'Shush,' whispered Belinda. 'She'll hear you. Heightened hearing, apparently, as well as sense of smell and taste.'

A slim woman – early forties, five foot five, ice-blond hair tied back in a ponytail – strode towards them. Her black court shoes clipped across the wooden floor, her navy skirt suit sharp and business-like to match her bearing.

'Hello again, Belinda,' said Sadie, embracing Belinda briefly before turning her attention to Harry.

'You must be the Harry Powell I've heard virtually nothing about,' said Sadie, fixing him with a stare before shaking his hand.

'That's me,' he said. 'I could say the same about you.'

Belinda thought about elbowing him in the ribs a second time but saw little point, especially as Sadie seemed to have turned her attention elsewhere.

With a rapid step closer to Cliff, which seemed to make him bristle, Sadie ran a well-practised eye over the top table.

'Mm,' she said, head on one side.

Harry copied her move but after a few seconds, put his hand up to support his neck before abandoning the pose altogether.

Sadie, on the other hand, was not to be so easily moved. After what seemed like an age, she sighed and said, 'It's flawless.'

In Belinda's peripheral vision, she saw Cliff pull a handkerchief from his pocket and wipe his brow before he hurried over to another table to perfect yet more immaculate settings.

Harry started to laugh at Cliff's reaction which he swiftly, and somewhat badly, attempted to turn into clearing his throat. The result was that he started to cough and had to lean forwards, hands on his thighs, to regain his composure.

'I think your friend's having a little trouble,' said Sadie, disdain owning her face.

'He's allergic to the, um, pollen,' said Belinda.

'I don't have hay fever,' said Harry, face now a softer shade of red, breathing back to normal.

'Allergies are the worst, aren't they?' said Sadie, as she opened the clasp on her black shoulder bag and took out a tissue with a flourish.

Harry put out a hand to take it, only to watch her dab at the corner of her eyes and put it back in her bag.

Out of the corner of her vision, Belinda caught sight of a barrel of a man entering the barn. She didn't have to turn her head far to see the gargantuan figure of Richard Duke, local busybody and human food hoover, as he made his way across the creaking boards towards them.

Sadie looked slightly startled at the sight of him looming towards her and stepped back a few paces towards the cheese and bread section of the farthest trestle table.

As Richard got within a couple of feet, Harry leaned across to Belinda and said, 'Sadie's so tiny, if she doesn't get out of the way of Richard's cheese stampede, he'll suck her up like krill.'

'Harry,' said Belinda, 'not now.'

'It's like watching a hippo running at a river of dairy goods,' said Harry. 'All that's standing in his way is Bambi.'

Belinda stepped towards them as Richard tried his best to tower over Sadie. Despite his height advantage, it didn't seem to be working.

'Why are you here already?' said Sadie, look of concern on her unlined face. Her eyebrows were arched, and the corners of her mouth downturned. Her body language could hardly be intended to take the edge off her expression.

It was a clear signal Richard failed to pick up on.

'Look here,' he said, 'as the regional product developer for Challham Frozen Foods, I was promised early access to the merchandise.'

He jabbed a podgy digit at the food and drink.

'Don't you think there'll be enough to go round?' said Sadie, arms folded and a vein to the side of her forehead looking like it was about to pop. 'We are trying to entice the local people to experience wine at its best and sample all that Little Challham's vineyard has to offer, not partake in a bun-fight.'

Belinda's attention was pulled towards the barn doors where a horde of thirsty people was jostling to get to the front of the queue.

'I had better go and speak to our customers,' she said to Harry. 'Can I leave you to deal with the fallout between Sadie and Richard?'

Harry gave her a look and said, 'Customers? More like freeloaders. But I'd probably rather take my chances with a crowd of fifty revellers than the bloated mongoose and the cobra.'

Belinda held up a hand, feeling the heat get to her. 'H, could I please leave this with you? I have to get outside and speak to the guests.'

Perhaps it was the tone of her voice, perhaps it was because Harry had got to know Belinda a little better over the past few months – whatever it was, he gave her a wonky smile and rushed towards the odd couple before more sparring started.

Relieved that there was one less issue for her to resolve, Belinda took a deep breath and stepped towards the staff trying their best to keep the baying crowd at arm's length.

'Ladies and gentlemen,' she said, allowing a hush to filter through the gaggle of people. 'Thank you all so much for coming along to Challham Valley's inaugural wine tasting event.'

Ever the show-woman, Belinda beamed her lipglossed smile at everyone as she stood at the barn's entrance. She felt a sudden swell of pride that the castle was her home, and one that welcomed guests from both near and much farther afield to enjoy all it had to offer. It was a brief and comforting distraction from the less than orderly gathering currently in front of her.

'If those of you with tickets numbered one to five would kindly make your way to the front,' she said, voice loud and clear. 'Those with numbers six to thirty will take part in the second tasting.'

Several people elbowed and edged their way forward, those at the front without the coveted first five tickets reluctantly moving aside.

'I've got number one,' said a voice as a hairy fist thrust a ticket in Belinda's face.

'Thank you for that, George,' said Belinda to the local village butcher, slowly easing his hand down with her own. 'Someone else minding the shop today?'

George shrugged. 'Pretty much sold out this morning and most of Little Challham seems to be here anyway.'

'Yes,' said Belinda, allowing herself to look pleased. 'I'm extremely happy with the turn-out.'

'It's free booze, love,' said George with a laugh. 'What did you expect?'

'Thank you for the feedback,' said Belinda, snatching the ticket from his fingers, surprised that a butcher would have such hirsute hands. Surely it was a hygiene obstacle?

'Go on in, George,' she said, forcing a smile. 'Cliff will show you where to go.'

'Hello, Belinda,' said Delia Hawking, one of the trustees of the local Women's Institute. At eighty, she ran the WI smoothly and with a level of vigour Belinda hoped she'd have at that age.

'Delia,' said Belinda. 'It's so good to see you. I couldn't have run this event without your help.'

They exchanged a brief hug and Belinda stepped aside to let her find her place.

Next to wave his ticket at Belinda was Steve Parry.

'Oh, hi, Steve,' said Belinda, with a glance over his shoulder. 'I thought that Kulvinder's name was pulled out as number three.'

'It was,' said Steve, as he handed her his ticket, 'but she's not feeling too good, so she told me to take it.'

'I hope she gets better soon,' said Belinda. 'I haven't seen much of her the last couple of weeks, and I wanted to catch up this afternoon.'

'Pop round and see her any time,' said Steve. 'She's working from home at the minute, so you'll find her in.'

It didn't take much to work out that Steve was trying his hardest to move round Belinda so he could get to the wine. Steve and Kulvinder hadn't been back from their honeymoon all that long, and now it appeared he was extremely keen to get a few hours by himself. Belinda had hoped their honeymoon period would have lasted a little longer. Still, Kulvinder's name had been pulled from the lucky dip, all fair and square. If she wanted to give the ticket to her husband, so be it.

With a smile, Belinda made small talk with those at the front of the throng and waited for Angie Manning, her tea room manager, to elbow her way through.

As she was watching Angie's mousy blond head bob along, Belinda was distracted by the heated debate taking place between Sadie and Richard, badly refereed by Harry. Belinda had underplayed Sadie's tendency to get under people's skin when giving Harry the low-down, and now wondered if she should have been a little more upfront. On the other side of the room, Steve Parry was giving Sadie a look that made Belinda think of pure, cold hatred.

'Sorry, sorry,' wheezed Angie as she reached the front, drawing Belinda's attention back. 'I didn't have time to change from work.' Her hair was making a bid for freedom from the clip she had used to secure it, and her tight white T-shirt and tiny black skirt were speckled with what appeared to be coffee stains.

'You're here, that's the important thing. Go on through.' Belinda gave her a cautious hug, keen not to cover her own outfit in spilled beverages. Once she had seen Angie inside, the ever-attentive Cliff appeared to seat the tea room manager on one of the two trestle tables flanking the head table.

Harry, who appeared to have all but given up on brokering peace between Sadie and Richard, looked at her pleadingly.

She stepped across the barn to help him out, amused, but was overtaken by Cliff, who was clearly determined not to skip any of his duties, even if his only motivation for ending Sadie and Richard's row was to ensure the right ambience for wine quaffing.

'I've already asked the gentleman to sit down,' said Cliff with an ill-disguised tinge of annoyance to his voice.

'I'll sit down when I've finished,' said Richard.

'I'm not going to have this discussion with you,' said Sadie, raising her voice. 'Not here, not in front of all these people. If you're not prepared to let this drop, I can walk out of the door right now. The alternative being that I ignore you and we sample the wine and enjoy the experience.'

'Exactly,' said Belinda. 'Let's enjoy the experience.'

She deftly stepped in between Sadie and Richard, put her arm around the other woman's shoulder and said, 'Now, please tell me more about the 2019 Sauvignon Blanc we spoke about on the phone.'

Belinda glanced over at Harry as she led Sadie away. Harry picked up on the hint and placed a hand on Richard's upper arm to cajole him towards his seat.

That was catastrophe number one out of the way, thought Belinda as she took her own seat at the top table.

The rest would surely be plain sailing.

THREE

Before long, Sadie Oppenshaw was on her feet addressing the five lucky winners enjoying their first taste of Challham Valley wine. The three tables had been arranged so that Sadie, Harry and Belinda sat at the head of the room with the two other tables facing one another. There were place settings the entire length of each table for those who would come later. Their experience was to be a briefer one, less guest speaking and more straightforward drinking. For now, Richard and Delia each took a place on one side, and Steve, Angie and George occupied seats on the other.

Harry sat as still as he could manage, trying to maintain an air of interest in what the shrill woman was saying. Her voice was beginning to sound like a seagull that had inhaled helium.

He couldn't for the life of him recall how he had allowed himself to be talked into this. He wouldn't mind so much but he didn't even drink wine. Give him a nice, chilled lager in a beer garden, or better still, a pint of bitter. Nothing could top a bitter made from the finest Kentish hops, with the taste of caramel malts and a peppery finish. The thought made him salivate.

It was cut short when he looked at the thimble of white wine that Cliff had poured for him.

Out of sheer boredom, Harry picked it up and held it,

wondering if it was a glass for a doll's house. Or perhaps he'd been stung by a bee and his hands had swollen up.

'... and Harry is clearly demonstrating for us,' said Sadie, her voice waking him from his reverie, 'the first part of the tasting – taking a good look at the wine before we go any further.'

This is why I drink beer, thought Harry. *Get it down your neck, marvel at its taste and order another.*

'Harry is clearly taking time to notice how the colour and intensity of the wine varies between different grape types,' said Sadie, giving him a proud teacher smile.

As he brought the glass up to his lips, Sadie's hand shot out and with a strength he hadn't expected, grabbed his forearm and said, 'What Harry will show you next is not step three – the tasting – but step two – smell!'

Harry looked up at her and saw a feverish delight take hold of her features. This was the last thing he needed – to get sucked into a wine cult. He rubbed his neck with his free hand, the one not being pincered by a claw. The woman was some sort of snake-pigeon-lobster. A snapigster. Hell, he was bored.

He used to be a detective inspector. He used to solve murders for a living and now he lived peacefully in a stunning part of the Kent countryside in a village so perfect it should be on a box of chocolates. His job was to deliver dog food to a round of lovely customers, stopping for tea now and again, advising them on the right flavour for their beloved four-legged family member. Compared to his former days of finding a dead body and working out who the culprit was, wine tasting in the grounds of Little Challham's castle should have been a wonderful way to enjoy his retirement.

Harry felt his attention wandering around the room, watching the rapt faces of Richard Duke, Delia Hawking, Steve Parry, Angie Manning and George Reid who had been fortunate enough to win a ticket to the world's most boring event.

On closer inspection, if Harry wasn't mistaken, Richard and Steve seemed to be paying Sadie rather a lot of attention, instead of concentrating on the wine. Harry welcomed the chance to find out what Richard and Sadie's earlier heated exchange had been about. Cliff, who was standing at a discreet distance, seemed to be fighting a battle with himself to hide his disdain behind a professional countenance. He constantly moved from foot to foot, tugged at his sleeves and made a visible effort to rearrange his unhappy features.

Fortunately for Harry's sanity, the arrival of Ben Davies, wine producer of Challham Valley Winery, prompted Sadie to take a break at the end of the white wine segment of the tasting.

He stayed in his seat and watched Sadie make her way to the back of the barn to speak to Ben. Their greeting was less than enthusiastic. He had expected them to hug, kiss, shake hands at least. Hadn't Belinda said that Ben had recommended Sadie? If that were true, why did Sadie look as though she were chewing a wasp and why did Ben's expression ooze hostility?

He studied their awkwardness, a little fascinated, but mostly worried. If things went wrong, it would reflect badly on Belinda, and that was the last thing Harry wanted. He supposed that a thirty-something man like Ben who could afford a 400-acre estate, winery and tasting room must have upset a few people along the way. All amassed vast fortunes hid a sorry tale. Sadie might well be a part of this particular tearjerker.

Ben was an average enough looking man: five foot ten, slim build, sandy brown hair, reasonably attractive in a slightly geeky way. His clothes were a modest choice of a pale blue short-sleeved shirt, black jeans and black brogues. Nothing about him said that the guy was worth a small fortune, and yet he was calm and self-assured. He was certainly holding his ground with Sadie. But despite Ben's stoic façade, Harry thought it best if he casually joined their conversation.

He made his way over to give him a warm welcome and see if he could be of more help than he was with Sadie's last heated debate.

'Lovely to see you again, Harry,' said Ben, stepping forward to take Harry's outstretched hand.

'And you too,' said Harry. 'Sadie's been talking us through the white wines. Are you taking over for the reds?'

Ben gave a sad shake of his head.

'No, I'll leave all that in her capable hands. We go back a very long way, and I know that no one can hold a candle to her zeal and fury. When it comes to wine, obviously.' He and Sadie were staring at one another with such intensity, it was almost too much to watch.

'Your wine does need an expert to put the right spin on it,' said Sadie. 'To be honest, it's not going to sell itself.'

'That's why I called on the best,' said Ben, unblinking, motionless. 'Where would I be without you to put me on the right track?'

Harry watched Sadie recover from the comments with lightning speed and perform a well-practised look of modesty that still failed to deliver.

'Then we're all in for another treat,' said Harry, wishing the entire thing were over.

'Oh, you stop it.' Sadie blushed, with a frighteningly bashful pose.

If Harry wasn't very much mistaken, Ben was stifling a laugh.

'Now, you two boys mustn't keep me,' said Sadie, waving a finger at them. 'I have to get back and make sure that the wines are all laid out properly.'

She beckoned them closer and made a poor attempt at speaking to them covertly, using the back of her hand as a shield. Even children at pantomimes weren't fooled by that one. 'Pays to check these things oneself, you know.'

Harry was beginning to wonder if she was either a tiny bit mad or had drunk more than her fair share of the produce.

Cliff was at Sadie's elbow before she had finished her stage whisper. So sudden was his appearance that Harry wasn't entirely sure whether he had overheard Sadie's criticism. His face gave nothing away, yet the edge to his tone was like a note chiming a little off key.

'Ms Oppenshaw, would you be so kind as to come and advise on a delicate matter with the red wine?'

Sadie, clearly not concerned whether Cliff had heard her disparaging words, said, 'You've always been the same, Cliff. I can't trust you to do anything. That's why you'll always be the *waiter*. Come on, let's see what you've managed to make a pig's ear of this time.'

As she stomped back to the tasting tables – a scarlet-faced Cliff wringing his hands as he trailed behind – Ben tapped Harry on the shoulder.

'Sadie seems to have taken a liking to you,' he said. 'As you can no doubt see for yourself, she's not that easy to get on with. You're clearly bringing out the best in her.'

Harry considered the shrewd businessman in front of him, shirt unbuttoned at the collar, one hand in his pocket, the other at his side. Weren't successful businesspeople good at reading others, not to mention playing them?

It wasn't only people of Ben's ilk who had such skills. As a retired detective inspector, Harry liked to think he knew a thing or three about working out who was really thinking what.

'I'm not sure what I've done to deserve her praise,' said Harry. 'To be honest, I didn't drink any of the wine.'

'Oh, I see,' said Ben, obvious annoyance on his face.

'There's nothing wrong with the wine,' said Harry, anything to end the pained expression he was seeing. 'I'm trying to cut down on my alcohol intake and offered to drop out. Belinda didn't take no for an answer.'

'Right,' said Ben, still not looking completely convinced.

'It's a warm day too,' said Harry, aware he was back-pedalling. 'Once I get started on your Challham Valley produce, I find it hard to stop.'

Ben's face seemed to soften at the overblown compliments. Harry was on the cusp of asking him if there was more to his history with Sadie than just wine, when he realised that Ben no longer seemed to be paying him much attention.

He followed Ben's eyes to Sadie, standing by the head table, chatting to Belinda. Belinda looked as if she needed rescuing. Harry knew he should be the gentleman and go and help her. He would make it his next priority. Right after he got over to the cheese table before Richard Duke inhaled the entire spread.

'Sorry, Harry, am I keeping you from something?' said Ben, a tinge of frustration in his voice.

Harry turned his attention back to Ben.

'No, I should apologise,' said Harry, trying to keep the peace. 'I was distracted by Sadie and Belinda's conversation over there. It looks a bit lively.'

'I see what you mean,' said Ben. 'That's one intense talk.'

The backdrop of their heated debate were several eight-foot-tall advertising posters adorned with photos of the vineyards in all their glory. The photos proudly displayed the verdant countryside with rows of vines centre stage, discreet Challham Valley Winery branding morphing so seamlessly into the picture. At first glance it was impossible to tell you were being sold a product – more like it was seeping into your subconscious than blatant advertising.

'Nice work on the adverts,' said Harry.

'I had some of my best people work on them,' said Ben. 'I think the result was worth the wait.'

Harry glanced at Ben and his designer smile. There was something about the way he kept staring at Belinda that made Harry feel uneasy.

Belinda was his friend, and he would be damned if someone as smarmy as Ben, with his chiselled good looks and impeccably nerdy dress sense, would breeze in and paw all over her.

A scream rudely woke Harry from his thoughts.

He turned towards the noise, the sight of something huge crashing to the floor having caught the corner of his eye.

Within a heartbeat, Harry had covered the distance between himself and the now collapsed enormity of Richard Duke.

FOUR

Belinda had taken less than a moment to register that Richard Duke had dropped to the floor. As she ran across the barn floorboards towards him, thoughts of how much this was ruining her inaugural wine tasting should not really have been so prominent in her mind. Even allowing these thoughts to creep in made her feel horrendously guilty. Little Challham didn't need another suspicious death, especially not when a local business had put its trust in her to help promote their products.

She raced to his side, kneeling next to Harry, who was already crouching down beside Richard.

'He's breathing, so that's good,' said Harry, as he fumbled with Richard's collar and tie, loosening them in an effort to liberate his many chins.

'Someone call an ambulance,' said Belinda. Cliff pulled a mobile phone from his pocket and got busy summoning the paramedics.

'We should put him in the recovery position,' said Harry.

Momentarily startled, glancing at the rise and fall of Richard's enormous stomach, Belinda said, 'Good luck with that.'

'I was counting on you helping me,' said Harry, annoyance creasing his face.

'Oh, yes, of course,' said Belinda. 'Which, er, end?'

With a splutter and a cough, Richard opened his eyes.

'Don't try to sit up,' said Harry. 'Stay still until you get your breath back.'

Richard put a hand up to his forehead, where beads of sweat were gathered. His complexion was a peculiar shade of puce.

'I – I felt faint and the next thing I knew, I passed out,' said Richard.

'The paramedics are on the way,' said Belinda, hoping that the rest of the guests weren't too distraught at Richard's collapse, and that help would soon be on its way. She had clocked the expression on Ben's face as he lingered at the back of the barn, looking as if he was having the worst day of his life.

'I'll go and make sure the stewards know where to send the paramedics,' said Harry, bracing himself to stand up.

'No, you stay here with Richard, and I'll go.'

Harry gave her a short smile before she was up and across the floor.

With a quick stop at the door to have a word with the two stewards, Belinda doubled back towards the vineyard owner, keen to reassure him that the tasting would carry on as soon as possible. Just then, something behind the top tasting table briefly grabbed Belinda's attention: Steve Parry was staring at Sadie. A slow smile played on his lips but it was lost on the way to his narrowed eyes.

Sadie had her back to Belinda and was fanning herself with one of the Challham Valley brochures, to little avail.

'Who holds a wine tasting in this heat in such unsuitable premises?' said Sadie to Ben.

The young man's face adopted an uncomfortable look as Belinda stepped into his field of vision.

'I'm so very sorry, Sadie,' said Belinda. 'If I'd have known that the day was going to get so warm, I would have moved the tasting inside. It shouldn't hold proceedings up too much if we were to do that, I wouldn't have thought.'

She looked round for Cliff who was dabbing at his forehead with his handkerchief again, looking very pale himself.

'Did you suggest moving the wine?' said Sadie.

Cliff gasped.

'Yes?' said Belinda.

'Move. The wine?' said Sadie. 'No, we're not doing that.'

Cliff let out a long slow breath, put his hand over his mouth and rushed out of Belinda's view.

'So, you're definitely all right to carry on?' said Belinda.

'Well, of course, dear,' said Sadie with a laugh. 'It would hardly be fair on these esteemed guests to cancel the event, would it? Besides, I simply can't let Ben down. He wanted to come along because he's desperately keen to see whether I'll be recommending his wine to local restaurants. One word from me can make all the difference.' She turned from Belinda, thought twice about dismissing her so readily and said over her shoulder, 'I would have thought you'd have a tasting room. After all, it *is* a castle.'

Belinda stood rooted to the spot, staring at the back of Sadie's head as she moved across the room in search of someone else to be rude to. Over in the far corner, the long-suffering Cliff was doing his best to hide behind a two-foot-high box of savoury biscuits.

'Cliff,' said Belinda, who normally would have been amused at the startled look on the middle-aged man's face, 'you do know that it's almost impossible to camouflage yourself with a box of crackers and water biscuits?'

'Has she gone?' he said, eyes swivelling left and right like Action Man.

'Yes, she's gone,' said Belinda. 'And the paramedics have arrived to see to poor Richard.'

She spent the next few minutes with them while they spoke to Richard, checked him over and helped him onto their stretcher. She couldn't fail to notice the looks of relief that passed between them when the trolley's hydraulics fulfilled their function and they were able to begin moving him outside.

'I'm feeling much better now,' he said, with a wistful glance back at the buffet. 'There's still several more goodies to try.'

'Perhaps they'll make you up a doggie bag,' said the exhausted-looking twenty-something paramedic, long brown plait down her back and beads of perspiration breaking out on her forehead. Her crewmate, a man probably twice her age, suppressed a smile and made his way to open the ambulance doors.

'I really do think I'm much better,' said Richard, trying to turn on the trolley to look back at the barn, and probably the food. 'I had a golden ticket, you know.'

Belinda stood in the doorway contemplating that if she were Willy Wonka, and Richard was Augustus Gloop, who on earth was Charlie?

'Belinda,' said Harry. 'Are you OK? Should we carry on?'

She regarded her friend for a moment then said, 'Of course. Richard will be fine: he was too hot and probably a little, well, over-excited by events. If we speak to Sadie and Ben, we can get the rest of the guests back in their seats and continue. The show must go on and all that.'

Belinda gave him a bright smile, one that she doubted fooled him at all. Over time, it had become easy for her to tell when he was hiding his feelings, so she supposed he had an idea of her real thoughts too. She didn't consider herself to be a complex character, merely better practised at pretence. Harry, however, usually wore his heart on his sleeve.

He knew how much work and preparation she had put into today and the angst involved in getting everything as perfect as could be. He'd know she'd now be more determined than ever to make it a day no one would forget.

'On to the red wines then?' said Harry, with what she thought was a twang of misery to his voice.

She leaned towards him, made sure no one else could hear. 'Are you actually enjoying yourself?'

'I wouldn't miss this for the world,' he said. 'Anything you host is bound to get the villagers talking about it for ages.'

'You really think so?'

'I have a feeling it'll be hard to forget today,' said Harry, stepping aside to let her return to the top table and the increasingly impatient Sadie Oppenshaw.

Belinda wasn't entirely sure whether she heard Sadie tutting, but there was no mistaking her looking at her watch.

As Belinda was about to gather together the rest of the guests, Steve Parry headed straight for Sadie. Fascinated, perhaps slightly concerned, something about his approach made Belinda wait a beat.

Sadie's head swivelled to the right, and she turned to face him. Her scowl might have stopped a less determined person.

'Sadie, long time, no see,' said Steve, mammoth arms crossed, feet planted a shoulder width apart.

For one horrible minute, Belinda remembered that Steve had been a boxer in his youth. If he uncrossed his arms, she was going to jump in between them, whatever the consequences.

'Ah, young Stephen,' said Sadie. 'I wondered if you'd make the time to talk to me today. How lovely to see you.'

'Is it really?' Steve chewed the side of his mouth. 'You put my brother's restaurant out of business.'

Sadie waved her slender painted fingers at him. 'That's the first mistake: it wasn't a restaurant. It was a roadside café with delusions of grandeur. And let's not forget, you invited me to *dine* there for an honest review. That's what you got.'

Steve's arms unfolded, his hands dropped to his sides and one foot inched back.

'Sadie! Steve!' said Belinda, rushing forward before things took a turn for the worse. 'Why don't we get back to our seats and see what splendours the red wines bring us, shall we?'

With a gentle steer in opposing directions, Belinda guided them to their separate tables. After two confrontations and a collapse, surely nothing else could go wrong?

FIVE

The warmth of the day was getting to some of the visitors as they tried to look as though they were enjoying the idea of sipping red wine. Steve Parry was repeatedly pulling at his shirt as the thin cotton material stuck to his chest. Patches of sweat appeared under his arms and when he could take no more and used the tablecloth to wipe his neck, Cliff, who was silently polishing glasses at the back of the room, gasped and squeezed so hard, the entire thing shattered in his hand.

Everyone looked round, Belinda with concern, Sadie with annoyance and George with more interest than he had shown in the last hour.

'It's OK,' mouthed Cliff with a fake smile, waving his blood-free hands for all to see.

'As I was saying,' said Sadie, 'this is the first of the red wines we'll be trying today, and I think you'll find it...'

Harry had forgotten to set the planner to record *Glimpses of Blackpool in 1974*. He loved old footage, especially black-and-white film. It seemed so innocent. It was probably the jaunty 'aren't we all having a lovely time?' music. He'd been meaning to ask Belinda if she fancied coming round at some point to watch some of the fascinating programmes he'd recorded. It had to be more interesting than sitting in a barn listening to a dullard banging on about wine, especially in this heat. It was a wonder more people hadn't collapsed. He would make a point of calling the hospital to check on Richard when this was all over.

He risked a peek down the table at Belinda, noticing that she had barely glanced at her first red of the day, let alone picked the glass up and actually taken a sip.

Suddenly, there was movement at the entrance. A young woman of about twenty-five or so had crept into the barn. She was around five foot five, her dark brown hair cut into what he thought would be described as a choppy bob and an angelic face that would stop traffic. He was so taken with her that he stared at her for several seconds until he realised that he was leaning around Sadie as she waxed lyrical about some grape or other, and Belinda was eyeing him suspiciously.

Harry watched the woman edge slowly around the room. It was like watching a terrible mime act as she inched her fingers along and side-stepped until she was within a couple of feet of Ben.

Ben had moved a seat from one of the tables and positioned it towards the right-hand corner. He sat with his forearms resting on his knees, a casual pose that was at odds with his expression.

Harry couldn't help but notice that Ben was going to great lengths to ignore the Marcel Marceau tribute act going on at his eyeline. Instead, he seemed to scrutinise every move, every word, every gesture that Sadie was making. It was as if he were deliberately concentrating so hard, he could only have room to study one person.

The vineyard owner was either truly fascinated with Sadie, possibly to the point of obsession, or he was avoiding acknowledging the newcomer's presence.

Now Harry could see the woman from head to foot, he took in her black jacket, fastened by two of its gold buttons, a green knee-length skirt and black open-toed sandals. She stood with one foot in front of another, and looked in danger of toppling over, so unsteady was her stance.

Despite her partially buttoned-up jacket, she still looked cooler than anyone else inside the uncomfortable heat of the barn. Harry wondered how she would fare in the next thirty minutes if the temperature went up. He supposed that she must be something to do with Ben or she wouldn't have sidled up to him, even if he was blanking her. Against the white noise of Sadie, Harry watched the young woman watching Ben and decided it must be Lucy Field, Ben's PA, event organiser and all-round general dogsbody.

'So, that's all we need to know about this Pinot Noir,' said Sadie, 'we should get on and savour it.'

Her nails-down-the-blackboard voice made Harry jump. He looked away from Lucy and caught Cliff's expression in the process.

The head waiter was looking at Sadie with such contempt, Harry wondered how the man managed to hold down a job. It was obvious Cliff was nervous and edgy around her but the hatred on his face now made it seem as if he would happily kill her.

Sadie seemed oblivious to it all as she held her glass in the air, spoke again about the look and smell and how it was time to partake in its wonders.

'Yes, yes,' she said, 'we all know that a full-bodied red such as this should be served at fifteen to eighteen degrees.' Sadie peered down her nose at Belinda. 'This is hardly a cool room temperature, but don't let that influence anyone's decision to stock up on Challham Valley wines.'

There was no way anyone was going to get Harry to drink red wine on such a hot day. He would rather mud wrestle a rabid alligator.

Or Sadie.

He smiled to himself at the thought, then realised what a weird thing he had smiled about and shook his head. Could alligators even catch rabies? Could anything bite alligators?

Sadie sat down next to him with a thump.

Startled at the noise and the whoosh of air as she plonked herself down, Harry turned to ask her if she was all right. She had beads of sweat on her forehead and her face was a terrible colour.

'I was going to ask if you're OK,' said Harry, frowning, 'but clearly you aren't. Do you need to go outside and get some fresh air?'

'I'm not sure that would help,' she said. 'The heat seems to have got the better of me.'

'Sadie,' said Belinda, leaning across from her own seat, 'you don't look very well. Can I get you anything?'

Cliff appeared between Harry and Sadie and replenished the water jug.

'Here,' he said. 'Have some water. There's ice in it. It's so stupidly hot in here.'

Harry couldn't fail to notice the look he gave Belinda. It wasn't as deathly as the one he had aimed at Sadie only seconds ago but gave it a run for its money.

'The weather is no one's fault,' said Harry, feeling he had to defend his friend.

Belinda gave him a grateful smile.

'Nothing wrong with the wine, I trust,' said Ben, appearing on the other side of the table and casting a shadow over them.

All four looked up at his frowning face.

'No, er, it's great,' said Harry, even though he hadn't touched his.

'I was talking to Sadie,' said Ben.

Harry couldn't be certain, but Ben appeared less than pleased with the way things were going.

'Oh, hello everyone,' said the young brunette Harry had watched only minutes ago. 'So so sorry I'm late. My mother's been ill and I couldn't leave her at the—'

Ben put up a hand to stop her. 'Lucy, I'll speak to you in a moment. Let's see to Sadie first.'

Harry saw Lucy's shoulders drop and heard a faint sigh.

'You'll be better off outside,' said Belinda, moving her chair back and putting her hand on Sadie's arm.

By now, Sadie's face came close to looking bleached and it seemed her eyelids refused to stay open.

'We'll take her outside and get a first aider,' said Belinda. 'The St John's Ambulance volunteers are around.'

Harry was relieved to hear he had swerved brushing up on his recovery position skills for a second time. He also wasn't sure if calling another ambulance after such a short time might put the drinking within the castle grounds in the wrong light.

'I'll go outside and see if I can find someone,' said Harry, glad not only to do something useful but also to move outside away from the still, stale air which was starting to smell like a hangover.

He made it as far as the doorway, sun in his eyes, temporarily blinded. But as he moved into brilliant daylight, from behind him came a gasp, a thud and then a cry of, 'She's collapsed, call an ambulance.'

Harry turned. Initially unable to see where he was going in the dim interior, he collided with a stack of boxed wine glasses. Then, without waiting for his eyes to adjust, he groped his way around the table to the small crowd standing around Sadie.

Belinda looked up at him from where she was crouching by the prone wine buff.

'I don't think we need the St John's Ambulance any more, Harry,' she said. 'Sadie's dead.'

SIX

Belinda stood and looked at the stricken faces of the small crowd. Three of the four remaining lucky five ticket holders had moved over towards Sadie's lifeless body, their faces ashen and frozen in horror. She couldn't help but notice – with a shudder at his callousness – that George Reid carried on drinking his wine and seemed to be scanning the table for a top-up.

'Can everyone stand back, please?' she said. 'And someone call the police.'

Harry already had his phone in his hand, but on seeing Ben pull his mobile phone from his pocket, he dropped down to the floor and began to check Sadie's vital signs.

Belinda said, 'She's definitely gone, Harry. Her eyes aren't moving, there's no sign of breathing and I've already checked for a pulse.'

'Shall I clear away the wine?' said Cliff. 'You know, to make room for the police and ambulance when they arrive.'

Harry stood up to his full height, and glared down at Cliff.

'Absolutely not,' said Belinda. 'If I've learned nothing else from Harry, retired detective inspector, it's this – we don't touch or move a thing in a potential crime scene.'

Despite the gravity of the situation, she couldn't resist the briefest of smiles at her friend.

'Belinda's right,' he said, taking charge, 'all move back, please, leave everything where it is and make your way to the rear of the room.'

'The thing is,' said Ben, pausing in his call to the emergency services, 'I've got another function I need to be at, so I'll be off in a minute.'

'A woman has died, and we don't know how,' said Harry. 'I suggest that no one goes anywhere.'

It was clear to Belinda that this would not pan out well if Harry lost his temper. Right at that moment, she wasn't feeling all that rational herself. It was most likely the shock that this was happening in her own home, and to someone she had invited.

'Hang on,' said Delia Hawking, who had been uncharacteristically quiet up until now, 'you said "crime scene", are you saying she was murdered?'

'Oh, my!' said Lucy. 'No, not murder. We – I – Ben...' She looked to her boss who was still holding his phone to his ear.

Ben's face was an angry picture as he relayed the information asked for by the 999 operator.

'All right, everyone,' said Belinda, not at all happy that so many people had, in fact, shuffled closer to the stiffening corpse. 'You all really need to do as Harry asked. Each of you go over there... if you'd be so kind.'

She clapped her hands and flicked her fingers at them, feeling like a schoolteacher, wondering if five-year-olds were as difficult to handle as wine quaffers. Sober tiny tots must be easier than drunken crime witnesses.

Belinda cast an eye around the assembled group. Some were doing as she asked and giving them room, George was still minesweeping the table, and another figure had appeared in the doorway.

Her brother Marcus stepped inside the barn, all blond hair, blue eyes and charm. His clothing was the kind only worn by the reassuringly rich: orange trousers, brown shoes, white cotton shirt and gold-plated aviator sunglasses pushed to the top of his head.

He waved at her briefly before he stepped to the side to allow the paramedics through. They were followed closely by the police who, Belinda couldn't fail to notice, eyed her suspiciously. Word had clearly got round that together she and Harry had solved several murders in the picturesque village of Little Challham in the weeks leading up to the wine tasting.

Perhaps it was paranoia... As she thought that, she saw Cliff creeping further away from the police officers, and indeed, the crime scene.

'Here we go again,' said Harry in her ear, sending a shiver down her spine, despite the despicable warmth making her feel as though her blood were gluhwein.

Getting herself embroiled in a murder wasn't something she had thought would ever happen again, and most definitely not in her own home. The idea was sickening and was beginning to make her head pound. Belinda battled against the notion that something so horrendous had happened right under her nose.

This felt personal.

'Once we've finished with the police, we should go somewhere quiet,' said Harry, a hand placed gently on her shoulder.

'What?'

'You know – you, me and the whiteboard! Work out who could have done this.' He gave an embarrassed little laugh. 'I'm not sure how Major Crime coped without me after my retirement. Though would you look at that? That's only one of my old team turned up. I'm off to say hello and let them know what's been going on here.'

And then he was gone.

SEVEN

It was some time before Harry caught up with Belinda again. He found her back at the castle coming from the kitchen where they had shared a coffee that morning. She looked as though the day had drained her of energy.

'There you are,' he said, wondering how she was going to cope with the added stress of a death in her home.

Police officers, paramedics and members of the public were milling around, some with more purpose than others.

She gave him a wan smile and said, 'I've been talking to the police for the last hour. What is it with you lot and all the questions? I clearly didn't kill her.'

That gave Harry pause for thought. 'Who said anything about murder?'

'If it's not murder, why are so many of your old friends here?'

Harry knew he looked embarrassed. 'To be honest, you're, well, how do I put it?'

She stared at him, her head tilted.

'The thing is, Belinda' – he gave a dry laugh – 'you're influential and not hard up for a couple of quid.'

'So that gets me better response than, say, someone who collapses in the street?'

'No, no,' he said, as he tried not to stumble over his words. 'It's not that simple. Everyone gets equal treatment.'

'Unless they happen to live in a castle?'

Knowing that this was an argument he wasn't likely to win, especially as it was with one of the most eloquent people he had ever met, and she did have a point, Harry changed the subject.

'Do you want to go and talk about what happened?' he said.

She looked over at the immaculate gardens, a dozen or so starlings landing on the lawn in front of them, each one getting straight down to the task of pecking at the ground with complete concentration.

'I probably could do with getting away from this heat,' she said, running her forefinger along the front of her dress. 'I think I'm starting to melt.'

'Don't tell me the castle has air conditioning?' said Harry, wondering how that would sit alongside Belinda's commitment to energy saving.

'Better than that,' she said, with the first genuine smile he'd seen since their coffee together some hours ago. 'Nature's air conditioning.'

He followed her through the door, past the security guard who was slumped in the chair, in brown nylon trousers with more creases than a concertina. The fifty-something man all but jumped from his seat when Belinda stepped back inside.

'He's with me, Stan,' she said. 'Don't get up.'

There was no hint of sarcasm in Belinda's voice, yet Harry couldn't help but smile at the reaction from the previously listless security man, no doubt relishing his tour of duty away from the crowds.

Harry upped his pace to keep step with Belinda as she strode across the tiled floor, into the carpeted corridor adorned with family photos – mostly of dogs the Penshursts had bred and loved over the years. She turned left and headed into a part of the castle Harry had not previously visited.

'You haven't ever had the full tour,' she said, pausing to punch a code into an electronic keypad beside a heavy wooden door. The door clicked open, and Harry saw a light come on as she pushed against it.

With a smile, and what he could have sworn was a twinkle in her eye, she added, 'You'll have to come over and use the pool sometime.'

The confusion must have been written all over his face.

'I've never seen a pool.' Harry thought of the parts of the grounds that he had walked around beside Belinda and her Labrador puppy. He had seen the rolling fields, the stables, the lake, the woods, but never a swimming pool.

'Yes.' Her attention was now back to the door and what lay beyond. 'It's indoors, around that corner and along a bit. Ideal for a late-night swim or early morning dip. Whichever you'd fancy.'

He was glad Belinda couldn't see the surprise on his face as she descended the stone stairs.

The chilled air engulfed him, and he felt a flood of relief at being able to cool down.

'Where are we going?' he said, ducking to avoid a brief encounter with the stone of the arched ceiling.

'The wine cellar, of course.'

He bit his tongue from saying something about how every home should have one. He had clearly touched a nerve earlier with his comment about the police response. The combination of the weather and upset of a dead body weren't bringing out the best in her.

They reached the bottom of the steps and Belinda turned the handle on a door almost identical to the previous one, minus the electronic keypad.

She stood aside and Harry stepped into an Aladdin's cave of wine. There was wooden wine rack after wine rack spreading as far as he could see. The soft lighting only allowed him to peer fifty feet or so into the dimness, but Harry knew there were a fair amount of bottles stacked along the walls; several hundred, if not thousands.

'Who drinks all this?' he said, his mouth hanging open.

'Most of it isn't for drinking, really.'

'That's the most insane thing I've ever heard.'

Belinda walked over to another door, a metal one this time, and was feeling around the top of the door frame.

'Please don't tell me you're looking for the key,' he said, watching her stretch her arm up, sleek black hair flowing around her shoulders as she tilted her head upwards.

'Where else am I going to keep it?' she asked as her fingers grasped the metal key. In one swift movement, she pushed the key into the lock and turned it.

With a flourish, Belinda pulled the door open and felt to her right-hand side for the light switch.

'Wow,' said Harry. 'When did you... Why did you...'

He walked into the fifteen-by-fifteen-foot space, with its stone floor, walls and ceiling, strip lighting above their heads, one wall adorned with a whiteboard. In front of that, an old wooden Jack Daniel's barrel had been given a new lease of life as a glass-topped table. Next to it was a pair of old wooden bar stools.

'Beer?' she said, walking over to a small fridge in the farthest left-hand corner.

'Er, yes, please,' said Harry. 'I don't understand. There's what I take to be some sort of tasting area out there.' He thumbed over his shoulder. 'So why this in here?'

'My father wouldn't allow beer in his wine cellar,' she said, passing him a bottle of Stella Artois.

Harry took it without trying to be too disappointed: he thought for a moment she had actual *beer*, not lager, but this was a vast improvement on wine.

'So,' she said, 'let's take a look at the murder suspects, shall we?'

'We don't know anyone's actually been murdered yet,' said Harry, unable to stop himself from sitting on one of the stools.

Belinda picked up a marker pen and wrote, 'Death of Sadie Oppenshaw – possible suspects' in large, bold handwriting.

'It was hardly likely to be natural causes, was it?' she said, compiling a list of names, 'especially after the way Sadie looked before she collapsed. My money's on poison.'

When she finished, she stood back and admired her work.

'Richard Duke, Ben Davies, Cliff, George Reid, Steve Parry,' read Harry, pausing at the question mark after Cliff's name and clattering the half empty bottle on the glass table top.

'Apart from George, all of them were arguing or having a tense exchange at some point with Sadie,' she said.

'Why have you added him, in that case?'

'Let's not forget he has a temper,' said Belinda. 'He's also very sarcastic.'

'It doesn't make him a murderer, especially when we don't even have a murder yet!'

'What else can it be?' Belinda tapped the marker pen against the board.

'I'm not sure we should be suspecting anyone of anything right now, not until we know more. We need to establish exactly how poorly Richard was before we go jumping to any conclusions about *him*. Someone might have tried to poison him. Alternatively, his collapse could have been solely due to heat exhaustion. That would take him out of the running.'

'True, true.' Belinda considered this thought process. 'Although it could have been a double bluff to get himself out of the barn before Sadie died. To throw the police off the scent.'

'Mm. He didn't appear to go anywhere near any of the food or drink that Sadie touched. In fact, I don't think she ate a thing, come to think of it,' said Harry. 'Sadie's drinks, like ours, were in front of her.'

'So, we're saying that Richard didn't slip anything into her drink,' said Belinda, drawing up the other bar stool and sitting opposite him. 'Then how did she die?'

'We won't know that for some time,' said Harry, 'but if, and I mean if, she was poisoned by someone else at the tasting, I think it's highly probable that the murderer would have wanted to be present to make sure she died. It wouldn't follow that they'd go to all that trouble and not see the outcome.'

'What makes you so sure? The sensible thing to do would be to get as far away as possible and give yourself an alibi while the poison was working through her system.'

'No,' said Harry. 'Too much could go wrong. One of the main reasons the police take names and addresses of people at or near the scene of an incident isn't just to get witness details.'

'I'm intrigued,' said Belinda, propping her elbow on the table and cupping her chin in her hand.

'It's because the murderer often hangs around afterwards or can't resist going back to see their own handiwork. It's very common. I think our killer was there all the time.'

'Then you agree it was murder?'

'If I were the attending police officer, I would treat Sadie's death as suspicious until the facts said otherwise,' said Harry, tearing the paper label from his beer bottle to avoid looking her in the eye. For Belinda's sake, and the reputation of her family's home, he didn't want to agree. But in his heart, he knew there was the slimmest of chances it was anything but murder.

'I can't stand the thought of someone doing something so barbaric in my home, H.' There was a pinch of disgust in her voice. 'If it does turn out to be murder, will you help me find out who's responsible?'

It wasn't how he would have liked to have spent his time with her, but she was a friend, and a dear one at that.

'You know I will. Let's start by talking to our suspects.'

EIGHT

Belinda and Harry emerged from the castle, both blinking at the bright sunshine as they made their way back outside. Belinda took great pleasure in giving him a 'told you so' look when they saw the barn was now cordoned off with police tape, and very much the scene of the crime.

'It's standard procedure,' he said. 'To begin with, a suspicious death would be handled in the same way as a murder. To be on the safe side.'

'Yes, you told me,' she said, with mixed feelings that she was right about something so macabre.

'It's probably just a precaution,' said Harry. 'Or even a health and safety thing.'

'Hello, ma'am,' said the young fresh-faced police officer standing guard at the barn entrance. 'I'm sorry but I can't allow you to go inside.'

'It's my barn.'

'And it's a crime scene,' he said, red tinge to his pimply cheeks.

'Well, your crime scene is in my barn,' she said, hands on her hips, 'and I suggest you move it somewhere else.'

'Belinda,' said Harry, touching her elbow, 'you know he's only doing his job and if we go inside, all we'll do is—'

'Contaminate the crime scene,' she said, not taking her eyes off the youthful PC. 'I know. You've told me often enough, Harry.'

The PC gulped and said, 'Blimey, you're Belinda and Harry. Everyone was talking about you at the police station. How you solved the murders and...'

It suddenly dawned on him that he had said too much and he gave a nervous glance over his shoulder. Behind him, through the wedged open door, Belinda could see the Crime Scene Investigators and officers in white paper suits checking for clues.

Belinda took a step to the side of the policeman, unsure herself whether it was to get a better view or to attempt to get inside.

'We'd better leave this alone for the time being,' said Harry quietly. 'Thanks, officer. We wouldn't dream of doing anything to interfere with the investigation, would we, Belinda?'

'You're such a drag,' she said to Harry, trying to keep her voice down so that the PC on the cordon didn't hear. His snort of laughter gave her every indication she had failed.

'I've a much better idea,' said Harry.

Slightly annoyed that Harry was simply killing the mood, she turned towards him and caught sight of his expression of concentration.

'There's someone we need to speak to,' said Harry. 'I don't think we should wait as he won't be as easy to track down as the villagers.'

Curiosity piqued, Belinda followed Harry away from the barn and back through the scattered mix of Little Challham folk who were meandering across her family's land towards the exit, the day having been brought to an abrupt end.

It took two or three steps before she caught up with him; it was her turn to try to match his purposeful stride.

'I thought you were suffering from the heat,' she said.

'Oh, I am,' said Harry, rolling up his shirt sleeves. 'But we don't want to miss him before he gets away.'

'Who gets away?'

They had reached the edge of the open field and come to a

stop. Here, the noise from the guests was more a background murmur: two hundred or so people in the distance, mingling, drinking and partaking of the barbecue Belinda's family had provided. Meanwhile, a handful of police officers were trying to pack them up and send them on their way.

There were twenty or so cars and trucks parked in the service area, a stark contrast to the backdrop of the castle's historic walls. It was where all the deliveries, both domestic and business, unloaded and loaded their goods. A shield of magnificent trees and rhododendrons two storeys high were doing their best to keep the vehicles hidden from view.

One of the catering trucks rocked slightly from the movement of the crew jumping in and out. This was the team of six employed solely for the private tasting. Belinda and Harry drew level to the rear of the truck, its doors pinned back, metal steps unfolded and taking the brunt of several pairs of sensible shoes as favoured by those required to stand on their feet for most of a ten-hour shift.

'Let's hurry up and get out of here,' said Cliff from inside the truck. 'I don't want to be here any long—'

Belinda stopped short of biting her lip. She had wanted everything to be so perfect for the guests. That was the least of her troubles now.

'Cliff,' she said, hands, once again, on her hips. She stared intently at the flustered face of the catering services manager. 'You seem to be rushing off before the police have had a proper chance to speak to you.'

He thrust the large plastic box of tablecloths he was holding at a startled young waitress and ran down the three steps. With a flourish of his forefinger to indicate they move a little further away, he brushed away invisible dust from his shirt and glared first at Belinda and then Harry.

'I don't get paid anywhere close to enough money to put up with someone trying to kill me,' he said, enunciating every syllable. 'Or even worse, giving A1 Catering a bad name. I simply can't have murder associated with *my* cheese and crackers. It's not on, not on.'

'Who said it was murder?' said Harry.

'Pleeease,' said Cliff, with a shudder and a shake of his head that would have stood him in good stead for a pantomime audition. 'All those police officers running around sending people home and the barn sealed off? Anyone can see it's more serious than someone collapsing in the heat, like that other man. Richard, was it?'

'See, Harry,' said Belinda. 'Even Cliff gets it.'

'Even Cliff?' said Cliff, his eyebrows trying to take refuge in his hairline. 'I take offence at that. Only a fool wouldn't see what was going on here.'

Belinda ignored the tutting noises from Harry and said, 'What I meant was, you were so busy keeping us all topped up with wine and your delicious nibbles, that you probably weren't able to fully focus on what was happening in the barn. And yet you still have your finger on the pulse.'

Cliff's eyebrows surrendered. Giving a tiny shrug, he said, 'I've known Sadie a long time and nothing would bring about her early shuffling off the planet unless it was at the hands of someone else. As in deliberate. As in murder.'

He gave another shudder, this one seemingly genuine rather than for their entertainment, and said, 'If you don't mind, I'd prefer to get out of here while I'm still breathing. If someone's managed to bump off Sadie, any one of us could be next.'

He took a step towards the catering truck.

'Hang on a minute,' said Belinda, putting out a hand to stop him. 'Before you go, exactly how long had you known Sadie for?'

For the briefest of moments Cliff looked as though he might start to cry, then he pushed his shoulders back and lifted his chin. 'I worked for her years ago at her restaurant in Dover, the Fish by the Sea. It was a total joy to work there, and we used to be booked solid for weeks at a time. Then, for no apparent reason, Sadie seemed to lose interest. I never really worked out why it happened, despite asking her on more than one occasion. She simply said it didn't have the same appeal for her any more and then she sold the business.'

'Who bought it?' asked Harry.

'It was bought by a coffee shop chain,' said Cliff. 'All very unremarkable but by that stage, Sadie didn't seem to really care who bought it or what they did with it.'

'So, what exactly did she do in the restaurant?' said Harry. 'Cook? Pour the drinks?'

Cliff found this extremely funny and rolled his eyes. 'Cook? Not on your life. She employed a Michelin star chef at the Fish who brought in no end of business. Sadie was a food critic with her own acerbic style; she would reject lots of seemingly fine wines in her restaurant. Oh, yes, she upset a fair few vineyard owners in her time, that's for sure.'

With a glance over Belinda and Harry's shoulders, Cliff stepped closer and said, 'One day, I went with her to a tasting for a local Kent vineyard who were trying to launch a wine and she turned their wine down flat.'

His face lit up as he recounted Sadie's rudeness. 'She said to the roomful of people gathered and awaiting her verdict, "I would rather serve a good vinegar than insult my clientele with this." Well, can you imagine? The embarrassment! I think the vineyard went bankrupt and not long after, Sadie sold the Fish by the Sea. Today was the first time I'd seen her in years.'

'What was the name of the vineyard?' said Belinda, watching Cliff as he kept one eye on the catering truck.

'I really can't recall,' he said, 'but it failed very quickly. It was its one and only harvest, as far as I know. I think they sold the land to the local farm. It's part of Wallop Orchard now. Still, if life gives you apples, make cider. Isn't that the saying?'

'No,' said Harry, 'it's not.'

This earned him a sideways look from Cliff.

'As much fun as it's been talking to you,' said Cliff, attention entirely elsewhere now, 'I really do have to get out of here before the staff stack everything in the wrong place and I have to spend half of the evening sorting out the mess.'

'What if the police want to speak to you again?' called Belinda after him.

'They'll find me at the same place that's on the invoice I'm going to post through your front door,' he said, waving over his shoulder.

'Well,' said Harry. 'That's obviously that.' He turned to her and smiled, before it was replaced by a frown. 'What?'

'Are you seriously suggesting we leave it there?' she said, aware her voice was an octave or three higher than usual.

'Sadie sold her restaurant to a coffee chain and was rude about some wine,' said Harry. 'It's hardly a motive for murder.'

'What if neither of those things have anything to do with her murder?'

'Then we're wasting our time because we've no idea why she was murdered – if in fact she has been murdered,' said Harry.

'Here we go again,' muttered Belinda, eyes closed to keep out the images of those who insisted on trying her patience.

'Why are your eyes closed?' said Harry. 'Did beer on top of the red wine give you a headache?'

'That's it!' said Belinda, eyes now as big as saucers. 'I didn't touch the red wine and neither did you. I had a sip or two of the white, but not the red. We won't get much else out of Cliff today; he can wait. Right now we have to go back and tell the police about the red wine.'

With that, Belinda turned in the direction of the barn, listening for Harry's heavy footsteps behind her.

'She never listens to me,' said Harry as he lumbered along behind her. 'What have I said repeatedly – let the police get on with their job and don't go interfering, but no, that's too easy.'

'Oh, try to keep up!' she said.

She strode back towards the barn, the touch of the sun feeling like a woollen blanket around her shoulders. Not letting the heat of the day get her down, she arrived in front of the young PC standing guard at the cordon.

'I'd like to speak to the officer in charge of the investigation,' she said, her smile as genuine as a liar's promise. 'Please,' she added.

'Miss Penshurst,' said a voice behind her. 'Can I help you?'

She turned and stared at a young man whose face looked familiar but which she couldn't immediately place.

'I didn't recognise you with your clothes on,' she said, head to one side, with a genuine smile this time. 'When I say clothes, PC Vince Green, I, of course, mean plain clothes.'

'Have you moved to the giddy heights of detective?' said Harry, staring down at the grey-suited officer he and Belinda had previously met over more than one dead body in Little Challham.

'I'm trying out a stint in CID,' said PC Green, 'although I've not made detective yet.'

'National shortage of detectives, you see,' said Harry to no one in particular. 'In my day—'

'Not now, Harry,' said Belinda, shielding her eyes from the relentless sun. 'Is there somewhere we can speak in private, please?'

With a look from PC Green that bordered on weary – perhaps it was the heat, so she'd cut him some slack on this occasion – Belinda allowed herself to be led across her own lawn to a makeshift mobile incident room.

The three of them clambered inside the metal trailer where the temperature was probably five or so degrees higher than outside.

'It's reassuring to see that the taxpayer still isn't footing the bill for you to cool down in the summer,' said Harry, loosening his collar, a bead of sweat breaking out on his forehead.

'What did you want to speak to me about?' said PC Green, deftly ignoring the retired detective inspector, his attention on Belinda.

'I would have preferred to talk to the officer in charge,' said Belinda, eyes narrowed, but seemingly to no avail.

PC Green's deep brown eyes stared back.

'Harry and I were talking, and I've remembered that I didn't drink any of the red wine at the tasting and neither did he,' said

Belinda, watching the officer closely in case he inadvertently gave anything away.

'So, you haven't been drinking?' he asked. 'At a wine tasting?'

His tone was a trifle more sarcastic than Belinda would have liked.

'That's not why I'm telling you,' she said. 'Neither Harry nor I drank the red wine from the same bottle as Sadie Oppenshaw. Does that mean she was poisoned?' Belinda was starting to feel exasperated at this young man's inability to falter from the path of professionalism and tell her what she wanted to know.

'It's too early to tell,' he said, watching Belinda as she threw herself backwards in the seat bolted to the trailer's floor, her hands flapping around to show her irritation.

'What I can tell you, though,' said PC Green, leaning forward across the tea-stained table, careful not to put the arms of his obviously new suit in the spills, 'is that someone had been in the barn before the tasting.'

Belinda and Harry exchanged a look, and said, 'And?'

'What do you mean, "And"?' said PC Green.

'There were people in and out all day yesterday and the catering crew were there early this morning setting up,' said Belinda, wondering why he thought this was a big reveal. 'It's my barn. I know who's been in there.'

PC Green was clearly an idiot.

'Do people usually make a habit of removing part of the barn walls and wriggling through them in the dead of night?' he asked with a satisfied nod.

Now this was something Belinda hadn't been expecting. Neither had she expected to take a sudden liking to PC Green, clearly an enlightened and gifted officer, especially if he was going to give her crucial information in a murder inquiry.

She treated herself to a long slow wink at Harry, delighted that they were getting somewhere and had their very first clue.

'We need to start talking to the suspects straight away,' said Belinda.

'*We* need to speak to the suspects,' said PC Green, tapping his police ID on the lanyard around his neck.

'Officer, this was on my land, in my home and happened to my guest,' said Belinda, ignoring the fidgeting from Harry.

PC Green sighed and looked down at his notebook. 'Anything anyone tells you – unsolicited, of course – you let me know.'

'Without question,' said Belinda. 'I wouldn't have it any other way.'

NINE

After a gruelling thirty minutes spent in the hot, clammy confines of the mobile incident room, Harry and Belinda were allowed to leave, PC Green watching as they made their way through the throng of happy drinkers who were ambling towards the gates.

The sun was starting to show some mercy and Harry was up for a drink in one of Little Challham's two pubs. The New Inn was partly owned by Belinda but the other was, in Harry's honest opinion, a much nicer boozer.

'I don't know about you,' said Harry as they walked towards the castle, 'but I could do with an actual pint in the Dog and Duck about now. You're welcome to join me if you can get away for an hour.'

He said it as casually as he could, aware that Belinda was unlikely to pass up the chance to discuss all things murder, not to mention see how the competition was doing.

They strolled along amicably, side by side, comfortable in the silence between them. They listened to the sounds of families and couples ending their day in the grounds, trying to grab a last-minute juicy burger from the barbecue or a succulent pulled pork bap from the hog roast stand before the police shut everything down.

'I'll go for a pint,' said Belinda, unable to see the triumphant smile on Harry's face as she spoke, 'on one condition.'

'Name it.'

'You're paying.'

'Wouldn't have it any other way,' said Harry, glancing across at her, smile still on his face.

They meandered along the driveway that took them from the Penshurst family home to the village of Little Challham.

'So,' said Belinda, 'what should we do next?'

'I thought we were going for a pint?' said Harry.

'You know I'm not likely to leave it there, don't you?' she said. 'I meant next about Sadie's murder. We still have the same suspects: Richard Duke, Ben Davies, George Reid, Steve Parry, Cliff, despite what he's told us. Add to that list, whoever owned the vineyard that went to the wall as a result of Sadie's scathing wine critique. The least we should do is speak to the five of them and pay Sadie's PA a visit, get some more background information.'

Harry loved this more than he wanted to admit. Since he had retired from the police where he had held the rank of DI and solved murders for a living, he had moved to Little Challham to start afresh. His dog food delivery round was doing well enough, but if he was being honest with himself, it wasn't truly the job for him. It had just been the welcome break from murders he was after – until Belinda Penshurst hurtled into his life.

He had never met anyone quite like her and couldn't completely fathom her out either. That was what made her so appealing, he supposed.

He had tried *not* to find her attractive, but other than the glaringly obvious fact that she really was stunning, he felt himself drawn to her. Her personality was bursting at the seams with quirks and kindness and her company was addictive.

The only thing stopping Harry from falling for her was Harry himself. His heart still hurt from a break-up, and that had been a relationship he should probably never have got involved in straight out of his divorce. He had thought that Hazel Hamilton was the love of his life at the time; he was too fragile to get it wrong again.

'What's with the sighing?' said Belinda. 'Or are you practising blowing out imaginary birthday candles?'

'It's not my birthday.'

'Good, I didn't get you a cake.'

Harry laughed and looked at Belinda. A pint in a village local and a friend that made him laugh. Who could ask for more in life?

They reached the end of the driveway and Harry glanced across their picture-perfect village. In front of them lay the green, a large open expanse for the community to stroll on, exercise on, meet with friends and chat on the benches, admire the hanging baskets laden with trailing flowers, all against the backdrop of the black-and-white seventeenth-century coaching inn, the New Inn. The parade of shops boasted a post office and general store, delicatessen, butcher's shop and, nestled around the corner, the Women's Institute, village hall and microbrewery.

Belinda and Harry were heading towards the far end of the green where the welcoming frontage of the Dog and Duck beckoned. There were only a few people around, unusual for a Saturday afternoon, but most of the villagers were currently wandering around Belinda's home as a handful of police officers tried their best to send them on their way.

Harry held back from making a comment about the freeloaders at the castle, milking Belinda's family for all they could. He rarely heard Belinda say a bad word about the locals, even when they were murdering one another. She was fiercely loyal to them, and they, in turn, hadn't tried to kill her. Yet.

The front of the building had recently been painted a soft green to match the wooden panelling of the bar area, which was visible as they got closer to the open doors. A couple of drinkers were sitting on the only bench on the pub's frontage; the rest of the outdoor seating was in the pub's ample rear garden, a suntrap that Harry knew Belinda wished the New Inn had.

Nodding hello to the two young women enjoying their gin and tonics, Harry noticed that one of the glasses seemed to have a bunch of dried flowers sticking out of it and the other contained more green than a shrubbery.

Why can't people just have a drink these days? he thought as they walked inside the pub's cool interior. *Why does it have to be such a rigmarole?*

'That's what I'm going to introduce to the New Inn,' whispered Belinda, the back of her hand shielding her words in case the landlord heard her evil plot to serve drinks in her licenced premises.

'Oh, yeah, right,' said Harry, with a feeling of impending doom that Belinda might make him try one of the alcoholic floral arrangements. Perhaps he could tell her he had hay fever after all. That was bound to do it.

'Frank,' said Belinda to the pub's latest landlord. 'How the devil are you?'

Frank Hartley was in his mid-fifties, sported a classic landlord's figure and a mop of white hair so thick that there had been speculation for some time that it was, in fact, a toupee. Other than his stomach putting his shirt buttons to task, he appeared to be in fine health. His ruddy cheeks were a sign of country living and a balanced diet rather than too many beers.

He flashed a smile and said, 'Hello, you two. How's the wine tasting going?'

They took a seat at the amply stocked bar, hops hanging from the ceiling giving the place an authentic Kentish air.

'Hi, Frank,' said Harry. 'It's taken a turn for the worse, so a pint of your guest bitter, if you would, and whatever Belinda would like.'

He put a twenty-pound note on the bar and looked around the virtually empty interior. The place had been decorated with soft tartan furnishings throughout the bar, the open fireplace area and through to the separate restaurant at the back. Harry liked the cosy yet modern feel to it.

Belinda had opted for some sort of Chelsea Flower Show of a drink, masquerading as a gin and tonic. Frank set the drinks on the bar after what Harry thought was an enormous effort. He was gasping for his pint and marvelled at how little change he had from the twenty-pound note. They decided to move over to one of the sofas.

'I have to confess,' said Belinda, 'I am rather jealous of this pub. This is what I'd always envisaged for the New Inn.'

'Well, things didn't exactly go as planned for your business investment over there, Belinda,' said Harry kindly. 'And, in all honesty, this sofa is playing havoc with my lower back and my knees are in my face, so whatever you do, don't buy any of these.'

'Would you prefer to move?' she said, gesturing with her bouquet-drink at the many empty tables.

'No, I'm loving the thought of the few coins I've got left after that round ending up down the back of the cushions.'

'So!' She bounced on the seat, causing Harry to clutch his pint. 'Who are we going to talk to next about the murder?'

Harry indicated towards the bar where Frank was busy taking bottles down and giving them a polish.

'The landlord of the Dog and Duck?' said Belinda. 'I hardly think so, and besides, he's been here all day. He turned down my offer to come along for a tour and a chance to sample the Challham Valley goods. He said he'd let the staff enjoy it while he held the fort. He seems decent enough too.'

'No,' said Harry. 'I was going to say we could ask him if he knows anything about Sadie Oppenshaw. He's bound to have crossed paths with her before. Don't forget he used to run the Watery Grave down on the seafront in Dover.'

'Good point,' said Belinda, about to call across to him.

Someone appeared in the doorway, momentarily casting a shadow and making both of them look over.

'Daisy,' said Frank, putting back the bottle he was midway through polishing. 'How goes things at Royal Mail?'

'Good, Frank, good,' she said as she sauntered across the wooden floor. 'How's things with you?'

She turned and smiled at Harry and Belinda as she crossed the twenty feet to the bar, gave them a small wave before sitting down.

'Wasn't she – you know?' said Belinda in Harry's ear, with a subtle nod in the young woman's direction.

'What?'

'You told me she was up to something?' said Belinda, staring unblinking at Daisy.

Daisy Thornton was twenty-five years old, with a mane of straight blond hair and gently freckled skin covering a confident nose. She rarely wore anything other than shorts or cut-off jeans, even in the winter. The snow had to be very deep for her to give in and wear trousers.

As she sat at the bar chatting amiably to Frank, Harry said, 'She is, but I don't think it's murder.'

'You told me that you'd seen her disappearing round the back of the delicatessen some mornings and taking much longer than necessary for a special delivery.'

Harry's laughter echoed around the pub, causing Frank and Daisy to look over.

'You know what I mean,' said Belinda, cracking a smile herself at her choice of words.

Wiping his eyes, Harry said, 'Yes, you're right. She usually comes back outside looking a little ruffled and with a spring in her step. I've always assumed she was there to see Martin, the owner, rather than the young lad he's got working there. He can only be about eighteen years old. I might have got that wrong, of course.'

'Tell you what,' said Belinda, putting her empty glass on the table, 'go and get another round in and see if you can drop it into the conversation. But could you get me the alcohol-free G&T this time, please?'

It took Harry about ninety seconds to get himself up and off the sofa, something that caused Belinda great amusement, as did the look on his face at spending another king's ransom on two drinks.

'The alcohol-free variety for Belinda, Frank,' said Harry when he had regained his dignity and checked the change in his pockets. 'A half for me and one for Daisy.'

'Thanks, Harry,' Daisy said, twisting in her seat to look at him. 'I'll have another of these, please.' She waved a bottle of Cobra at him.

Harry put down another twenty-pound note and appeared as casual as he could manage, which wasn't very casual at all. He would never have made an undercover officer, especially with red hair, being over six feet in height, and having a tendency to barge into other people's conversation. He was no James Bond.

'Are you and Martin Box in a relationship?' said Harry. He wasn't very tactful either, but he liked the element of surprise.

Daisy almost spat out the mouthful of beer she had glugged down. She regarded Harry, wide-eyed and grabbing for a tissue to wipe her chin.

'How do you know about that?' she said, composure almost regained.

'I know the kinds of things that go on in a small village,' said Harry, sounding more insightful than he was. If truth be told, he had watched from his bedroom window as Daisy disappeared round the back of the Boxed Larder for up to half an hour, emerging much more dishevelled than she'd arrived. One or two of her shirt buttons were usually undone, and frequently her hair was shaken free of its ponytail.

Frank came back with the drinks and placed them down in exchange for the note.

'You're single, he's single,' said Harry. 'It's no big deal.'

'He still lives with his mum,' said Daisy. 'I've got a cat and he's allergic.'

Frank looked momentarily confused at the conversation and

then pulled the disinterested face of good bar staff everywhere and headed to the till.

'That is a dilemma,' said Harry, glancing across at Belinda who was craning in her seat to make out what was being said. 'You're welcome to come and join Belinda and me if you'd like.'

'Thanks,' said Daisy, 'but I've a bit of business to discuss with Frank.'

'Postal service paying you overtime?' said Harry, picking up the drinks.

'No,' she said with a laugh. 'Not that sort of business. Wine home brew business. I brew it and Frank's thinking of stocking some.'

Harry raised an eyebrow at Frank, who nodded.

'Really?' said Harry. 'You're not tempted to stock Challham Valley?'

'I can't afford to fill the pub with wine that costs that much,' said Frank. 'No one would buy it.'

'You mean it's dearer than a G&T?' said Harry, tone incredulous.

'Belinda had the craft gin with the trimmings,' said Frank. 'And the alcohol-free is the same price.'

'The same price *without* alcohol? With the trimmings?' said Harry. 'At that price, I expect it to be free-range and bottled by blind llamas.'

'Why would llamas work in gin production?' said Daisy.

'I was just thinking that,' said Frank, turning his attention to Daisy.

'Just one more thing, Frank,' said Harry, 'when you ran your pub in Dover, did you ever get to know Sadie Oppenshaw?'

'Can't say that I did,' said Frank, barely glancing at Harry. 'So, tell me more about this home brew wine of yours, Daisy.'

With that, Harry was clearly dismissed, so he made his way back to Belinda.

'You should have spoken louder,' said Belinda. 'I could hardly hear you.'

'Apart from Daisy confirming that she's in a relationship with Martin Box, who's allergic to cats and lives with his mother, Daisy makes home brew and Frank won't stock Challham Valley wine because it's too expensive.'

'Was that all you found out?' said Belinda, stirring her drink with what looked like a crystallised crocus.

'Yes, and I can't afford to find out any more, either,' said Harry. 'Paying informants is cheaper than this lark.'

'Here's what we need to do,' said Belinda before taking a tentative sip. 'We have to find out what happened to Richard Duke and whether someone tried to poison him, or if he genuinely collapsed.'

Harry put his hand up to his forehead. 'How could I have forgotten! Sorry, Belinda. When I tried to get between Sadie and Richard, you know, before we had the white wine and then he hit the deck, I heard him say to her that one of the reasons he left Dover was to get away from her. He said there was no way she was going to do it to him all over again and couldn't believe his luck that she'd turned up again in Little Challham.'

'His luck?'

'Yes,' said Harry, trying to make himself comfortable on the sofa, his bulk making it seem like he was sitting on a child's seat. 'Richard clearly meant it sarcastically, and I got the impression he didn't know Sadie would be there.'

'She did confirm some weeks ago,' said Belinda. 'I know how busy she is, and I didn't want to miss out on her coming along. Something I obviously regret now.'

'It's not your fault this happened,' said Harry, reaching out and touching her arm.

'Thank you, but it won't stop me feeling guilty.' She took a deep breath and continued. 'Anyway, I hadn't advertised it was Sadie, so not many people could have known to expect her.'

'Ben and Cliff both knew she was coming,' said Harry, 'even if Richard didn't know.'

'We still don't know if Sadie was the target or someone else, such as Richard,' said Belinda. 'George Reid, Steve Parry, Angie

Manning and even Delia Hawking knew that Richard was going to be there. It was supposed to be an important product launch for Challham Valley wine, and someone seemed to take exception to that. This was either about poisoning Sadie or ruining the big launch, possibly with the added bonus of killing her.'

'You spoke about Peggy Abnett, Sadie's PA,' said Harry. 'She should have an idea of who else knew Sadie was going to be there, plus she can tell us who Sadie's cheesed off over the years.'

Belinda nodded again. 'I know that Peggy was out of the country until after the wine tasting, so she'll have to wait. It could never have been Angie or Delia, and even George has no motive. Perhaps, tomorrow, we should pay Ben Davies a visit at his vineyard. I should apologise to him for, well, you know, someone having been murdered in the middle of his product launch. But we could see what else we can find out.'

'I hate to say it,' said Harry, 'but we should leave this to the police. I know how you feel about Sadie's death happening on your land, but that's more reason for us not to interfere.'

'Actually, as far as I'm concerned, it's the opposite: this feels as if I couldn't walk away now if I wanted to. It happened right in front of us.'

The words sat between them until Belinda spoke again. 'Not forgetting, I invited Ben to *my* home and arranged an event that didn't turn out well. I should at the very least speak to him. In turn, he can tell us what else he knows about Sadie.'

Harry eased back with caution, his arm on the back of the sofa. 'I suppose someone may have wanted to see Ben's business go down the pan. Asking a few questions probably wouldn't hurt.'

The smile on Belinda's face was fleeting but it lingered in her eyes as she spoke. 'I can't see that Ben would kill Sadie for saying something bad about his wine. After all, he recommended her, something he would hardly do if she hated his produce. While we're there, we can see how easy it would be to get hold of a bottle of Challham Valley wine to put poison in.'

'OK, OK,' said Harry. 'You win, we'll go tomorrow.'

Belinda opened her mouth to speak. Harry held his palm towards her.

'On one condition,' he said. 'If we find out anything worth knowing, we tell PC Green immediately.'

'Done.'

'I think I have been,' said Harry.

TEN

Belinda was up bright and early on Sunday morning. She wasn't one to lie in much later than 7 a.m., even on days when she had little to do, although they were few and far between. Today, however, she wanted to give Horatio a good long walk, to run an eye over the grounds and make sure the clean-up crews had done their job properly. She also wanted to check with the police still on the cordon at the barn if there was any likelihood of her having access any time soon.

Once she was ready to leave to meet Harry, Horatio in the safe-keeping of the gardener, Belinda walked to her Land Rover. She usually parked it in the lean-to next to the barn but fortunately she had had the foresight to move it to the front of the castle. The police had also cordoned off the two other cars her family kept parked in the lean-to. Why they had done that, heaven only knew. She might have asked Harry, only he was bound to draw her a diagram or something else tedious to demonstrate why she couldn't get to her own garage.

Belinda smiled at the thought of seeing Harry two days in a row, before getting distracted by her phone alerting her to a message.

It was from her scatty but loveable brother Marcus who had

left for the airport late yesterday. All he had told her was that he was going to Morocco to sell a large quantity of bone china teapots complete with tea cosies. It had 'disaster' written all over it, but there was little point in her telling him that. He was quite the nightmare.

With a heavy heart, she opened the video message.

Her heart was no longer laden – for a moment, she thought it had stopped. There on the screen was her brother, grinning at the camera in full selfie mode, standing next to Ivan Brenner, the man she had loved like no other.

Her fingers shaking, she pressed play.

'Hi, sis,' said Marcus. 'Took a tiny detour on my way and look who I bumped into.'

Ivan's oval face filled up the screen as Marcus repositioned the phone. Ivan still had the same dark brown hair, shaved at the sides, receding but slicked back to one side, deep blue eyes and a beard that gave the appearance of casual stubble. Belinda knew the effort that went into it.

'Hello, Bel,' said Ivan. 'Marcus tells me you're doing well. That's good.' His South African accent sent a chill down her spine. Or was it a thrill? It upset her that she couldn't decipher the feeling. Why couldn't she move on?

Marcus then went on to ramble incessantly about something or other, but she wasn't listening. Her breath had caught in her throat and she steadied herself against the side of the car.

Why now? She had started to get herself back together and no longer felt emptiness stretching before her like a chasm. And there was Harry. Wonderful, reliable, trustworthy Harry. He would never put her in the predicament Ivan once had.

Aware her mascara was about to run, and that she had business to attend to, she pulled herself together and got in the Land Rover.

First stop, the Gatehouse to pick up Harry.

There was no parking at the front of Harry's home as the road was narrow and ran alongside the green. Belinda, and every other guest with a car, always drove past the front door and round to the garden and parking area at the rear.

The couple of minutes it took her to get there had given her time to compose herself. Usually, she would chat something over with Harry if it were preying on her mind.

As Belinda sat in the car, fingers strumming on the steering wheel, she was forced to admit to herself that she simply didn't want to tell Harry about Ivan. Harry wouldn't understand. Or even worse, he would.

The kitchen door opened, and Harry stuck his head out. He gave her a thumbs up and she waved back.

A few seconds later, he was in the car beside her.

'Everything all right?' he said, concern on his low-maintenance stubbled face.

'Absolutely it is,' said Belinda. 'Sorry I'm bit early. The thought of Challham Valley estate and a chance to watch you sampling the wine made me keen to get here.'

Before she had a chance to manoeuvre out of the parking spot, a Citroën C1 of dazzling blue turned into the entrance behind her. The driver pulled the car to a stop, slowly got out and, with an embarrassed wave, stood next to the door.

'It's Peggy,' said Belinda, clambering down from the Land Rover and rushing towards the thin figure of Sadie Oppenshaw's personal assistant.

Belinda embraced the gentle-faced woman, Peggy's heavily lacquered light brown hair crunching on her shoulder.

'Peggy,' said Belinda, holding her at arm's length to take in her tired and washed-out face. 'I'm so sorry.'

Peggy's expression didn't change and for a hideous moment Belinda wondered if she didn't know what had happened to Sadie. Then her lip trembled and the tears welled in her eyes.

'I know, I know what most people thought of her,' stuttered Peggy, 'but she was good to me. I don't know what I'll do without her.'

Aware that Harry had crept forward, Belinda indicated behind her and introduced him to the distraught woman.

'You're welcome to sit inside,' said Harry, still a couple of feet away from them.

'Thank you,' said Peggy, 'but I'm not staying long. I got back from my brother's villa in Mallorca late last night. I went to the office first thing this morning to make sure everything was how it should be – I like to be ahead of the game as I never know what Sadie's going to...'

She dabbed at her reddening eyes with a handkerchief. 'Sadie worked me hard but paid me damn well. She was kind to me too. This last week away was my brother's fortieth birthday, and despite the tasting this weekend and other events she had on, she insisted I take time off and go and spend time with him and his family.'

'That was sweet of her,' said Belinda, feeling even worse that she had only got to know Sadie's gnarly side, not the softer edges.

'She had no family of her own, you see.' Peggy smiled. 'She didn't really have any friends either, not real, actual "shall we go out for a coffee?" friends.'

'That's such a shame,' said Belinda. 'I'm sure she could be very pleasant.'

Peggy looked to the sky as slender planks of sun broke free from the clouds. 'No, not really.' She gave a dry laugh. 'Sadie was abrupt to the point of being rude. She told me that the main reason she gave up her restaurant was because people wound her up and she hated being polite to the guests.'

Belinda tried her hardest to share a giggle about Sadie's contempt for her paying customers but failed. There was nothing funny about any of this. 'You do know that the police think there was more to it than an accident, don't you?'

The PA gave a minuscule nod of her head. 'Yes, I've been told they think it's something untoward. I can't see who'd want her dead.'

'No one?' said Harry.

'Really, no,' said Peggy, turning her attention to Harry for the first time. 'She could be difficult, even obnoxious, but she ran the Fish by the Sea for years before she sold it, without any issues.'

'Other than her disdain for the customers?' said Harry, earning him a look from Belinda.

'Her father died when she was only twenty years old and left her a reasonably wealthy woman,' continued Peggy, seemingly unperturbed. 'There were no other family members to stake a claim on her inheritance. All she ever wanted was her own restaurant, so at the age of twenty, she bought one.'

'How long was she there?' said Belinda, aware that Peggy was on the verge of breaking down at any minute.

'When I started working for Sadie, some twelve years ago, she told me that she sold it on her thirtieth birthday.' Peggy gave a soft sigh. 'I think that was one of the reasons she was so insistent that I visit my brother: one of her few indulgences was milestone birthday celebrations.'

'Are you sure that you don't want to come inside and have a cup of tea or something?' said Belinda, feeling fairly useless, aware that she was asking a lot of questions, yet not feeling that she was getting anywhere.

'Quite sure,' said Peggy, with an empty smile and another discreet dab at her eyes. 'I should be going. I have so many functions to cancel. I only dropped by because I wanted to see if I could get her handbag and other personal things from the police. They told me they couldn't release anything, and then I saw your Land Rover drive off. One of your ground staff told me where you'd probably be headed. I hope you don't mind me following you.'

'Of course not,' said Belinda. 'And if there's anything I can do, you only have to say it.'

'Find out why this happened,' Peggy said, her long, thin arms dangling awkwardly at her sides. 'Please.'

'I – we... Of course,' said Belinda, her voice almost a ghost of its usual self.

As Peggy made a move towards her Citroën, Harry said, 'Is

there anyone you can think of who might have wanted Sadie out of the way?'

'Like, kill her?' Her face went grey.

'What Harry means,' said Belinda, 'is – can you think of anyone whose business or livelihood she might have damaged, who would take extreme measures?'

For the briefest of pauses, Belinda thought that the answer was going to be a guarded one. Peggy thoughtfully tapped her fingers on her lips. 'There was a guy who worked for Challham Frozen Food who called up the office once and left a very shouty voice-mail. It was something about his prawns being the finest in the county and Sadie was the real bottom feeder. It was so unpleasant. I asked her to call the police, but she wouldn't hear of it.'

'And you've no idea of his name?' said Harry.

A hunching of Peggy's shoulders was as much as he was going to get. 'Then there was a vineyard owner who was supposedly put out of business by Sadie after one terrible harvest. It's part of Wallop Orchard now. I'm pretty sure that couldn't be anything to do with her death though.' She chewed on her lip, her face crumpling as she spoke.

'Please call me if there's anything else you can think of. It would be a great help,' said Belinda, keen to end the conversation, all too aware how exhausted Peggy was looking.

Belinda and Harry stood to the side to give her room to get her car out. They both put their hands up to wave when she hopped back out of the car again and, face more animated than before, said, 'Oh, I've thought of something else.'

They took a step closer.

'There was another man a couple of years back who invited Sadie to his brother's restaurant. By all accounts, it was a little grim and Sadie's review reflected that. I think his name was Steve Perry, or Parry, or something like that. He came to the office and was livid. He said that Sadie was an abomination of a woman and how dare she say such things.'

With a weary hand on her cheek, Peggy added, 'How I could

have forgotten that unpleasant scene, I can't imagine. It's all been such a shock and my mind can't function properly. Where was I? Oh, yes. He looked as though he could handle himself too. Not that it stopped Sadie. She invited him in, had tea with him and sent him on his way. What a woman!'

'Yes, indeed,' said Belinda, ruing the day she had invited the renowned wine connoisseur to her home.

'I should really go now,' said Peggy. She climbed back into the car, blowing her nose as she went, and gave a wretched smile as she put the Citroën into reverse and executed a clumsy three-point turn.

'You know what I'm thinking?' said Harry.

'Go on,' said Belinda as she waved.

'It's time to get *my* whiteboard out.'

ELEVEN

Before Belinda had the chance to interrupt him, Harry took his keys out of his pocket and unlocked the kitchen door. With a bow and a sweep of his hand, he guided her inside.

'I wasn't going to show you this yet,' he said. 'It was going to be a surprise, but Peggy's visit has changed a few things.'

Belinda stood agog, her mouth a tiny perfect O for the briefest of times. Then, she regained her composure and gave him a long, slow sideways stare.

'What?' said Harry, hairs on the back of his neck standing up. 'Did I do something wrong?'

'Far from it. You're as determined as I am to find out who poisoned Sadie.'

He shuffled his feet, leaned gracelessly against the kitchen worktop and said, 'I could see how upset you are and thought I'd do all I could to help.'

Harry watched her approach the six whiteboards strewn around his kitchen, resting on the counters, one propped up on a chair, one hanging where the clock usually resided, another suspended from the coat hook on the back of the door.

'When did you do all of this?' she said.

Even though he wanted her to be impressed, he didn't want to tell her that he had been up half the night trying to figure out who killed Sadie and how they did it. 'I woke up a bit early and started thinking about what we discussed yesterday, and so I thought I'd put together a board for each of our suspects: Richard Duke, Steve Parry, Ben Davies, George Reid – there are no obvious links whatsoever that we've found between George and Sadie so far – and Cliff...?'

'Cliff Barnes,' said Belinda. 'As promised, he put his invoice through the door. It was waiting for me when I got home last night.'

Harry busied himself adding the surname to Cliff's board.

'Tell me,' said Belinda. 'When did you buy all of these?'

'Oh, I've had them ages,' said Harry, taking his time writing a six-letter word so she couldn't see the tinge to his cheeks as he lied about the late-night online order he had placed complete with exorbitant special Sunday morning delivery costs. 'I started to clear out some stuff a week or so ago.'

She peered intently at the board headed Richard Duke. 'What have you added here?'

Feeling a tad smug about his insider's knowledge, Harry said, 'I managed to find out from an old colleague that Richard's collapse was purely caused by heat exhaustion. He wasn't poisoned; toxicology showed there was nothing in his system that shouldn't have been there. If you don't count the extra ten thousand calories a day.'

'But it was definitely due to the heat?' said Belinda, moving back so she could study all of Harry's notes more easily. 'It wasn't him pretending to collapse to get him out of the tasting before Sadie... well, was no more?'

'I don't think we can completely rule it out,' said Harry. 'That's why I dedicated this laminated space to him.'

Belinda crossed her arms and concentrated on what he was saying. 'That would scupper your earlier theory about the murderer wanting to hang around and make sure that Sadie was dead.'

'Yes, yes, it would,' said Harry. 'I don't think at this stage we can say one way or the other, hence, this.' He stepped towards the board and made a 'ta-da' noise that he was sure would make Belinda smile. It didn't.

'So there's no doubt that Sadie was the intended victim after all?' said a po-faced Belinda.

'Er, yes, I'd say that's the case,' said Harry. 'It's still very much a leap of faith right now that Sadie was poisoned, although I'd say there's limited ways to kill someone in a roomful of people without it being obvious.'

'And as we were sitting either side of her – and it certainly wasn't one of us – I'd say it could only have been the wine.'

'Yes,' said Harry, leaping over to the wall where his masterpiece whiteboard of all things Sadie Oppenshaw was hanging. 'I found out everything about her online that I could, printed off all of this lot – the opening of the Fish by the Sea, the closing of the Fish by the Sea, some of her highs and some of her lows. I couldn't find any reference to family or friends, but Peggy confirmed that she didn't really have either.'

'This one looks like it could have something to do with Steve Parry's brother's diner,' said Belinda, looking at one of the articles taped to the board. 'THE BACTERIA MOVES FASTER THAN THE STAFF: Hilltop diner slammed by local food critic and brothers forced to sell up.'

'It mentions Adrian Parry and his brother Steve, so yes, that's them all right.' He pointed to the article to the left. 'This one is about Challham Frozen Foods, Richard Duke's company, although to be fair, they're still going from strength to strength, so she didn't put them out of business.'

'What's this one here?' said Belinda, her attention drawn to a photo of a man ladling liquid into pots.

'This was really interesting,' said Harry. 'It appears that Sadie was instrumental in getting local restaurants and other eateries to donate their left-over food to the Salvation Army and other charities who run soup kitchens and food banks. She's quoted at the bottom as saying that "the worst crime against food is to throw it away when so many are starving".'

Belinda turned to Harry. 'Wow.'

'Wow, indeed,' said Harry. 'She really could be a decent person when she wanted to be.'

'If we look at this a different way,' said Belinda, taking a seat on one of the chairs that wasn't housing a whiteboard, 'perhaps Sadie simply adored food and wine, and hated it being disrespected.'

'Disrespected? I'm not with you.' Harry sat in the chair opposite her.

'That's not quite right word.' She pursed her lips. 'Mm, Sadie was so impassioned about good food and wine that anything that wasn't up to par, she felt a burning desire to put right.'

'It's a plausible train of thought,' said Harry. 'The feedback she gave was honest, even if it did cut to the quick.'

'Which didn't help those she put out of business.'

'Hence my list,' said Harry, leaping to his feet. He grasped the Sadie Oppenshaw board and twisted it over to reveal a list.

'Number one,' said Harry, with an open-palmed gesture at the top of the line-up, 'find and speak to the Kent vineyard owner Sadie O put out of business.'

'OK.'

Harry could tell she was impressed. 'Number two, speak to the other suspects.'

'That's it?' said Belinda. 'We were going to do that anyway.'

'I've put it in a list, though. I don't know why you think that's funny. Lists are helpful.'

'Yes, yes, you're absolutely right, they're very useful, H. But where should we start?'

'If we're saying that Sadie were poisoned—'

'Something I've been stating all along.'

'Yes, thank you, but I prefer not to jump to conclusions,' said Harry, excitedly brandishing the marker pen. 'Then we have to ask *how* she was poisoned.'

'It was in the wine! We've already established that Richard

wasn't poisoned, merely collapsed, Sadie didn't eat anything that we know of, and I drank some of the white wine. Neither you nor I touched the red. Sadie did and collapsed.'

'Now you're looking at me as if I were dense,' said Harry. 'I mean, how did the poison get inside the bottle?'

'Oh, sorry. I get that.' She glanced at her watch. 'Luckily, we've had some time to go through all of this, but if we want to get to Challham Valley Winery before it gets too busy, now's a good time to go. We can find out how difficult it would be to get hold of a bottle and add something to the contents.'

'If we take a tour,' said Harry, 'we can find out how easy it would be to get to the bottles during the production process.'

'That sounds more difficult and a lot riskier,' said Belinda.

Harry held his index finger up. 'Doesn't stop me adding both to the list.'

He started to write with a pen that clearly refused to work any longer. Try as he might, it wasn't relinquishing its ink for anyone. Slightly embarrassed that his slick operation was coming apart, Harry said, 'I've got a spare in the hallway.'

As he shuffled off to get a replacement, he thought he heard a yawn from Belinda. He scrabbled around in the two-drawer unit by the front door until he found what he was after, then he rushed his prize into the kitchen.

'I'm back,' he said as he bowled through the door. 'Oh, you've moved.'

Belinda had got up and was standing over by the window, beside the pile of papers and free magazines he had been meaning to clear away for ages. There was also an assortment of post, both things that had been delivered by Daisy Thornton, and items that Harry had yet to take to the post office.

With his back to her, he completed their short agenda of upcoming enquiries and stood back to admire his handiwork. 'First stop, Ben Davies, to find out what he can tell us about Sadie and have a recce around his property.'

He glanced over his shoulder at Belinda. Her face had taken on a distressed look, one Harry took to be a sign that she was suffering from an overabundance of whiteboards.

'Er, perhaps we should get going,' said Harry, placing the lid back on his newly located pen.

'Yes, great idea.'

And Harry found himself staring at the back of Belinda's head as she turned and walked back outside. It was as if something had jolted her in the short time he was rummaging in the hallway. He glanced around the kitchen, unsure quite what had happened.

TWELVE

Belinda drove them through the countryside, sun hidden beneath a thick blanket of cloud, a slight breeze making the temperature feel several degrees cooler. The Land Rover took them along winding single-track lanes, short stretches of dual carriageway and finally to the entrance to the Challham Valley estate.

The entrance was impressive: huge metal gates with the logo incorporated into the railings were pushed open across the forty-foot-wide entrance. A short distance along the driveway, carefully placed beyond the first speed bump so drivers would have to slow, was a large sign welcoming visitors with Ben Davies's chiselled good looks smiling sweetly down.

The tasting room and bar were at the top of the half-mile-long driveway, between the tour booking office and a shop and off-licence. All three buildings were clad with horizontal wooden slats and gently sloping roofs that wouldn't have looked out of place in a ski resort. The four-hundred-acre estate consisted of wildflower meadows, an ancient oak woodland, orchard, a nature trail, and, of course, vineyards. The gentle rolling green hills enveloped the stylish buildings, making them appear as if they belonged. Nothing looked out of place.

Belinda drew the car to a halt in front of the bar and its large open terrace, and sighed.

She felt Harry shift in his seat beside her.

'I know I've stopped right in the way,' she said, still staring at the buildings. 'I'm very much in awe. Do you think we could ever do something like this in the castle grounds?' She tucked a strand of hair behind her ear and added quickly, 'On a much smaller scale, obviously.'

'Belinda, if anyone can, you can.'

She smiled at him and drove towards the visitors' car park.

The journey had been a relatively short one and hadn't given her enough time to fully digest what she had seen amongst Harry's correspondence in his kitchen. She could hardly confront him about it. It was none of her business, and it would surely demand the question of why she had been paying his private affairs so much interest. For now, it was best she kept it to herself. They were friends, that was all. He had never indicated anything else.

'I think we should take the tasting tour first,' she said as they walked back towards the buildings. 'What do you think? Get a feel for the place before we speak to Ben?'

'Good idea,' said Harry, 'except the last thing I fancy is drinking more wine, especially as it's barely past noon. And you're driving.'

'Let's see if they do a teetotal tour,' said Belinda. 'Try saying that when you've had a few.' She added a laugh that felt false even to her ears.

'That'll make us stand out like a sore thumb,' said Harry, struggling to keep up with her purposeful walk. 'And are you sure you're all right? You don't seem to be yourself.'

Belinda gave Harry her best smile, bubblegum pink lip gloss and all. 'Oh, Harry, you're always looking out for others. I'm with my favourite retired detective inspector, about to learn more about vineyards and—' With a glance in the direction of the ticket office, she lowered her voice and said, 'Trying to solve a murder that someone thought they could get away with committing in front of us. I couldn't be more focused.'

They had reached the booking office, a small building that could comfortably house six people, including standing room on the veranda. The door was propped open and a young man of about eighteen was sitting behind the wooden counter reading a paperback. As soon as he heard them approach, he put the book down next to a hardback about twentieth-century British prime ministers and stood up, waiting for them to enter his domain.

Belinda made her entrance, pink wedge sandals leading her to the counter where she greeted Greg, according to his name badge, alongside another badge that declared 'I Love History', and asked about the next wine tour.

'I'm sorry,' said Greg, 'but we have to have at least six people to run a wine tour and nobody's made a booking so far. If you'd prefer, you can visit the shop, it's extremely well stocked and there's no obligation to buy by the case. There's a chance to buy pre-launch Pinot Noir, too. We sell individual bottles if there's something special you're after. You'll find it just across the other side of the tasting room and they'll have plenty of other information in there. They have all sorts of visitors' guides or, even better, the tasting room itself is open.'

He looked at them both eagerly. There was something about him that was familiar; Belinda couldn't put her finger on what it was. His slim figure was unremarkable and his height was average. His sandy brown hair had a little too much product to be safe near an open flame and a large spot on his left cheek and another on his forehead added to his nerd costume.

'What's your connection to Challham Valley Winery?' said Harry, thumbing through the leaflets on the counter.

'My dad Ben owns the estate,' said Greg with a mixture of pride and embarrassment. 'That's how I got a job here so easily.'

'And get away with reading sci-fi novels on duty,' said Harry, with a wink at the pimply young man.

'Oh, you noticed that?' said Greg, a blush – embarrassment was the most human of all emotions – creeping across his face. 'If you see my dad, please, do me a favour and don't tell him.'

'Wouldn't dream of it,' said Harry. 'I don't suppose he's here on a Sunday, anyway, is he?'

Greg chuckled. 'My dad is always here, unless he's at an event somewhere. He's rarely at home. He's a workaholic.' His face clouded over as he spoke. 'It's one of the reasons I love coming to work, so I can get to talk to people.'

Belinda fought the urge to glance around the otherwise empty office.

Harry was less subtle. He leaned back on the counter and said, 'Can't see how sitting here on your own reading *Star Trek* is going to sharpen your social skills. It's even less likely to have you beating the girls off with a shi—'

'Yes, thank you, Harry,' said Belinda. 'So, your dad is around here somewhere today?'

'By now, he's probably finished down at the beehives, so I would expect him to be in the tasting room or bar,' said Greg, demeanour returned to normal. 'He likes to make sure eveything's set up and then head home. Why are you asking?'

'If we see him,' said Belinda, 'we'll let him know how helpful you were.'

Belinda was aware that Harry was already making his way towards the door and she was keen to get out before Greg asked who they were. She still wanted the element of surprise.

With a smile and a nod, she made after Harry.

'Terry Pratchett,' said Greg.

Harry stopped and looked round. 'Sorry?'

Greg was waving the paperback book at them.

'It's not *Star Trek*,' said Greg, 'it's Terry Pratchett.'

'Girls like Terry Pratchett, don't they?' said Harry as they walked to the tasting room.

'I suppose some might,' she said. 'Why do you ask?'

'I'm worried that Greg'll die a virgin.'

'I don't think that's any of our business, do you? Let's see if we can find Ben.'

. . .

A couple of minutes later, they found themselves on the first floor of the tasting room. The newly renovated building had a large bar of forty feet or so along the left wall, dozens of tables with four chairs at each one, carefully placed so that no one party was too close to another, and a handful of tall tables with three or four bar stools.

Most impressive of all was the scenery. Belinda hoped she had only gasped in her head and not out loud. As someone who woke every morning to breathtaking vistas, she thought she was used to feasting her eyes on the gorgeous Kent countryside.

Two of the walls were made of glass, showing the full splendour of the estate. Immediately in front of them was row upon row of vines – neat, straight and uniform, all bursting with green. Just beyond the vines was the ancient woodland, a large house tucked on the edge. The window to their right gave a similar view, except the apple orchard peeked at them in the distance.

'They look like the beehives Greg mentioned,' said Belinda, feeling herself fall head over heels in love with the place. 'Bees, of course. What an inspirational idea.'

'Belinda,' said Harry, touching her sleeve. 'It's Ben.'

She turned towards the bar where Harry was pointing. Ben was standing there, dressed in black jeans and a polo shirt with the Challham Valley Winery logo proudly displayed.

'Nice T-shirt,' said Harry, in what she couldn't help notice was a tone of envy. His own work T-shirts were a trifle tacky, featuring a somewhat surprised cartoon dog looking over-excited at a bowl of kibble.

'He seems to have spotted us,' said Belinda, thinking that Ben appeared firstly taken aback and then a little annoyed that they were in his bar.

'Of course he spotted us,' said Harry. 'We're staring straight at him in an almost empty room.'

'Come on,' she said, breezing over towards Ben. 'Let's find out what he knows about Sadie's background.'

'Belinda, Harry,' said Ben, gesturing towards the far end of the bar, away from the staff checking the stock. 'It's so lovely, and unexpected, to see you both.'

They walked the length of the bar until they reached the enormous window.

Even Ben seemed to take stock of the green and pleasant land before him.

'Wonderful, simply wonderful to see you,' he said. 'Wait there, I know just what you'd like.' He rushed away to speak to one of the bar staff, with urgent whisperings and a little bit of pointing.

'What's he up to?' said Belinda.

'Perhaps he's planning how to poison us next,' said Harry.

'Don't be absurd,' she said. 'Who'd kill anyone in premises as plush as this?'

Harry leaned towards her ear as she drank in the scenery.

'You're convinced that someone did exactly that in your castle grounds.'

Trying not to bristle, Belinda said, 'I do know that. Let's just soak up the ambience and see what we can find out.'

'Here we go,' said Ben, appearing before them with a tray of drinks. He handed a pint of bitter to Harry and a glass of rosé to Belinda. 'From the hundred thousand bottles we're producing this year, this is one of our bestsellers.'

'Thank you,' said Belinda, holding her glass up to the sunlight. 'One thing we didn't sample yesterday was the rosé.'

'To be honest,' said Harry, 'it was more than one thing. We most certainly didn't try the bitter.'

With ill-disguised excitement, he took a large gulp.

He smacked his lips and said, 'Now, that's a cracking pint.' His face was almost glowing.

Ignoring Harry's noisy enjoyment, Belinda moved her attention to Ben.

'We weren't sure whether we should stop in unexpectedly.' She smiled, taking a tentative sip of her rosé. 'Having said that, we knew that if we called ahead, you'd probably take valuable time out of your day to talk to us.'

'And yet here we are,' said Ben, with the start of a smile.

'Yes, here we are,' said Belinda. She leaned across the table and lightly brushed Ben's hand. 'We wanted to make sure you were OK after the shock of what happened with poor Sadie yesterday. I – I don't know what to say. It was simply too awful.'

Ben looked down; Belinda noticed that his hair was thinning.

'It was a shock, a horrible shock,' said Ben. 'Made even more unbelievable when the police said they thought someone had killed her. Who would poison someone like that, especially so publicly? The humiliation for poor Sadie. She hated anything that lacked decorum. Collapsing and dying in public, now *that* lacked decorum.'

'Who said anything about poison?' said Harry as he cradled his diminishing pint.

With a simmer of self-possession, Ben said, 'What else could it be? If she was murdered, she definitely wasn't shot, stabbed or strangled. We were all sitting there watching.' His calm gave way to a shudder. 'Anyway, I have a fair bit to get on with. If you'd like to eat here, I can recommend the seafood risotto. Please, just tell them to put it on my personal tab.'

'That's very kind,' said Harry. 'We'd love to have lunch here.'

Belinda should have foreseen Harry would never turn down food even with the horror of a murder investigation.

'Thank you so much,' said Belinda. 'Before you go, we'd appreciate anything else you could tell us about Sadie that would help us understand her better. For example, did you ever visit the restaurant Sadie used to run in Dover?'

Ben paused, hands resting on the back of his chair. 'Can't say that I ever *visited* it. It had a good reputation, but Sadie was capable of creating a whirlwind around something, whether it be good or bad. I heard she really went to town on a restaurant in Upper Wallop, the Horseshoes. Shame, really, as I think it took them some time to get over the bad press, but I ended up supplying their wine, so it was a bonus for me.'

'I wouldn't have thought you'd want to be associated with a restaurant that Sadie had panned,' said Harry.

Ben tapped the side of his nose. 'Always pays to help turn a bad situation into a good one. You see, with Challham Valley wine behind the restaurant, Dan Windsor, the owner, was able to build on that. People love all that "I've seen the error of my ways and listened" nonsense. His business is thriving like there's no tomorrow.'

With that, Ben started to walk back towards the bar.

Belinda and Harry watched him return to place their orders, ask a few questions of the team of three behind the bar and chat about the stock.

A few more customers drifted through the door, some picked up menus and others sat at the bar.

'You know what we should do?' said Belinda when the background noise meant being overheard was less likely.

'No brainer,' said Harry. 'Have a few more drinks here on Ben's tab, get the risotto and call a cab.'

'No, Harry!' said Belinda. 'Go to the Horseshoes for a meal.'

'Are you nuts? We've got free tuck here, and you want to go somewhere else and part with good money for it. I'll tell you something for nothing, you would not have lasted very long in the police.' He shook his head at her as if she were insane. 'Walk away from a freebie and pay for a meal. I've never known the likes.'

'Did you ever eat for free on a murder inquiry?' she said, not sure she'd like the answer.

'Not in restaurants and pubs, obviously,' said Harry, sounding a little hurt. 'That's completely out of line. But when a friend like Ben offers up the goods, you never say no.'

'He's hardly a friend, though, is he?' said Belinda, watching the businessman as he charmed a young couple into buying one of the more expensive bottles of wine. Still, he had to recoup his losses on Harry's bar bill somehow, she supposed.

'You were keen to have him at your home,' said Harry, putting his pint down at last. 'I know you, and you wouldn't have got on board with him in any capacity whatsoever, if you didn't think he was trustworthy. Perhaps we'll have lunch, enjoy ourselves and use the chance to chat over everything we've found out so far.

'Besides, not only is he very unlikely to poison his own wine to kill Sadie at a tasting for his own vineyard, young Greg said that the shop sells the stuff by the bottle. It would be very easy for someone to get hold of one legitimately and doctor it, much easier than tampering with a bottle amongst the thousands being produced.'

Belinda tapped her fingers against the base of her wineglass, thinking this over. She had done her research on Ben and Challham Valley, Harry was correct there. But that was before someone was murdered during her wine tasting.

She got up and moved seats so that she could sit closer to Harry.

He raised a quizzical eyebrow at her.

'What if Ben *is* involved?' said Belinda. 'What if he poisoned Sadie in plain sight? It's thrown us off the scent, since we're dismissing him as not wanting to jeopardise his own brand.'

Their eyes followed Ben who had moved to another table and was advising a family of four on what wine would complement their meal.

'He's slight enough to fit through the gap someone made in the side of the barn,' said Belinda. 'He knew where the tasting was going to be held and he would have known which wine Sadie was going to drink.'

'The most worrying thing about all that,' said Harry, now with one hand on his throat and the other on his stomach, 'is that he knew you and I were also supposed to drink it.'

'Two seafood risottos,' said the young woman from the bar as she placed steaming plates of food in front of them. 'Compliments of Ben. Please let me know if I can get you anything else?'

They both stared down at their meals.

'Do you think this is safe to eat?' said Harry.

'You go first and let me know how it goes,' said Belinda.

THIRTEEN

Once Belinda had finished watching Harry eat his food with obvious discomfort – although the possibility it was going to kill him wasn't completely putting him off – they left the vineyard and headed back to Little Challham. The windows were open, and the sound of the car's engine echoed off the trees and thorny bramble bushes on either side of the empty country lanes.

'As good as it was to see Ben in his natural habitat, we didn't really learn a great deal,' said Belinda as they got closer to home.

'Well, we've ruled out the suspect needing exclusive access to the winery,' said Harry. 'Which, of course, whittles our list down to the entire population with a small waist who are capable of breaking into your barn and knew Sadie would be there to drink the wine.'

Belinda gave due consideration to Harry's less than helpful point before she said, 'That rules out Richard Duke, probably Steve and George too.'

'That leaves Ben again, and the snake-hipped Cliff,' said Harry.

'What do you think?' said Belinda, taking her eyes off the road long enough to see Harry's expression. 'I've got Cliff's address. Up for a detour?'

'It beats going home to tidy the house and fill the recycling bin with my clutter of magazines and other nonsense.'

Without realising, Harry had reminded her of the envelope she had seen on his windowsill. The thick padded envelope addressed in Harry's messy scribble to his ex-girlfriend Hazel Hamilton. His supposed ex-girlfriend.

'Do you need me to put the address in my phone?' said Harry, taking his mobile out of his pocket.

'No, thanks. I've already looked up his street. I know where we're heading.'

They were both silent until a cluster of houses came into view. They made their way past a bustling convenience shop and headed in the direction of the church.

Belinda indicated and pulled over in front of the iron railings.

'Don't tell me Cliff is also the vicar?' said Harry, undoing his seatbelt and twisting around in his seat.

'No,' she laughed. 'Far from it. His place is down that footpath to the side of the church.'

The pathway leading to Cliff's home and three other small bungalows was narrow, so Belinda walked ahead of Harry, forging her way through the litter of dead leaves and twigs that had fallen from the bushes and shrubs on either side.

'A bungalow?' said Harry. 'Do you think he lives with his mum?'

'Why would he live with his mum?'

'I don't know, but it's a bungalow.'

'Is there something wrong with bungalows?'

'No, they're great, but it's something you usually associate with older people.'

'Perhaps he likes living here,' said Belinda. She put a finger up to her lips as she used the other hand to unlatch the waist-high wooden gate.

They walked along the short, cobbled path from gate to neat white front door. Either side of the front step, clumped lavender leaned in the soft breeze as they waited for someone to answer the doorbell.

Before long, a figure appeared on the other side of the frosted glass panel. Whoever it was called out to someone else, 'It's all right, I've got it.'

'He's talking to his mum,' said Harry, earning himself another warning glare.

The door opened wide, revealing Cliff Barnes in a straw hat, a gardening glove on one hand, the other tucked under his arm as he held on to the latch.

'What are you two doing here?' he said. 'I've given you twenty-eight days to pay my bill. There's no need to rush round.' His eyes narrowed and he moved across so that he could pull the door behind him slightly. It was probably a futile attempt to stop anyone inside from overhearing.

'Hello, Cliff,' said Harry. 'Can we come in?'

'No, you can't. I was in the middle of sorting out the vegetable patch, or else I get it in the ear.' He folded his arms across his chest, dropping his gardening glove as he moved.

Belinda bent down to pick it up. 'Sorry for the intrusion, but we really could do with your help.'

He jutted his chin out slightly and said, 'Go on.'

'Harry and I were wondering about the wine that Sadie drank that caused her to collapse,' said Belinda. 'Was there anything unusual about it?'

'Apart from killing her, obviously,' said Harry.

'It was nothing to do with me,' Cliff said, snatching his glove back and tucking it into the waistband of his pink cotton trousers. 'I made sure everything was perfect – you heard Sadie say so herself – then I served the drinks and she was on the floor. That's it. I've already told you, not to mention the police, all about it.'

'I understand that,' said Belinda, wondering why he was being so tetchy if he had nothing to hide. 'What we could do with is your knowledge and insight into how someone could interfere with the wine. You know, add something to it to make it lethal.'

'Well,' said Cliff, with a quick flutter of his eyelashes as he looked towards a sweep of birds taking flight from the direction of the churchyard, 'what I can tell you, *and* told the police, was that I personally opened all of the bottles and allowed them to breathe. As I always do, I did it with one of my apprentices watching.'

He held his palms skyward. 'I can't begin to tell you how many times I've asked one of them to open a bottle of wine and they've made a complete fiasco of it. I mean, how difficult can it be?'

Cliff realised he was getting no reaction and lowered his hands again. 'So, there was definitely nothing to suggest that anyone had already opened one of the bottles and resealed it. I'd say it was someone who had either tinkered with the bottle before it was sealed, or who had a way of making it appear that no one had done anything untoward.'

'I'm not sure I get this,' said Harry. 'The wines were screw top, so what's difficult about that?'

'The white wines were screw top,' said Cliff, giving an almost imperceptible shudder at the word. 'The red wines were not. They had a cork.' He leaned closer to Harry. 'I thought you used to be a policeman. You're not very observant.'

'I didn't drink any of it,' said Harry.

'I noticed,' said Cliff, whose eyebrows were gathering together at the very thought of wasted wine. 'I kept clearing your glasses away.'

'Can we please get back to the matter of the corks?' said Belinda. 'You're certain that the reds didn't look as though anyone had – I don't know – injected anything into the bottle via the cork?'

'No,' he said. 'I didn't notice anything like that, and I would have noticed, mark my words. No one went near the bottles once they were opened. For a start, you would have seen them do it. If you want my opinion, you're looking for someone who has the capacity to recork and reseal the bottles.'

'With all of your knowledge, how do we know it wasn't you?' said Harry.

Cliff placed his gloveless hand on his heart. 'I've been embarrassed by Sadie many times in the past – what with her acid tongue and intolerance of imperfections – but do you know what? She was always right. If you're going to serve someone a meal, let them savour a fine wine, do it properly, for goodness' sake.' He rolled his wrists, hands flapping in the air. 'It's a show! You wouldn't put up with going to the theatre and halfway through a scene, the actors got bored and decided they couldn't be bothered with the rest of the script, would you?'

'Not unless it was improv,' said Harry.

'He's really not that helpful, is he?' said Cliff to Belinda.

'We understand your point about theatrics, Cliff,' said Belinda. 'We want to know how the contaminated wine got inside the barn.'

'Well, it wasn't on my watch,' said Cliff. 'It must already have been there. Think it through: if I'd have taken poisoned wine in, I would have had to mark the bottle or it could have ended up anywhere. No one would take that risk. It must have already been on the top table before any of us even turned up.'

The hole in the barn wall wasn't something that Cliff could have known about, unless of course, it was Cliff himself who had made it.

'If, hypothetically, we were trying to find out who could have got into the barn during the night, would you have an alibi?' said Harry.

'Yes, I was here, all night,' said Cliff. 'With my girlfriend.'

'Your girlfriend?' said Harry.

'Yes, my girlfriend,' said Cliff. 'What's wrong with that?'

'I thought you might live with your mum,' said Harry.

'Why would I live with my mum?' said Cliff.

'It's a bungalow,' said Harry.

'Is he a bit of a wally?' said Cliff.

'Only at weekends,' said Belinda.

'Lucky it's a bank holiday, then,' said Cliff. 'There's more to go around.' He stepped backwards and pushed the door open behind him. 'April!' he called into the hallway. 'Would you come here, please?'

A head appeared from a doorway further down the corridor. A woman in her early thirties emerged, with happy green eyes and a sad mouth.

'This is my girlfriend April Baby,' said Cliff, unamused look on his face. 'And she's having our baby.'

'Sorry?' said Belinda.

'Pardon?' said Harry.

April stepped towards them, her rather large tummy engulfed by folds of pink floral material. 'Yes, I know. April Baby sounds a touch strange, but I was born in April.'

'Ah,' said both Harry and Belinda.

'Fortunately, though,' said April, 'our baby isn't due in April.'

All four of them laughed the strained laughter of the embarrassed.

'On Friday evening, I told her not to eat two boiled eggs and a tub of Häagen-Dazs washed down with two pints of lemonade,' said Cliff, shutting his eyes and shaking his head. 'She wouldn't listen and so we were both up all night. She was moaning, fidgeting and—'

'Yes, thanks, Cliff,' said Belinda. 'We've got the idea.'

'We were most definitely here until Cliff had to leave for work,' said April. 'Sorry we can't help you any more.'

'Thank you both,' said Belinda, feeling a little more deflated than she would have preferred. 'We'll leave you to it.'

Harry unlatched the small gate for her and waited while she made her way back to the Land Rover, feeling as if she would never find out who had killed Sadie Oppenshaw right before her very eyes.

FOURTEEN

Belinda drove them back to Little Challham, feeling downhearted. Harry hadn't said very much; she felt exhausted at the constant thoughts in her head about who was behind Sadie's death and why. To add to her angst, Harry was in touch with his ex-girlfriend. It was none of her business, she knew that. She was also aware how much Hazel had hurt him by turning down his proposal of marriage. Belinda's eyes started to glisten, the start of salty tears, at the image of her friend going down on one knee in front of a Las Vegas crowd to ask Hazel to marry him. If Harry was sending her envelopes stuffed with who knew what, he hadn't severed all ties. His heart was still bruised.

'Here we are,' said Belinda, pulling the Land Rover to a stop at the back of the Gatehouse.

'Are you sure you're all right?'

'Please don't worry about me,' she said, painting a smile on her face.

'I know what the problem is,' said Harry, pausing as he opened the car door.

'Do you?'

'You're worried we won't ever find out who's behind this, but we will.'

Belinda's eyes met Harry's. He was right about that, but murder she could try to do something about. The personal side was likely to be out of her skillset.

'Tell you what I'll do,' said Harry. 'I'll add everyone else who might have had a grudge against Sadie to the whiteboard – the owner of the Horseshoes, the owner of the Kent vineyard – and I'll send you a photo. That way you'll know I've got your back and we're in this together.'

He waited for her to say something.

'Harry, you're a true friend. That's a weight off my mind. Perhaps later this evening, we can talk it through again.'

She resisted the urge to lean over and kiss his stubbly cheek, wondering how things might work out between them. Happily, he hopped out of the car before she could embarrass them both.

Belinda was keen to get home and put some distance between herself and the perpetually rolling thoughts of the last twenty-four hours. But it was bound to be impossible. Even so, she couldn't wait to pick up Horatio and take him to the local nature reserve where she was joining her friend Dawn Jones and her daughter Alicia. They had a gorgeous Great Dane called Colonel who had taken to Horatio and tolerated the younger pup's antics.

Horatio leaped up excitedly in his cage in the back of the Land Rover as Belinda slowed at the entrance to the car park. Dawn was already out of the car, trying her best to contain her over-excited dog, who was straining at the lead in his quest to seek out smells in the undergrowth some feet away.

Dawn's daughter Alicia waved frantically as Belinda reversed into a space, alerting Colonel that something even more amazing was happening than rabbits or foxes or squirrels. He began to bark and pull Dawn back across the tarmac in the other direction.

'Colonel!' said Dawn. 'Will you please calm down?'

Even though Dawn was wearing old combat trousers and a green short-sleeved T-shirt, she was far from camouflaged. Her brown wavy hair was pulled back into a ponytail and her sunglasses bounced on her nose as she tried to keep hold of her dog.

Alicia was dressed in shorts, a T-shirt adorned with black-and-white spots and a pair of supermarket trainers. She hopped from foot to foot with the excitement only a nine-year-old child could convey at the thought of walking in the woods with two happy hounds.

To prevent Dawn's shoulders popping out of their sockets, Belinda hurried from the car, made a quick fuss of Colonel, said a rapid hello to Dawn and Alicia and rushed to the back of the Land Rover to let Horatio out.

Once everyone – humans and canines – had calmed down and stopped sniffing each other – canines only this time – they started their thirty-minute circuit of the woods.

'I'm sorry to hear about Sadie Oppenshaw,' said Dawn, when Alicia was a few feet ahead with the dogs. 'I'm so sorry I couldn't be there.' She put her hand up to her mouth, her brown eyes widening. 'That sounded very macabre, and I really didn't mean it to.'

'It's OK,' said Belinda. 'I know you weren't being ghoulish. I had enough support from Harry and then dozens of his old colleagues.'

They continued walking further into the woods, sunlight breaking through the branches, temperature reducing the further they went. A squirrel ran across the path some feet in front of them; Colonel barked joyfully and ran towards it, Horatio following suit, probably not fully understanding what he was chasing.

'Come back,' shouted Alicia, trying her best to keep up until the squirrel disappeared up the nearest horse chestnut tree. The two dogs stood at the bottom, looking left and right, clearly flummoxed as to where it could have gone.

'Do the police have any idea what happened?' said Dawn, a watchful eye on her daughter and the dogs.

'They've told us it's a murder investigation and I can't see that it's anything other than poison. The police haven't confirmed that, but I think it's only a matter of time.'

'What about Harry?' said Dawn. There was a different tone to her voice.

Belinda concentrated on the scenery. 'What do you mean?'

'Is he keen to investigate another murder with you?'

'Oh, I see,' said Belinda, suddenly not sure what to do with her hands. 'I think he can be persuaded, although in typical Harry style, he's waiting on the police's official version of events.'

'He'll learn,' said Dawn.

'We've made a start on our enquiries.' Belinda shielded her eyes from the sun as they walked out of the trees and into the meadow. 'We popped to the Dog and Duck yesterday afternoon and spoke to Frank, the new landlord.'

'He seems decent enough,' said Dawn. 'A very much *what you see is what you get* type person.'

'True,' said Belinda with a nod. 'Daisy Thornton dropped in for a drink while we were there too.'

'I haven't seen her for, well, I can't rightly remember,' said Dawn. 'I'd have to guess it was the last home brew group get-together at her place.'

Now she had Belinda's attention. 'I didn't know there was a home brew group, let alone that you'd been part of it. She was in the pub yesterday trying to sell some to Frank.'

'Was she? It was never that good, which is the main reason I decided to give it up. I left some fermenting in the airing cupboard once, and it exploded. A couple of my best pillowcases still had a faint whiff of wine after four or five washes. It was pretty unpleasant.'

By now they had walked across the meadow and were heading back towards the woods. Belinda was aware that Horatio was wearing himself out, even if he didn't seem to realise it, and she was keen to get him back to the car and his water bowl.

'She must have improved the quality,' said Belinda, 'especially if she was thinking of selling it.'

Dawn chewed on her bottom lip. 'Mm, I'm not convinced she would have been the driving force behind it, to be honest.'

'I'm not sure what you mean.'

'Daisy has never struck me as someone with entrepreneurial skills,' said Dawn, 'she simply isn't all that money orientated.'

'Then why was she trying to talk Frank into stocking her home brew?'

'It's more likely to have been one of the others in the group,' said Dawn, searching in her pocket for a gravy bone for Colonel, who always came for a biscuit when they reached the edge of the meadow.

Horatio had learned the new trick from the older dog. He sat gazing up at Belinda, love in his puppy eyes. Until he had the tasty snack in his mouth and then he was off like a rocket.

'Who else is in the home brew group?' said Belinda, rubbing her fingers free of dog saliva.

'John Farthing, the retired bank manager, for one,' said Dawn. 'He's a fairly shrewd old boy, so I wouldn't put it past him to send Daisy to do the hard work and reap the profits.'

'Isn't he the one who owns the big house in Sellindge Close?'

'Yes, that's the one. It's the largest and grandest of the six houses in the close; I was never fully convinced he didn't have his finger in other financial pies.'

'Anyone else?' said Belinda.

'When I was in the group, it was only the three of us. Another reason I decided to leave was because they were about to recruit a new member. And the person they asked to join was someone I didn't think all that much of.'

'Go on,' said Belinda.

'They invited Richard Duke. And although I can't give you a reason, I always think there's something very odd about him. The whole thing was supposed to be for fun, and I didn't want to spend time with people I really didn't care for.'

Belinda considered her friend's words. 'I found him very helpful in setting up the wine tasting event, what with all the local contacts he has. I truly would have loved for you to come along to it. Not only to help out with the murder investigation, of course.'

They both laughed and immediately put their hands over their mouths, a little taken aback that they were joking about such a serious matter.

'I suppose as a food product developer, Richard does know a lot of people all over the catering business,' said Dawn, 'so I can see why he was useful.'

'You've reminded me about their row,' said Belinda. 'Sadie and Richard exchanged words before the tasting and I haven't had a chance to get the full story from Richard.'

Talking through the events of yesterday afternoon clarified matters for Belinda. 'Harry and I both dismissed the notion it could be Richard, and I'm not convinced he poisoned her. He wouldn't have got through the hole in the barn wall, for a start, not to mention the fact that he seemed surprised to see her there. But since they knew each other, it puts a different light on things.'

'Any idea who might have poisoned her?' said Dawn.

'None whatsoever, at the moment,' said Belinda. 'But I think I'd better get back to Harry and see if he fancies visiting Richard with me and finding out what he knows about Sadie and why they were arguing.'

Belinda called for Horatio and bent down to clip the lead on his collar.

'Dawn, I hope you don't mind if I take a short-cut through the trees,' said Belinda, patting Horatio and tickling the soft fur under his chin. 'I want to catch Harry now to talk things through.'

Belinda wasn't totally certain about Dawn's expression: the sun was in her eyes, and Dawn's features a touch obscured in shadow, but Belinda thought she detected a knowing look. 'What is it?'

Dawn shrugged. 'Nothing, nothing at all. Say hello to Harry for me.'

Belinda stood up, Horatio happily wagging his tail, tongue

lolling from the side of his mouth. 'Will do. Enjoy the rest of your walk.'

She turned to go. Dawn called out, 'There is one other thing, Bel.'

Belinda felt panic take a hold. She knew that this was a ridiculous situation to find herself in: Dawn was her friend and if she had got hold of the notion that Belinda had feelings for Harry, stressing about it was not the way to proceed. When the time was right, she would confide in Dawn and ask for her advice. Only not just now, when everything was so unsure.

She smiled and looked round at her. 'Yes.'

'It's to do with Harry,' said Dawn.

'Go on.'

'Alicia really is taken with him.' Dawn put a hand up to fiddle with her ponytail. 'She's got it into her head that he can teach her how to be a spy.'

'A spy?'

'Yes, I know. I tried to tell her that he was a police officer and not 007, but she won't have it.'

With what was probably a bit too much enthusiasm, Belinda nodded eagerly and said, 'I'm sure he'd love to, absolutely love to. Leave it with me and I'll get back to you.'

Belinda let out a sigh of relief and walked towards her Land Rover, Horatio unaware that his owner's face was the colour of Challham Valley rosé.

FIFTEEN

Somehow the day was slipping away from Harry, especially after the unscheduled visit to Cliff Barnes and his pregnant girlfriend. Since Belinda had dropped him home and he had had time to update their potential lines of enquiry as he'd promised, he'd started thinking about how Sadie was poisoned. He couldn't conceive of a scenario where Ben Davies, owner of a multi-million-pound wine estate, would use his own brand to kill someone. Despite these thoughts, something wasn't sitting right with Harry. He was keen to keep moving after his lunch at the tasting room. He didn't *feel* ill, as much as *thought* he felt ill. Surely, that was as bad.

Perhaps this is how voodoo works, he thought as he rummaged through the piles of junk in the garage.

Harry wandered around in his garage, unable to recall bringing all this stuff with him from his house in East Rise, a seaside town on the Kent coast. He had, somehow, managed to accumulate a plethora of useless and random rubbish in only the couple of months he had been living at the Gatehouse.

Taking a short break, he walked to the end of the garden.

He tilted his face to the early evening Sunday sun and blush-tinged clouds dotting the sky and knew that he was extremely lucky to be retired, to have found another job – admittingly one that left him cold – *and* live in the Gatehouse of Little Challham castle with wonderful neighbours like Belinda.

The fragrance of the nearby lemon verbena floated across to him as the breeze picked up and he took the briefest of pauses to stop worrying that someone had poisoned his seafood risotto.

'Harry, I—'

The sound of Belinda walking into his garden brought him back to earth. He was taken by surprise; the simplicity of her elegance took his breath away, from her black hair to her corn-flower blue ankle-skimming trousers.

He gawped at her, unsure what to say.

'What?' she said, appearing a little perplexed by his reaction.

'Did you shrink those trousers in the wash?' As soon as the words were out of his mouth, Harry knew he had said the wrong thing. 'I don't know what I'm saying. I'm telling you, it's the risotto making me talk this way.'

'Really?'

'Goes without saying,' said Harry, a hand going up to scratch at his stubble. 'Let's be honest, you live in a castle, so you probably don't put on a wash yourself.'

Please let this be voodoo, he thought. *At the very least food poisoning.*

'I was coming to tell you something about the murder,' said Belinda, one hand on her hip, the other pulling her sunglasses down from the top of her head. 'It seems you'd rather comment on what I'm wearing.'

'I'm – I'm sorry,' said Harry. 'It had slipped my mind that you said we could have a catch-up, that's all. I was so caught up with clearing out the garage, I said the wrong thing.'

'You are aware that you were staring at the trees when I arrived, and not doing anything of the sort?'

'I was taking a break,' said Harry. 'Chewing the fat.'

'Thinking up insults.'

Harry rubbed at his eyes. 'I'm making a hash of this, aren't I?'

He gave her a smile that he trusted would do the trick.

Belinda dropped her shoulders, and a smile tugged at her mouth as she said, 'Do you want to know what I've found out or not?'

'Absolutely, I do. I can put the kettle on or I've got some beers if you'd like one?'

Belinda considered his offer for longer than he would have liked. 'Would it be disturbing your spring clean if we went to the pub? That way, I know I've got your undivided attention and you won't be distracted by that Hornby train set on the top shelf, for example.'

'Let me grab my wallet and keys, and you'll have my full concentration,' he said, walking towards the kitchen door.

Harry left her in the garden, heading for an expanse of crimson dahlias, their flowers perfection itself. His fingers crossed, metaphorically speaking, that she would approve of the beer traps he had left out for the slugs. As an animal lover, he wasn't sure whether Belinda would detest how he had saved the prize blooms, or begrudgingly admire that the gluttonous gastropods had had a happy send-off.

He closed the kitchen door behind him, tempted to lean back against it to give himself a breather. The problem was that the top panel of the door was frosted glass. If she realised he was composing himself in the doorway, she would think him even weirder than she already did.

As distracting as he had found Belinda's sudden appearance, there had been a reason for his bizarre behaviour: an unexpected voicemail had been waiting on his mobile phone, one that filled him with feelings of despair he hadn't thought possible. He wasn't sure what to do or how to react. He had no right to be jealous, least of all upset. The truth was, he was both. The last thing he should do was to try and get in the way of two people who had unfinished business. He knew he wouldn't be the victor here.

With a quick glance out of the window to check that Belinda was still engrossed in his perennials, he scooped up his keys and wallet from the kitchen worktop and held a hesitant hand over his mobile phone.

Another glimpse into the garden; he reloaded the saved voice-mail and pressed play.

'Harry, how the devil are you? Marcus here. Listen, I've got a bit of a surprise planned for Bel. Be an old sport, would you, and play along? I've managed to persuade Ivan – she's probably told you all about him and their escapades saving animals all over Africa – to come back and pay us a visit at Little Challham. She and Ivan have unfinished business to attend to, if you know what I mean. I'll let you know the time and place, if you could make sure she's there for the big surprise. Thanks so much, more soon. I'm off to Casablanca now.'

One more peek out of the window to where Belinda stood cupping a Japanese anemone, and Harry took a deep breath, ready to go to the pub.

He glanced back at the pile of papers and flyers on the counter-top. He stopped short. At the top of the pile was an envelope addressed to his ex-girlfriend Hazel Hamilton, her name and address bold and clear in capital letters. He thought back to earlier that day when he had left Belinda in the kitchen to seek out a marker pen. Was this what had made her appear on edge?

Harry had to accept that for now Belinda wasn't going to be in his life the way he would like her to be. If he had to settle for being friends at this moment in time, so be it. Whoever this Ivan bloke was, he wasn't going to stop them solving Sadie's murder together. After all, half of something was better than all of nothing.

SIXTEEN

'So, which pub do you fancy?' said Belinda as they strolled across the green. It was particularly splendid. Dozens of people were taking advantage of the pleasant early Sunday evening weather and the next day's bank holiday.

'I'll let you choose,' said Harry.

Belinda was briefly distracted by the abundance of hanging baskets adorning every lamppost around the green. They were kept in all their glory by the local volunteers who made a special effort this time of the year to water them and see to their upkeep. Both of the village pubs, the Women's Institute and village hall had similar displays of vibrant flowers, giving Little Challham a burst of colour against the black-and-white façade of its sixteenth- and seventeenth-century buildings.

But despite all this beauty, something seemed wrong with Harry, and Belinda was determined to find out what it was.

'How about we give the New Inn a try?' she said.

'Sounds good to me.'

They walked the last few feet in the same silence that had mostly dominated their journey since leaving Harry's garden. Usually, Belinda would have found it comforting. This evening, it unnerved her. He had seemed reluctant to catch her eye when he had walked out of his kitchen door, keener, in fact, to concentrate on locking up and pointing out the plants she knew were in his garden. Belinda's family owned the Gatehouse and it was rented out to Harry. She was well aware of what was growing there, most of it planted by her team of gardeners.

'Is everything OK?' she asked as he held back in the pub doorway, waiting for her to walk inside.

'An evening pint with you?' he said. 'Fewer things in life could give me greater pleasure.'

As she entered, fully aware that Harry had deftly avoided answering the crux of her question, she scanned the pub and its clientele. It pleased her to see the place doing a reasonable trade. She had invested in it heavily, after all. Recent events meant she had played a more hands-on role in its running, which she was keen to delegate to the new manager, Freddie Laker. She had poached him from the Dog and Duck, something she had been surprised that she had got away with so easily, but the landlord at the rival pub had been out of town and not able to object too strongly.

A handful of the local regulars and one or two of the neighbouring villagers sat at the bar which dominated the back wall. The rest of the bar had nooks and crannies, some behind pillars and a chimney breast. It gave it a cosy atmosphere but without the modern feel of the Dog and Duck. Belinda wasn't sure it would pay to have the entire bar renovated, but it was on her agenda. Perhaps she could discuss it with Harry, if he was in the mood for talking anything other than murder.

'Evening, Belinda,' said Freddie. 'What can I get you, Harry?'

'I'll have an orange juice, please,' said Harry.

Freddie and Belinda exchanged a glance.

'Really?' said Freddie, his thin black eyebrows rising above the top of his glasses, though they weren't agile enough to reach the gelled-back black hairline. 'Is that all?'

'Sorry, sorry,' said Harry, taking his wallet from his pocket. 'Whatever Belinda would like and have one yourself.'

Freddie shrugged and went off in search of the Sauvignon Blanc.

'I'm not sure that's what Freddie meant,' she said. 'It must be the first time you've resisted a one-liner about, "Oh, yeah, and a cheap flight to Miami while you're at it."'

'He's probably had enough of the wisecracks,' said Harry, watching Freddie pour the drinks and chat with the other customers. 'The kid's not even old enough to get the joke.'

'Neither am I, but I still laugh. Anyway, he's almost thirty, not a kid.'

'So, tell me,' said Harry, 'what was it you found out?'

Freddie came back with the drinks before Belinda could answer.

'Would I be able to put them on my tab, please?' said Belinda. 'I think Harry and I could do with a couple of sandwiches too?'

She looked across at her friend's lined face, the corners of his mouth turned down, the crow's feet around his eyes. She took in the flecks of grey in his neatly combed red hair, forcing her to tilt her head upwards.

'Cheese? Ham? What do you fancy?' she said, Freddie waiting to punch the order in the till.

'Either will be fine,' he said. 'I'll find us a table over there.' He indicated a far corner behind a pillar where the rest of the pub was largely out of sight. He picked up the two drinks and wandered off.

'What's up with him?' said Freddie, leaning across the taps to speak to Belinda. His voice was surprisingly deep and loud for someone of such slender proportions, something that frequently took Belinda by surprise. She might even have been startled by it, but rather childishly, she and Harry often laughed about it.

'I'm not really sure,' said Belinda. 'It's probably the thought of another murder in Little Challham and the whole him not being a policeman any more thing.'

Freddie made a tutting noise which sounded more alarming than it should have done – so much so, Belinda wasn't convinced that she hadn't moved back slightly.

'Tell you what,' said Freddie, 'when your sandwiches are ready, I'll bring him over something I've got up my sleeve. Not literally, obviously. There's just a used tissue up there. He won't want that.'

'No, Freddie, I don't think he will.'

Belinda wondered if her new bar manager was a cause for concern, but she knew she had more important things to worry about – a murder to solve and more pressing right at this moment: what was eating Harry Powell?

Belinda made a point of taking a seat on the bench next to Harry, rather than the softer cushioned chair he had left free for her.

'I thought you'd rather sit on that one,' he said, picking up his drink without enthusiasm and taking a sip. He took his time repositioning the glass until it was exactly in the centre of the beer mat and said, 'So, what's happened?'

To make up for the complete lack of excitement in Harry's tone, Belinda said with more animation than it warranted, 'The wine home brew group that Daisy Thornton is a part of has three members. She's one, clearly, but the other two are John Farthing, as we know, and drum-roll, please...'

Harry made a *go on* gesture, accompanied by a hang dog expression.

'Richard Duke!' Belinda sat back on the hard wooden bench and took a sip of her white wine, the crisp, dry drink hitting the spot.

For the first time since meeting up again, Harry gave the impression of interest, at least, Belinda hoped that was what she was seeing.

'Richard Duke?' Harry picked up his drink again and took another tentative sup. 'That's very refreshing. Not the same as a beer, but it's about time I cut back.' He turned sideways to her, sitting with one leg bent, his foot resting on the back of his other calf.

She smiled. 'I thought that would get your attention. Let's not forget that Richard is a food product developer. He's—'

Harry started to choke as he fought the urge to laugh and spray Belinda with a mouthful of orange juice.

'I'm sorry,' he said, composure regained, mouth and eyes dabbed dry with a paper serviette from the cutlery holder on the table. 'Your comic timing is wonderful, Belinda. I can only guess from the size of him that he seeks out perfection wherever he goes.'

'You're being mean.'

'Then why are you trying not to laugh?'

The tension in the air was gone: her wonderful Harry was back.

'We're drawing a blank with Ben, as well as Cliff and his alibi,' said Harry. 'Not forgetting that it would have been possible to get hold of a bottle of Challham Valley Pinot Noir before the tasting on presale at the winery.'

The realisation that the home brew group could well hold the key to this occurred to them simultaneously.

Both of them looked at one another.

'That must have been how they did it,' said Belinda.

'They've got the equipment to reseal a bottle of wine,' said Harry.

'One of them must have bought the wine,' said Belinda, 'opened it, put the poison in and sealed it back up so no one was any the wiser.'

'We should tell the police,' said Harry, moment of euphoria clearly short-lived.

'Tell them what, H? They'll know sooner or later exactly what killed Sadie and we've already told them it must have been in the red wine. If we can dig around a bit more and find out something more solid, your old friends won't think we're wasting their time with dead-end leads.'

Harry downed the rest of his drink and said, 'Annoyingly, I think you're right.'

'I see you're enjoying the OJ,' said Freddie, appearing from behind the pillar, two plates stacking up his left arm and a pint in his right hand. He put the bitter in front of Harry and two plates of sandwiches between them. 'I ordered you one cheese and one ham. Thought you could share, you know, mix it up a little.'

'And an actual alcoholic drink for me,' said Harry. 'If I carry on like this, I'll end up like human foie gras.'

'I can take it away again,' said Freddie, hand reaching towards the newly delivered pint.

'No, no,' said Harry, pulling the drink towards him. 'I don't want to waste your time, and besides, I made the effort with one soft drink.' He held the glass up to the light.

'I'd love to know what you think of it,' said Freddie, schooling his features as Harry took a tentative sip, followed by a much less inhibited taste.

'What is it?' said Harry.

'It's a new local craft beer.' Freddie looked to Belinda for approval. 'Providing it's OK with you, I'm thinking of stocking it regularly. Anyway, enjoy.'

'Right,' said Harry when the bar manager had left them to it, 'what's this about Richard Duke and his food product developer job?' He couldn't stop himself chortling as he said it.

'We know from what Peggy the PA told us that there's no way it can be a coincidence,' said Belinda, pulling the sandwiches closer and picking up one of the ham triangles. 'He's involved in the food industry – selling substandard prawns according to Sadie, which may be what they were rowing about. Sadie used to run a restaurant and was lately involved in giving the thumbs up – or thumbs down – to English vineyards' wine, meaning local eateries stocked it or didn't.'

'How does this fit in with the home brew, do you think?' said Harry, making short work of a cheese quarter.

'I'm not entirely sure, although at a guess, perhaps she put local businesses off the idea of stocking their wares,' said Belinda, swallowing a delicate nibble of her food and picking up her glass of wine. 'We should speak to Richard Duke and John Farthing, find out if she'd angered them in the same manner as most others she encountered. It wouldn't hurt to speak to Daisy again either in case the three of them are working together.'

Belinda watched him chew, his jaw working overtime so he could carry on the conversation.

At last, he said, 'It's bank holiday Monday tomorrow. I'm not working; they may all be at home. It may be worth trying all three of them. See if any of them were definitely holding a grudge. What do you reckon?'

She beamed at him. 'I reckon that's a great idea.'

An entire day with Harry Powell would be her idea of heaven.

If only he knew it.

SEVENTEEN

Although Belinda didn't get to the bottom of what was irking Harry – it wasn't through lack of trying – they still had an enjoyable couple of hours together. Belinda decided that it was time to call a close to the evening and, despite Harry's protestations that he should contribute, went to the bar to pay her tab.

Since Belinda and Harry had arrived and settled themselves in a remote spot of the bar, the butcher George Reid had taken up a stool at the counter and was drinking a pint.

'Evening, George,' said Belinda as she made the universal 'bill' sign at Freddie with her imaginary pen. 'Anita not joining you tonight?'

'Belinda.' He inclined his head as if it was an effort. 'I know, right? Two days on the trot she's let me out. You on your own? Feel free to join me.'

There had been no hesitation on Belinda's part to make George part of her small wine tasting group at the castle – he had come through with cut-price meat for the barbecue – yet she still couldn't warm to the man.

'Thanks, that's kind, but I'm with Harry and we're calling it a night. I'm about to settle up and head home.'

She didn't like the smirk on his face when she mentioned

Harry, or the part about heading home. 'Harry, being a gent, is bound to insist on walking me,' she added.

George waved his palms at her in a placatory manner. 'Never said nothing about nothing.'

Starting an argument with the village's butcher was probably not a good way to end her Sunday. If nothing else, despite his brusque, often rude attitude, he did run a drop-off service from his shop for the elderly and less mobile at no extra cost. He had even been known to throw in a few freebies if he thought the customers were struggling. Belinda gestured towards his almost empty beer glass.

'Can I get you a drink before I head off?' she said as she took a handful of notes from her purse.

'That's very kind of you,' said George, then turned his attention to Freddie who was waiting with Belinda's bill. 'I'll have another of this guest ale, please, Fredders.'

Belinda thought she saw a twitch in Freddie's eye, but his demeanour otherwise gave nothing away.

'And add it to my bill, if you would, before I settle up.' She glanced up and down the drinks on display. 'By the way, what is it? I suppose I should know if we're going to stock it.'

Freddie paused, one hand on the guest ale pump, the other holding a pint pot. With a minuscule movement of his head, he beckoned Belinda closer and said, 'You'd never know it,' he glanced up and down the bar, 'but right at the moment, it's a freebie, until they get approved to sell their brew.'

After the briefest of pauses, Belinda realised that her mouth was hanging open. Forcing her lips into a smile, she said, 'Home brew?' with more venom than she'd anticipated. 'They brew beer as well as wine?'

Freddie's face clouded over. 'I thought that you were OK with me making some decisions if you weren't around.'

'I'm happy to drink it,' said George, staring at Freddie, who seemed torn between wanting to keep his customer happy and not infuriating his boss.

'Then don't let me stop you,' she said, counting out ten-pound notes and concentrating on the bill, her mind buzzing. 'That should cover it, and have one yourself, Freddie. When you've closed up for the night, obviously.'

Her bar manager had gone back to pulling a pint but was still casting looks at Belinda. 'You are all right with this?' he asked again.

'If it's good enough for George, it's good enough for the rest of the pub.'

'Harry enjoyed it too,' said Freddie.

'What did I enjoy?' Harry said, joining them at the bar, attention switching between the three of them.

'Your drink,' said Belinda, her tone neutral. They'd both narrowly avoided death by red wine the day before – in addition to Harry's claim to being poisoned at lunch – now here was Freddie revealing the last pint was home brew of dubious origins. This probably wasn't going to help his mood.

'Can I ask who's been making the beer?' said Harry, cutting straight to the centre of matters.

George snorted into his beer. 'You'll never guess, not in a million years.'

'Daisy Thornton, Richard Duke and John Farthing?' said Harry.

'Fair enough.' George shrugged. 'It didn't quite take a million years.'

'I heard about your detective skills,' said Freddie, as he pushed his glasses back up his nose, 'but I had no idea you were *so* sharp.'

Harry managed to bristle with pride. 'I was top of my game.'

Belinda busied herself picking up her change from the bar so he couldn't see the start of a smile.

'As long as the punters are happy,' she said, 'we can discuss a regular supply at a later date. Did they say how much they could provide?'

Freddie said, 'John seemed to think it would be around seventy-two pints every week, if we wanted that much.'

'Less guest beer, more permanent resident,' said George, wiping his mouth with the back of his hands.

'Any idea where they produce this?' called Belinda as Freddie stepped towards the optics.

'At the biggest house,' he said, pushing a glass against the vodka optic, ice cubes rattling. 'John Farthing's home. Or more accurately, a shed in his garden, as far as I know.'

Keen not to show anything other than mild interest, Belinda put her change into her purse. She knew how much people gossiped in a small village, and the last thing she wanted was anyone to know what she and Harry were up to.

'When you next see John, congratulate him on his achievement, would you?' she said. 'We're off now, so see you all another time.'

'Night,' said Harry, the quizzical look he was sporting ill-disguised as he followed her outside.

At a safe distance from the pub, Belinda checked over her shoulder and said, 'That's settled that, then. Tomorrow, we visit John Farthing and find out a bit more about the home brew and anything that connects it with Sadie.'

'I don't think I feel very well,' said Harry.

'H, I'm sure there's nothing wrong with you or the beer.' Belinda took a couple of steps across the green. 'What time do you think we should—'

Harry was still some feet away.

'What's the matter?' She walked back and joined him.

'Doesn't it seem a little bit odd that only yesterday, Daisy was in the Dog and Duck trying to sell the home brew wine in there, and today the New Inn is giving away booze from the same home brew gang?'

'Not really. If anything, I'm pleased that the good folk of the parish are keen enough to try any avenue for a living.' She held her purse out. 'Besides, it was free and in due course, should bring in a tidy profit. I'm all for that.'

'Sadie was killed on Saturday afternoon after arguing with

Richard. He's involved in making money from the home brew. Just as sales were about to take off, in walks Sadie Oppenshaw to take it all away again.' Harry's face was a tad difficult to read in the fading light.

'You think that Sadie was that much of a threat to them? It's home brew!'

'Remember I heard Richard telling Sadie that he wouldn't let her do it to him again?' said Harry. 'What if she was threatening him? Or planning on doing something to put them out of business?'

'How much money would they stand to lose?' said Belinda. 'As far as we know, this is three friends making beer and wine in a garden shed. How could Sadie possibly put paid to that?'

He looked at her for a brief time and then said, 'Come on, I'll walk you home. But I think you've got the right idea. First thing in the morning, we'll go and pay a visit to John as he's the one housing all the gear. We can naturally drop into the conversation that we know Daisy Thornton is also trying to peddle their goods in the village. According to Freddie, they don't have the paperwork at the moment to sell it, so something tells me John has no idea.'

They fell into step as they walked in the direction of the castle, an impressive sight in spite of the rapidly increasing darkness.

'How are you feeling, H?' said Belinda as they got past the Gatehouse and onto the long driveway taking her home.

'Er, not too bad, thanks.' He was silent for a moment and then said, 'I was probably worrying about nothing. As you've said, I would have been dead by now if there was anything dodgy about the lunch, or that pint of home brew I all but downed back there.'

'Good,' she said. 'You're the last person I'd want anything to happen to.'

Belinda threaded her arm through his, not sure whether she imagined his momentary recoil at her touch, but reassured when he relaxed and leaned in against her.

'Nightcap?' she said when they reached the front door.

Harry studied the end of his size ten loafers. 'Not tonight, thanks. I've had enough for one day.' He went to meet her stare but thought better of it. 'And John might make us taste the home brew in the morning. There's only so many toxins I should pump around my system.'

'I'd never do anything to put you in any danger, you know?'

He smiled his wonky smile, the one that reminded her heart to beat that little bit faster.

'Belinda, I—'

She leaned across and kissed his cheek, this time without hesitation. 'Thank you for walking me home. Goodnight, Harry.'

The security light at the front door came on as Belinda moved closer to the imposing wooden entrance, key in hand. The brilliance of it lit Harry up in his full startled glory. He stood on the gravel driveway, his face a mixture of surprise and confusion.

'I'll see you in the morning,' he said. 'And I'm glad you've stopped leaving the key under a flowerpot.'

He shuffled backwards, watching her unlock the door and disappear with a wave.

The door shut and bolted behind her, she regained her composure. It was only a peck on the cheek, yet Harry had seemed – horrified? Bewildered? It was hard to tell, but perhaps she should back off. After all, they had a murder to solve, that was what mattered here.

A bleep from her phone brought her back to reality.

The text from Marcus read:

See you in a day or two, sis xx

If nothing else, Marcus might bring a welcome distraction to her week.

EIGHTEEN

'I don't think that we should leave it much longer before we go and see John Farthing,' said Belinda. 'I'm concerned he might go out for the day, seeing as it's a holiday.'

Harry gave it serious consideration for longer than Belinda's patience had time for. She tapped her fingernails – red today – on Harry's kitchen table. She had walked down to his house early and now she was here, had persuaded herself that he was being off with her. Did the peck on the cheek the night before unnerve him that much? Perhaps he was thinking about Hazel. She really should just come out and ask him what was in the envelope, but then he would know that she had been looking at his private corre-spondence.

'No doubt you're right,' he said, giving his chin a scratch, one of his quirks that Belinda usually found endearing, but not right now. 'If they've got as much of the stuff as we think, they're hardly likely to pour it all down the drain. The merest hint of an open flame and the entire village will end up engulfed in a fireball.'

'I don't really see why that's amused you so much.'

'No,' he said, sitting up straight in his chair. 'Do you know what? Since I had that pint of home brew in the pub last night, I've not been myself. Do you think it's made me a bit, well, odd?'

'I'm not sure I'd be able to tell the difference.'

'I'm being serious.'

'So am I.'

Harry leaned across the table, folded his arms and said, 'I was in the garden this morning before you got here, sorting out my supply of Doggie Delight. I heard a collared dove calling out and it sounded as if it was singing "Gudbuy T'Jane". You know? The one by Slade.'

'What are you saying?'

'Well, of course, I know it wasn't really singing that! It was a bird. I'm not crazy.'

'Sorry,' said Belinda, pinching the bridge of her nose. 'You thought a bird was singing a rock song from the 1970s, and you want clarification from me that you're perfectly sane?'

'When you put it like that, I can see the problem. I thought I'd been poisoned by the home brew.' He waved his fingers to emphasise his point. 'If I've only had a mild dose, perhaps instead of killing me, it's merely given me some sort of brain malfunction.'

'It's not the beer.'

'How can you be so sure?' said Harry, moving back in his chair.

'I don't think one pint would take something like twelve to fifteen hours to make you hallucinate,' said Belinda. 'Besides, a collared dove has a three-syllable call – coo-coo-coo. See?'

'I see what you're saying,' said Harry. 'More Alvin Stardust.'

'What?' said Belinda, blowing the air from her cheeks.

'"My Coo Ca Choo".'

'Harry, I really don't think the beer is the issue,' said Belinda. 'Let's go.'

By the time they arrived at Sellindge Close on the outskirts of Little Challham, Belinda had decided to find Harry's weirdness charming. He seemed to be in a better mood, so that was a real plus. At one point, while Harry's Audi idled at traffic lights, Belinda had caught him from the corner of her eye, finger on his neck checking his pulse, silently counting while peering at his watch. She had to bite her lip at his paranoia. Sadie had died quickly, whereas Harry had gone home, slept, then, mercifully, had got out of bed again and spent the morning lugging dog food around. Of course he was fine.

The thought struck her that if Harry wasn't around, she didn't know what she'd do. Here they were, standing on John Farthing's doorstep, waiting to talk to a man about his home brew, while surreptitiously questioning him about any knowledge of a murder or his involvement in one. She felt as if she could tackle anything with Harry by her side. On her own, it would all be so much harder, if not impossible.

'What's the matter?' he said, concern racing over his face. 'Is it a bee?' He flapped his hands around his head.

The sight was too funny, too precious.

'Stop laughing,' said Harry. 'John'll come to the door at any minute and wonder why we're larking around.'

'I was thinking how much I enjoy your company,' said Belinda. 'I'm sorry I laughed.'

'As it's you, I'll let you off.'

They both turned their attention back to the door.

'Perhaps he's not in,' said Belinda. 'Though the car on the driveway would suggest otherwise.'

Harry ran a well-practised eye over the front of the two-storey detached brick house. The porch was a modest affair which was more than could be said for the rest of the building. It bordered on garish, but the beautiful wisteria making its way from the space beside the porch somehow rescued it from ugliness.

Belinda watched Harry as he moved back away from the house, hand up to shield his eyes from the morning sun.

'Top windows are open,' muttered Harry, more to himself than anyone else. 'Car's here and curtains are drawn back.'

Belinda followed him as he stepped delicately through the well-maintained beds of dahlias, lobelias, petunias and begonias.

With a hand pressed to the windowpane, Harry said, 'That's strange,' before moving a couple of feet to his left for a better view.

'What's strange?' said Belinda, as she, too, placed the side of her hand against the glass to fend off the reflection. 'Is that...?'

'Yes,' he said, as he ran for the side of the house. 'It is.'

Luckily, the metal lattice gate was unlocked. Harry raced to the kitchen door. He put his hand on the handle and pressed down.

Worryingly, this one was also unlocked.

Harry gave Belinda a wary look and said, 'We both saw the bottles and glasses on the floor. It seems that something's gone on in there, so before we go inside, I think—'

She pushed past him and stepped inside.

'John, John,' she called, heels clacking on the ceramic-tiled floor. 'It's Belinda Penshurst and Harry Powell. We've popped round to see if you're all right.'

The noise of her Valentino kitten heels was muted as she reached the carpet. The sound of her voice was silenced as she saw the corpse slumped in the armchair.

Harry ploughed into the back of her as she stopped, knocking what little air was left in her body clean out.

'Why did you stop...' Harry paused for only a split second and then leaped across the living room towards the cadaver that used to be John Farthing.

Taking only a heartbeat longer, Belinda knelt down beside Harry as he felt for a pulse.

'Harry,' she said, 'I'm going to call the police. From his terrible colour, I don't think there's much we can do for him.'

Harry gave a long slow breath. 'You're right. He's very cold too. From the number of empties lying here on the ground, perhaps he drank himself to death?'

Belinda leaned in closer to Harry. It seemed to have upset him. She doubted it was another dead body – he had seen plenty of those in thirty years as a police officer. No, this was something to do with the home brew Harry had consumed and his fear that someone was trying to bump him off as well.

With a gentle touch to his arm, she said, 'Going by the volume of glasses and bottles, I'd say he had some help. It doesn't seem likely that he drank all of this by himself until it was too late to stop. We need to find out who plied him with drink before they hurt someone else.'

'Who on earth are you?' thundered a voice behind them.

Belinda screamed and Harry jumped up, knocking the table next to John's body over. Beer poured all over the floor.

NINETEEN

'Are you trying to frighten us to death?' said Harry, wondering why neither he nor Belinda had heard the approaching stranger.

'Me?' said the man of eighty years or so, dressed in brown moleskin trousers, white shirt and a tweed jacket. 'You, young sir, are more likely to have scared the living daylights out of me, rather than the other way around,' he went on, peering intently at the pair of them, and then looking at the body in the chair. 'Good grief, he's dead. What have you done to him?'

'Us?' said Harry, as he helped Belinda to her feet. 'Don't touch him, or the rest of the bottles or the other, well, stuff.'

'What's the matter with you?' said the octogenarian. 'Are you a bit slow? It goes without saying that I'm not going to touch him. John's clearly past the kiss of life.' He gave them both a suspicious look. 'I suppose you're both off the hook as I saw you arrive a couple of minutes ago and thought to myself, *now, what can this young lady and her stooge be up to in my neighbour's house?*'

'Oh, you're a neighbour,' said Harry.

'Of course I'm a neighbour! Have you called the police? And by the way, it's not "other stuff", it's a potential crime scene.' He gave the rest of the room a once-over and said, 'It doesn't seem like anything's been taken, not from in here, anyway.'

'We were just about to call the police and then you arrived,' said Harry.

'I'm Belinda Penshurst,' said Belinda, 'and this is my friend, Harry Powell.'

'Penshurst, as in the castle folk?' said the man. 'I know some of your family, but it would be difficult not to living round here. Are you the one who disappeared abroad for years?'

'And you are?' said Belinda, hand thrust forward. Harry knew this wasn't the time, but Belinda seemed to want to get him off the topic of her wanderlust.

'Sorry, sorry, where are my manners? My name is Donald Faraday and I live at Sunny Bank, the house opposite poor John.'

'I recognise your name,' said Belinda. 'My father's spoken about you several times, but I've never had the pleasure.'

'Give my regards to the old boy when you see him.' Donald gave Belinda's hand a brief shake and then turned his attention to Harry. 'I hope you're going to tell the police that it was you who knocked the table over and spilled beer everywhere.'

'I wouldn't dream of doing anything else,' said Harry, gathering himself to his full height. 'I was a detective inspector before I retired earlier this year.'

'Then you should have known better,' said Donald, with a shake of his head. 'I'll give them a call now.'

He wandered in the direction of the kitchen to call 999 from his mobile, a phone that Harry couldn't fail to notice was somewhat more modern than his own.

Harry opened his mouth to say something but was interrupted by Donald shouting, 'And don't tread beer all over the carpet. There may be fibres or footprints and we don't want your size tens – oh, yes, police, please.'

'As I was about to say,' said Harry, flicker of annoyance on his face as he listened to Donald's vociferous instructions to the police operator, 'if he saw us arrive, there's a good chance he saw anyone else who's been here recently.'

'Agreed,' said Belinda. 'My money's on poor old John having

snuffed it last night after unwittingly drinking poison. That's if these empties are anything to go on.'

'Someone seems to have made it look like a social gathering. Or else it's the same person who murdered Sadie plying John with poisoned beer.' Harry tried his best to take everything in during the short time he had before the police arrived and took over. Dead body aside, nothing seemed out of place, assuming he'd spent a night drinking with friends. There were seven bottles, five empty and the other two half full, three dirty wine glasses and three used beer glasses. It gave the impression that two other people had been in John's living room but had left their beverages unfinished when they decided to call it a night.

'None of these bottles have labels on them,' remarked Belinda. 'Is someone in the home brew group behind Sadie's death and covering their tracks or are they now the target?'

'It could be either,' said Harry. 'I'd say that a second death – presumably poisoning – points towards Sadie's death being connected to what's happening now, rather than something lurking in her past.'

'Do you think someone sat here and watched him drink the poisoned wine?' said Belinda with a shudder.

'I'd say so, yes,' said Harry. 'Some of the bottles are empty, two aren't.'

'To be fair, H, two are only empty because—'

'Because this clumsy clown knocked the table over,' said Donald, as he stomped back into the living room.

'Only because you sneaked in behind us and—'

Belinda stepped between them and, with a placatory palm outstretched, said, 'I think the best thing we can do is to wait for the police, rather than try to second guess, or blame one another for anything that's happened before we know all of the facts.'

'Hear, hear!' said Donald.

'That's what I was going to say,' said Harry, with a touch more of a sulky tone than he would have liked.

'Perhaps we should wait outside,' said Belinda, taking a quick peek over at John's lifeless face, his open eyes and his head resting at an unnatural angle against the high-backed armchair.

'That's a marvellous idea,' said Donald.

'We should wait here,' said Harry. 'Now we've found him, we shouldn't leave him. I'll stay, you two go outside if you're feeling a bit queasy.'

'Nothing of the sort,' said Donald.

'I'm doing all right, thanks all the same,' said Belinda.

'OK then,' said Harry. 'Donald, who's been in John's house in the last day or so?'

Donald crossed his arms and rocked backwards and forwards slowly. 'That postwoman, Daisy, was here Saturday morning, dropping off some post.'

'She was here as a postwoman?' said Harry.

This earned him a withering look from Donald. 'Yes, man, or else why would I have said "that postwoman"?'

'You weren't clear,' said Harry, 'you really should have explained better.'

'You didn't give me a chance,' said Donald, raising his magnificent bushy eyebrows.

'Who else was here?' said Belinda.

Harry couldn't fail to notice that Donald responded more favourably to her.

'Who else, indeed?' he said, uncrossing his arms. 'Let me think.' He tilted his head back and inspected an invisible spot on the ceiling. 'The home brew group was here last night, without a doubt.'

'We guessed that much,' said Harry.

'And yet you still asked? Interesting, interesting.' Donald took a step towards the large bay window. 'The police are here.'

Harry was mildly interested to see Donald push the sleeve of his tweed jacket up and check the time on his gold wristwatch. He would have been less surprised to see Donald pull out a pocket watch, but then Harry supposed that would have meant limited space for his dapper pink pocket square. It was all quite charming.

Donald muttered something that sounded like, 'Not bad even for these county mounties,' and marched to the front door, unlocking it and pulling it wide open.

'He should have gone out through the kitchen door,' said Harry, more to himself than Belinda, who was busy staring out of the window at the officers getting out of their cars.

'How lucky is this?' she said to Harry, as she smoothed down her skirt and ran a hand over her hair. 'It's only PC Green.'

'He's going to love this one,' said Harry, trudging after Belinda. It was only a matter of time before PC Green's suspicions turned towards the two people who continually stumbled across the bodies.

TWENTY

'Belinda Penshurst and Harry Powell,' said PC Vince Green, dressed in an even sharper suit than the one he had been wearing on Saturday. 'I thought that yesterday was a quiet day, what with the lack of corpses turning up.'

Belinda thought about commenting, but unusually for her, decided against it. She was feeling curious as to how Harry and Donald were going to thrash this one out. Sooner or later, she knew she would have to intervene in the clumsy dance of the testosterone-fuelled donkeys – especially given Harry's sombre mood – but it would be amusing in the meantime.

Several officers, both uniformed and plain clothes, filed either side of PC Green as he stood on the driveway talking to the witnesses. 'And who might you be, sir?'

'Donald Faraday. I live over there at Sunny Bank. I saw this pair, here, knock on the door and disappear round the side. I hadn't seen John – that's the homeowner, poor old John Farthing – this morning. Just to be on the safe side, I came over to see what was up and found these two standing over the body.'

'Pardon?' said PC Green.

'Sorry?' said Belinda and Harry in unison.

'He was dead, quite dead, I'm sure, before this brace of trespassers stumbled their way in.' He paused to lean towards PC Green, although he made no attempt to keep the volume down. 'The taller one claims to have been a police officer, some sort of detective, but I have my doubts. He knocked a table over and the beer's now soaked into the carpet. Criminal. Anyway, I'll leave it to you now. Off you go.'

Donald stood aside to allow room for the many officers and staff who were busy cordoning off the crime scene.

'You three,' called PC Green, as they made to move away. 'Don't go too far; I still need to talk to you.'

Harry opened his mouth to speak but was interrupted by Donald who bellowed, 'No problem, officer. We'll be at Sunny Bank with the kettle on for you and your colleagues.'

Belinda was alive to Harry's growing annoyance at Donald taking charge of the conversation, when it should naturally have been the retired detective inspector. 'Are you OK?' she whispered as they crossed to the other side of the cul-de-sac, keeping up with Donald's brisk stroll.

'Yes, thanks. Any reason I shouldn't be?'

'No, not at all. I was—'

'Come on, you two,' Donald called. He had opened the front door to an immaculate two-storey house, pink roses climbing up each side of the porch and along the top of the windows.

He disappeared inside, followed by Belinda and Harry.

'I guess he's hardly likely to try to kill us with half of the constabulary outside,' said Harry in Belinda's ear.

She put a finger up to her lips, which were breaking into a smile.

'So,' said Donald, coming to a stop in the long hallway. He clapped his hands together with ill-disguised excitement. 'Tea? Coffee? Lemonade?'

'Er, do you want me to shut the front door?' said Harry.

'No, don't bother with that, man,' said Donald. 'Nothing ever happens around here anyway.'

'Your neighbour's just been murdered,' said Harry.

'Perhaps his heart gave out,' said Donald, peering towards John's house where more police had arrived, along with the paramedics.

For a few seconds, he stood watching the comings and goings.

'I've lived here almost my entire life,' he continued, 'and the last time I saw this many people in the street was when the king died.'

'Elvis?' said Harry.

'No, King George VI. What is the matter with you?'

Still shaking his head, Donald went off to the kitchen, leaving Belinda silently trembling with laughter, trying her best not to antagonise Harry further. He really did amuse her.

Harry mouthed 'What?' at her which made her giggle more uncontrollably.

'Perhaps the young lady would like a brandy,' called Donald from the kitchen. 'You know, for shock?'

'No, no, I'm fine, but thank you,' she said. 'I take it you've lived here a very long time.'

'Yes,' he said over the noise of the kettle boiling. 'This used to be my parents' house, who inherited it from my grandparents. I like the area, so I stayed. The house has been renovated so many times, it's almost a new build.'

Donald edged back to where they both stood awkwardly in the hallway. 'Where are my manners? Come and sit down while we wait for the plod. Isn't that what you're called?' He aimed the last remark at Harry.

'Not since the eighties,' said Harry.

'What are you saying?' said Donald as he rattled teacups and saucers from a large white modern dresser. The entire back of the kitchen was fitted with bi-folding doors, opening to a pristine garden bursting with plants. The kitchen seemed to be a fairly new installation, with the sink on an island in the centre of the room. 'What was that about the eighties?'

'This is quite some kitchen,' said Harry, ignoring the question.

'One of my sons – the one who's not a scientist – is a builder,' said Donald, smiling for the first time since he had scared the life out of Harry over John's corpse. 'He insisted it needed an upgrade about five years ago and took care of this for me.'

'That's quite some son,' said Belinda, taking her time to appreciate the room. 'Are you here on your own? If you don't mind me asking.'

Donald paused, teapot in hand. Worrying that she had said something to upset him, Belinda was about to apologise when he set the teapot on the large round wooden table and said, 'Yes, I am. Sadly, I lost the perfumed dictator some years ago. Remarkable woman, and I'm beside myself without her. Still, she wouldn't have wanted me to mope around, so I get on with life. The life I have without her, anyway.'

He turned his back on them as he got the cups, sugar and milk together, giving Harry an opportunity to pull a face at Belinda and her to shrug in a 'how was I to know?' way.

'Sit down, sit down,' said Donald. 'Let's have some tea. Most things are better after a cup of tea.'

A few minutes later, Donald had given them a slightly more detailed outline of his life. Belinda was amazed to learn that he had never been in the military or armed forces of any kind. He had a background in working for the government that he skirted round. She got the impression that there were things about his past he wasn't going to share.

'Donald,' said Belinda, when enough time had elapsed for her to broach their grim discovery again, 'before the police get here, is there anything else you can tell us about John and any visitors he had? You said that the home brew group were here, but exactly who was at his house last night?'

'After they'd all gone home, Daisy, the postwoman, she came back.'

'When you say, she came back,' said Harry, 'do you mean as a part of the home brew group or otherwise?'

'She came back a second time on her own,' said Donald. 'She was here the first time with that Richard Duke fella – not a real duke, you know.' He shook his head as if this were the worst news imaginable.

'Daisy's not really a flower,' said Harry, the start of a laugh dying as quickly as the joke. 'Tough crowd.'

'You could do better than him,' said Donald to Belinda, nodding at Harry.

'We're not a couple,' said Belinda, instantly feeling disloyal. 'We're business associates.'

Why on earth she said that, Belinda failed to fathom. Harry was so much more than a colleague, and she would like him to be in her life in other ways. Her clumsy words this morning certainly weren't going to help that along.

Aware that their time unchaperoned by PC Green was close to its end, Belinda hoped she could build bridges with Harry afterwards. For now, she had to plough on.

'Did you notice anything strange about the time they arrived or left, or anything at all?' she said.

'Can't say that I did.' Donald sat back in his chair, arms folded across his chest. 'Their get-togethers are usually alternate Mondays but I suppose they changed it as today's a bank holiday. They go to John's mostly, sometimes to the pretend duke's place. The postwoman only has a flat with no room to store the stuff, so John once told me. I'm going to miss that cantankerous old—'

'Hello,' shouted PC Green from the doorway.

'Anything else?' said Belinda. 'Please.'

'Daisy has a distinct walk.' Donald sat upright. 'I would have known it anywhere after all the years she's delivered my mail. She came back very late last night, but I assumed she'd forgotten something. I saw her disappear around the side with some bottles and when she came out some time later, she was empty-handed.'

'Mr Faraday,' said PC Green, who had taken it upon himself to locate his witnesses in the kitchen. 'I'm going to have to stop the three of you from talking until we've got statements.'

'Absolutely, no problem,' said Harry.

'Whatever you need, officer,' said Donald.

'Can we have five more minutes?' said Belinda.

'No, you can't,' said PC Green. 'After all of the murders you keep finding yourself involved in, Ms Penshurst, you should know the drill by now.'

'Aha,' said Belinda, 'so this is a murder too?'

'I never said he was poisoned like Sadie Oppenshaw,' said PC Green, turning the colour of a beetroot when he realised what he had said.

'Aha,' Belinda repeated.

'Good grief, officer,' said Donald. 'You've the breaking strain of a KitKat. Work in Intelligence much?'

Even Harry found that funny.

'OK, I'm really going to have to ask you to sit in separate rooms,' said PC Green, trying to puff himself up to full single-breasted jacket size. 'Ms Penshurst, how about the living room? Mr Powell, the police car.'

Dutifully, Harry stood up and walked outside.

Belinda, with much more reluctance, pushed her chair out and allowed herself to be shown to the sofa in the next room.

TWENTY-ONE

When the police had at last finished asking them endless questions, Harry and Belinda walked outside into the afternoon sunshine and headed across the road to Harry's Audi.

'At least they're letting us leave the crime scene,' said Harry when they were both in the car. 'There's something positive, even if we can't get any further information out of Donald right now. He'd be our best bet.'

'Who do you suggest we try to see before the police get to them? Daisy Thornton or Richard Duke?'

Harry considered her suggestion: he really should leave this to the police, only he knew how much it meant to Belinda. The horror of murder should never be used to his advantage, but once Ivan was back in her life, Harry might never have the chance to spend so much time with her.

'What?' said Belinda. 'Is it a bee?'

They both smiled as she waved her hands around her head in an exaggerated fashion.

'I think we should find Daisy and ask her why she went back there late last night,' said Harry. 'Once we've spoken to her, we can ask Richard what was behind the row they had on Saturday and whether it was to do with the prawn debacle Peggy Abnett told us about.'

'We need to explore the possibility that one of the home brew group resealed the poisoned bottle that killed Sadie,' said Belinda.

'Perhaps Richard or Daisy are now covering their tracks by killing off anyone who knew what they were up to,' said Harry, worried about what they might be walking into.

'Also, we shouldn't overlook that it could be someone else entirely, trying to wipe them all out for some other reason,' said Belinda.

'Good point. If they were on the cusp of releasing their wine and beer and making their fortunes, possibly we're miles away from the truth.'

This was a sobering thought.

'You know,' said Harry, engine idling, 'one possibility is that Richard and Daisy were looking to increase their profit margins.'

'Splitting the profits between two instead of three would make murder a little more lucrative,' said Belinda. 'We know that Richard genuinely did collapse, rather than fake it. However, perhaps it was nerves and he's right back at the top of our whiteboard's Most Wanted.'

'Sadie's death might have been a way to throw the police off course,' said Harry.

Belinda shuddered. 'The thought that she was collateral damage is even worse than her being an intended victim, surely?'

'We'll see what Daisy's prepared to tell us,' said Harry, pulling away from the kerb.

Belinda opened the car window and waggled her fingers at PC Green.

Ordinarily, Harry would have told Belinda not to wind the officer up, only he didn't get the chance. PC Green stepped out into the road.

'Just when we were home and dry,' muttered Harry, with more volume than he'd intended. He slowed down to allow the police officer to talk to them through the open window.

'I trust that in the five minutes you had alone with Mr Faraday, he didn't tell you two anything about any of the other witnesses,' Vince Green said, casually leaning against Harry's car.

'Er, no, no, he didn't,' said Harry.

'Glad to hear it. Bye, both of you.' PC Green stood back from the car and watched them as Harry pulled out of the close, indicating left towards the village.

'That was close,' said Harry.

'Yes, I know,' said Belinda. 'I don't think that PC Green's warming to us. Are you thinking what I'm thinking? We should definitely go and see Daisy next.'

Harry headed in the direction of the small block of flats where Daisy had a top-floor apartment.

'Any news from your brother?' said Harry as he navigated a bend in the road, a tractor travelling from the other direction making him raise his voice.

'Not for a bit,' she said. 'Why do you ask?'

'No particular reason,' said Harry. 'I thought that a sideline in selling home brew might be right up his street, that was all.'

Belinda let out a long, slow sigh.

Harry glanced over at her and said, 'Want to talk about it?'

Now he'd come to think about it, Belinda had dark rings under her eyes and he was sure she had been chewing her bottom lip.

'There's not much to talk about really, H. He's off on one of his get-rich-quick schemes that normally end up with a financial loss for the Penshurst family. You know – the usual.'

As Harry drove into the small residents' car park, he sought out the first space he could find and then put his hand on hers.

Momentarily surprised by his touch, Belinda stared at him, unblinking, unmoving. For the shortest time, they locked gazes, his hand still on hers. Harry drank in the deep colour of her eyes and the tiredness etched on her face.

He opened his mouth to speak when a banging on the window made them both jump.

'You can't park there,' said Daisy, fist still up against Harry's window. 'That bay's for Darren at number six. He'll be home any minute.'

'You gave us a fright,' said Harry, opening the door to get out and speak to her.

'What are you doing here?' said Daisy, eyes narrowing. She was dressed in her Royal Mail shirt and shorts, and a pair of Timberland boots that had walked most of the postcode area. Her blond hair was forced into a clip that was refusing to cooperate.

'Are the police already here?' called Belinda from across the car roof, using a little less tact than Harry would have liked.

Daisy clutched the front of her blue shirt. 'The police? No, why? What's happened?'

'You've gone very pale,' said Harry, noticing she was wearing her uniform on a bank holiday. 'Something you want to tell us?'

He stepped closer to her. Nothing stirred in the car park other than a solitary ginger cat that wandered by and gave them the feline glare of contempt. The parking area was tucked back from the main road, and as there was not so much as a corner shop or bus stop nearby, the sound of any traffic approaching was easily apparent. The nearby parked cars were empty of people and only one or two of the flats had their windows open. Daisy, however, appeared to be on full alert, as if Harry and Belinda were about to snare her.

'I – I don't have anything I want to say, thank you,' she said. 'I was waiting on someone and when I saw you drive into my neighbour's space, I thought I'd do the decent thing and ask you to move, that's all.'

'So, why, when I mentioned the police, did your face turn paler than the bride of Frankenstein's best wedding frock?' said Harry.

'Because no one wants the police knocking, that's why,' said Daisy.

'Harry,' said Belinda, 'I can hear a car coming.'

'If I'm not mistaken, Daisy, that's the distinctive sound of a well-loved diesel engine with over 100,000 miles on the clock, or

CID, as we like to call them,' said Harry. 'I'll ask you again – is there something you want to tell us?'

'Why should I tell you anything?' she said, standing firm.

'Because we may believe you, whereas the police are most likely to arrest you,' said Belinda.

'She's right,' said Harry. 'I used to investigate murders for a living – thirty years of professionalism behind me – and, if I do say so myself, Belinda and I make a very good pair of amateur sleuths.'

'You had to get that in, didn't you?' said Belinda, toe of her Valentino tapping on the tarmac.

'It adds flair.'

'When you two have quite finished,' said Daisy. 'If you want to know about last night, I met Richard here. His wife drove us to John's house so we could both have a drink, and she came back and picked us up about ten o'clock. That's all there is to it.'

'So when you left, he was still alive?' said Belinda.

'What?' Daisy said. 'Who? Of course Richard was still alive. His wife drove us – oh, wait a minute. You're talking about John. What's happened to John?'

Harry had to hand it to her – she looked horrified.

'You tell us,' said Harry as the sound of a car pulling into the entrance made the hairs on the back of his neck stand up. He knew the police were about to descend and more importantly, he knew he shouldn't be speaking to a witness in a murder investigation. But right now, finding out who was responsible seemed more important than anything else.

A car door slammed and PC Green's weary voice called out, 'Not you two again!'

'John was fine when I left, I swear,' said Daisy. 'You have to believe me. How did he die?'

Any answer Harry or Belinda might have given was lost in the melee of the second police car arriving and its occupants reaching them.

Two uniformed officers flanked Daisy. PC Green stood to one

side of them, and a woman in plain clothes stood on the other, like detective bookends.

'I know I won't get a straight answer,' said PC Green, 'but what are you doing here?'

'Us?' said Harry, moving his index finger between him and Belinda.

'Yes,' said PC Green.

'We got our post nice and early today,' said Harry, 'so we thought we'd say thank you to Daisy. We know how seriously she takes her job.'

PC Green looked skyward. 'Arrest her for John Farthing's murder and put her in the car,' he said to the two uniformed officers.

He watched as they took a bewildered Daisy towards the police car, then turned back to Harry. 'You must think I've just fallen out of the Christmas tree. No one's stupid enough to be taken in by a blatant lie about early post on bank holiday Monday. Take this as your final warning.'

He looked at them both and added, 'For your own sakes.'

TWENTY-TWO

'Next port of call – Richard Duke.' Belinda gave Harry her best smile. It didn't seem to be working today: Harry's face clouded over.

'Really, Belinda. I think we should do as Vincent of Dock Green asks and stay away from this for a bit.'

'Firstly, H, you're showing your age there, and secondly, you've told me how long it takes to book a prisoner in, let alone interview them for murder. Therefore, PC Green is hardly likely to show up at Richard's house in the next half hour, is he?'

For less than a second, she thought that Harry's resolve was about to crack. Then he said, 'No, there'll be another patrol on their way there now. At the very least, they'll be asking him questions. I can only assume that Daisy was arrested because Donald told them he'd seen her return last night.'

'But why would she go back?' said Belinda. 'That doesn't make any sense. If it was poison, she could have slipped it into John's drink and then left.'

Harry mulled this over for a moment or two. 'You know what would make me think more clearly about all this?'

'Let me guess,' said Belinda. 'Would it be food by any chance?'

He rubbed his hands together with glee. 'I know a clifftop café in Capel le Ferne. You'll love it. The sea views are amazing.'

'Come on then,' she sighed.

It took Harry half an hour to drive to the café, which turned out to be most definitely closed. The door was shut and the place was deserted. They sat at one of the empty tables outside, a cool sea breeze reducing the temperature by several degrees.

'I thought it was bound to be open on a bank holiday,' he said, misery finding a home in every syllable.

'Never mind. We can find somewhere else.'

'Suppose so,' he said, as if this was the most depressing news he had ever heard.

Belinda had hoped to use the time to broach the subject of his job. Ordinarily, she would have thought that was what was niggling at Harry. There was nothing wrong with selling dog food, not at all. In fact, she ordered her own pet's tuck from him. But it simply didn't seem to suit Harry. At times, he gave her the impression that he lacked purpose, and this wasn't enough for him. Only now, she was worried it was more to do with his ex-girlfriend. Perhaps she was about to put in an appearance in Little Challham? It was a conversation she was summoning the courage to have. Her fear was, she might not like the answer. Maybe she was better off not knowing.

'The view is spectacular,' she said, more for something neutral to say than anything else.

'On a clear day like today,' said Harry, 'you can see straight across to the burger van miles over there. That looks shut too.'

'Can we stop talking about food? Please.' Belinda turned her attention away from the continent in the distance, sunlight glinting off the top of the silver burger van catching her eye.

'You're right,' he said, giving her his full attention, 'I'm sorry. We should talk murder and wine. Not forgetting the home brew.'

Belinda's nerve failed her; it would wait for another time.

'So far,' she said, getting down to business, 'we've got Sadie being poisoned at the wine tasting, possibly by someone who broke into the barn, plus Richard Duke collapsing, and we're taking that as genuine heat exhaustion.'

'Or even that he over-exerted himself by stampeding at the cheese goods.'

'I hadn't forgotten.' She gave his arm a squeeze. 'And then we have John Farthing, probably poisoned by the same person who killed Sadie, dead the morning after his home brew group met at his place.'

'And the group consists of John, Daisy and Richard Duke,' said Harry. 'The only connection we can see at the moment between Sadie and the home brew group – other than the poisonings, obviously – is the chance that she was in some way a threat to them.'

'That works if it was Daisy or Richard who used their rebottling skills to kill Sadie,' said Belinda. 'And now they're covering their tracks.'

'Daisy looked genuinely terrified,' said Harry. 'That takes us back to Richard.'

'And from what PC Green told us, the police are already on their way to pick him up,' said Belinda. 'Rather an anti-climax, but at least it's all over.'

'Richard had the capability to poison the wine and reseal it,' said Harry. 'He seemed genuinely surprised to see Sadie on Saturday, but I guess he fooled us.'

'He couldn't have got through the hole in the barn wall,' said Belinda. 'He either had an accomplice or it was a red herring.'

'At least Steve Parry's in the clear,' said Harry. 'As angry as he was at the demise of his brother's café, there's no connection between him and the home brew group.'

They sat in companionable silence, their attention drawn to the sounds of a plane dragging across the wide, blue sky.

'If this really is all over, I might get away for a bit,' said Harry. 'Change of scenery.'

'Oh?' said Belinda, eyes following the trail the plane churned out into the atmosphere. 'Anywhere in particular?'

'I'll give it some more thought, but I've somewhere in mind.'

Belinda feared her time with Harry was drawing to a close.

'Come on,' she said, standing up. 'We can't possibly get this close to the seaside and not have fish and chips. My treat.'

'Now you're talking,' said Harry, moving at an alarming speed towards his car.

They headed towards Dover seafront, Harry managing to find a parking space surprisingly easily on a bank holiday afternoon. Several bars were open and a large number of pubs, with all-day drinkers taking advantage of the pleasant weather and the patios and balconies.

They made their way along Marine Parade, ambling towards the marina, seagulls screeching above their heads and the grey, angry sea swirling the other side of the wall.

'Good place to dump a body,' said Harry. 'Did I ever tell you about the murder I worked on—'

'The Watery Grave,' said Belinda.

'Well, I suppose that's one way of putting it,' said Harry as he paused to take a deep lungful of salty sea air.

'No,' said Belinda. 'Not that. This. This pub is the Watery Grave, the one Frank used to run, before he took over the Dog and Duck.'

'Come on,' said Harry, absentmindedly patting his stomach, 'it wouldn't hurt to drop in.'

Belinda had seen the 'We serve food all day' sign.

They walked into a pleasant enough pub, one that paid homage to all things seafaring: the walls were adorned with sailing paraphernalia and old photos of the seafront, while ships' lanterns and messages in glass bottles dangled from the ceiling.

The place was, by and large, empty. This was fortunate as

Harry failed to keep the volume down as he said, 'I haven't seen this much old tat since I last did a boot fair.'

'Shush,' said Belinda, watching the young barmaid's face. Barely old enough to serve alcohol – yet at an age where nose and lip piercings were encouraged – she didn't react as if she had taken offence at Harry's insult. In fact, she hardly glanced up from her phone as they walked across the mostly empty room. An elderly couple were sitting at the table closest to the door on the right-hand side. They smiled and nodded hello and then went back to their hushed conversation and glasses of orange juice.

By now, the short walk had taken them to the counter. The barmaid put her mobile phone in the front pocket of her denim dungarees and peered out at them from under her blond fringe, an immaculate shiny bob framing her round face.

'Afternoon,' she said, her eyes softening, even if the rest of her features didn't fancy joining in. 'What can I get you?'

'A tonic water for me, please,' said Belinda.

'A half of bitter, please,' said Harry. 'And is there any chance of a couple of cod and chips?'

'Not a problem at all,' said their server, who poured the drinks, put the food order through and presented them with a bill in less time than it took Belinda to find her bank card and scan the tables for the one with the least sticky residue.

They sat side by side, so both could soak up the ambience of two pensioners eating out of a packet of peanuts.

'Those two have brought their own snacks,' said Harry. 'See. They're supermarket own.'

'What are we now? The nut police?' said Belinda. 'And keep your voice down, they'll hear us.'

'They can't hear us over the rustling,' said Harry. 'Ah, great, here comes the fish and chips. That was quick.'

'Yes, it was, wasn't it?' said Belinda with a bad feeling, one she hoped didn't manifest itself as an actual physical one.

While Harry chowed down with genuine excitement, Belinda

picked at her own food. The chips were pleasant enough, but the fish was a touch too off-white for her liking and possibly had been lurking at the back of the pub's freezer for longer than it really should have.

'This isn't bad, is it?' said Harry, face full of glee and mouth full of cod.

'Bad is one word,' said Belinda, chasing a piece of crisp batter across her plate. 'I doubt this is the sort of thing Sadie served in the Fish by the Sea.'

'No, it wasn't,' said the woman on the next table.

Startled, Belinda glanced over, and even Harry paused mid chew. The couple were late-sixties, early-seventies, with short grey hair, black-framed glasses and dressed in brown trousers and light blue rain jackets. They could have been a couple who had morphed into almost identical versions of each other over the years, or siblings with the same dress sense. It was hard to tell.

'I'm sorry, what was that?' said Belinda.

'I said that the Fish by the Sea served much better quality food, but it is a pub,' said the woman.

'You used to eat there?' said Harry, setting his knife and fork down.

'Oh, yes,' said her husband/male clone. 'We ate in there often, even worked there for a short while.'

'You did?' Belinda was hardly able to contain her excitement.

'It was a short time too,' said the woman. 'Sadie, she was the manager, sacked us within the week.'

'So you weren't fond of her?' said Belinda, wondering if they had inadvertently stumbled across more suspects, just when they thought the case was closed.

'No, we got on fine, didn't we, Malcolm?' she said. 'The problem was us – we were utterly useless.'

'Sheila here only went and dropped an entire trifle,' said Malcolm.

'And Malcolm caused a power surge that shorted out the electrics!' said Sheila.

They both shrieked with laughter.

'Well, the ovens went off, the lights went out and the fridge was on some sort of time-lock, so Chef couldn't get anything else out for over an hour,' said Malcolm.

Sheila pulled a small plastic bottle from her pocket. She poured a generous amount into both hers and Malcolm's glasses.

'The orange juice here is a touch on the strong side, you see,' said Malcolm when he saw Belinda and Harry looking. 'We like to water it down.'

'And the nuts?' said Harry. 'Or do you pay corkage?'

'They turn a blind eye in here due to my allergy,' said Malcolm.

'What to?' said Harry. 'Nuts?'

'When did you last see Sadie?' said Belinda, desperate to get back on her agenda.

'Quite a few years ago now,' said Malcolm, who looked at Sheila for confirmation, delivered with a nod. 'We stopped working for her – we had to after she fired us – and ate in the restaurant a handful more times before it closed.'

Sheila drained her glass and set it down.

'We'll get you another two orange juices, won't we, Harry?' said Belinda, nudging his foot.

'Oh, yes, that's not a problem,' said Harry, easing himself off the hard wooden chair.

'May as well stick a vodka in each of them as it's a bank holiday,' said Malcolm, pushing the empties across the table.

Harry huffed, but went and got another round in, listening from the bar as Belinda tried to glean more information about the former restaurateur, food critic and wine buff.

'Was there anyone around here she was particularly close to?' said Belinda, trying to concentrate.

The couple looked at one another and both shook their heads.

'She was a bit of a loner,' said Malcolm. 'The only one I used to see her talking to outside hours was that young waiter – so much so, I used to wonder if there was something going on between the two of them, if you know what I mean? What was his name?'

'Bill?' said Sheila.

'No, that wasn't it,' said Malcolm. 'Burt, Bob.'

Harry almost dropped his change as the barmaid yelled across the pub, 'It was Ben, Grandad.'

'Grandad?' said Harry, attempting to identify the family resemblance.

'Thanks, Jenga,' said Malcolm.

'They're my grandparents,' said Jenga.

'Am I in the Twilight Zone?' said Harry.

'Come and sit down, H,' said Belinda, not wanting Harry to upset things now they were getting somewhere.

'You were talking about Ben,' she went on, doing her best to ignore Harry, his chair creaking as he sat back down, drinks safely delivered.

'Yes, we called him young Ben, but of course, he was probably in his late twenties or even early thirties,' said Sheila. 'He was a good waiter, worked his way up to head waiter and was about to take the front of house when he and Sadie had a bit of a falling out.'

'Go on,' said Harry, after Malcolm paused and shot his wife a glare.

'Ought we?' said Malcolm. 'We don't like to gossip.'

'Would it help if I told you that Sadie was dead?' said Harry.

Gasps came from Malcolm and Sheila. 'She's not?' said Sheila. 'I've gone all cold. How did it happen?'

'The police are looking into it,' said Belinda before Harry could respond. For an ex- detective inspector, he was showing little in the way of compassion. 'Where was her restaurant?'

'It's a Starbucks now,' said Jenga, still tapping away on her iPhone. 'I use it all the time.'

'Sadie was only too glad to sell up in the end,' said Malcolm. 'I remember how pleased she was to be moving on. She told us she did well out of it financially, it allowed her a new lease of life.'

'I wonder if young Ben knows about Sadie,' said Sheila to Malcolm, scrunching up the nut bag out of sheer angst.

'Let's not worry ourselves about that, my love,' he said, putting his hand over hers, which mercifully stopped the sound. 'I expect he does.'

'He does, he does,' said Harry.

'He had that lovely young son too,' said Sheila. 'He used to help out with the washing up at the Fish sometimes. I've got no chance of remembering his name.'

'It was Greg,' said Jenga, and then immediately looked as though she wished she hadn't.

'Aw. I'd forgotten how great you two used to get along,' said Sheila, playing the role of embarrassing nan. 'You'd come to the restaurant and wait at the kitchen door until he came out with two cans of Lilt and sat on the steps with you. It was so sweet.'

'Leave it, Nan,' said Jenga, disappearing further under her fringe.

The door opened and three fifty-something men walked in, talking nineteen to the dozen and greeting Jenga as if she had the elixir of life – or at least the ability to serve them alcoholic drinks.

'Anything else that you can tell us about Sadie or Ben?' said Belinda, raising her voice to make herself heard over the newcomers, and craning to hear their reply.

The couple exchanged another look and Sheila said, 'Nothing in particular. Ben never did anything daft like drop the dessert or short the electrics, but he seemed to have a close relationship with her. They were often chatting together before or after work. He left for another job, and it really didn't go down very well with Sadie. That was why they fell out in the end. Sadie thought he'd let her down and told him so.'

'That's right,' said Malcolm, casting annoyed glances at the men at the bar who were getting louder and louder as they placed their order. 'Sheila and I'll be off in a minute. We always call it a day when it gets this packed.'

'What happened when Ben said he was leaving?' said Harry, leaning across the table.

'Sadie shouted a bit and said he'd never make a go of it on his own,' said Sheila. 'She said his idea of opening a vineyard in Kent was daft. No one would be prepared to pay three times the price for English wines as they would French or Italian. It was all a fad, would never catch on, it wasn't something she would ever sell in her award-winning restaurant, that sort of thing. It was quite the carry-on, wasn't it, Malc?'

A huge roar of laughter went up from the bar, followed by much back-slapping. The door opened and a fourth man came in to join them.

'That's it,' said Sheila. 'We're off. No idea how Jenga puts up with this.'

'It was nice to meet you,' said Malcolm, getting to his feet and pulling his wife's chair out for her.

'We're here every Monday,' said Sheila, stepping away from the table. 'Perhaps we'll see you again soon.' She leaned closer to Belinda. 'Keep this to yourself, but we have it on good authority that next week's special is scampi and chips in a basket. Ta-ra.'

'Oh, er, ta-ra,' said Belinda. She watched them leave, weirdly jealous of a couple with a shared history and love of cagoules.

The four men had, by now, got their drinks and sat down at the table next to the bar. They had quietened enough to allow Jenga to retrieve her mobile phone from her pocket and give it the full attention it had been lacking for the last five minutes.

'You know what this means, don't you?' said Belinda, inching across in her seat towards Harry.

'That this probably isn't the end of it,' said Harry. 'We need to find out why Ben lied to us about how he knew Sadie and what he knew about the Fish by the Sea.'

'Exactly,' said Belinda, casting her eyes down to the congealed remains of her lunch.

'I'll take these back,' said Harry. 'I'd hate it if Jenga exerted herself too much today.'

He picked up the two plates, one picked clean, the other less so, and carried them to the bar.

'Thanks, Jenga,' he said. 'That meal was absolutely average.'

He pointed at her phone. 'I don't suppose you're reading a book on that thing, are you?'

She looked up long enough to scowl at him.

'Because if you are,' Harry continued, 'and you happen to be reading a Terry Pratchett, I think you've already met your Dover sole-mate.'

Belinda loved it when she and Harry shared a joke.

TWENTY-THREE

Back outside in the late-afternoon sunshine, a breeze picking up across the white-tipped waves, Harry and Belinda stopped to consider their options.

'I can see the Starbucks a few doors down, on the next corner,' said Belinda, peering a little further along the street.

Harry nodded. 'And little point in standing outside it for no reason. From what Malcolm told us, Sadie had no regrets about selling, so that's not going to take us any further forward. We have to speak to Ben again. It's convenient he failed to mention that he used to work for Sadie and they'd had a row about him leaving.'

'Do you think there was more than a working relationship between them?' said Belinda. 'It might explain why he didn't talk to us about it, opening old wounds and suchlike.'

'He'd still have to be pretty miffed to use his own wine to kill her,' said Harry. He tried not to stare at Belinda. Her hair was ruffled by the fresh sea air and her linen dress was full of creases. Between the two tonic waters she had drunk and the little she had eaten, her lip gloss had worn away, leaving her as the natural and striking beauty she was.

He had noticed that she hadn't enjoyed the food and wanted

the chance to tell her his news somewhere less greasy pub grub and more Michelin star.

'What is it?' she said, attempting to smooth her hair down with her hand, despite the strengthening wind. 'Don't tell me that pesky bee's followed us.'

Harry grinned and was about to answer her when his phone bleeped. Shielding the screen from the glare, he unlocked it and read a message that made his stomach tie itself in knots:

Harry, old chap, any chance you're with my sister and can bring her back home pronto? I've something that can't wait. Thanks, M.

'Er, I've an idea,' said Harry, locking his phone and fleetingly allowing himself the idea of ignoring Marcus. 'It's still incredibly warm out here. Why don't we get back to your wine cellar and see what the whiteboard has to say about all of this?'

'Oh, goody,' said Belinda with a certain childish glee, 'a briefing. You know I love a briefing.'

She threaded her arm through his and they walked back to the car.

If Belinda noticed that Harry was quiet on the way back home, she had the good grace not to mention it. He listened to her chat about the coastal road and how infrequently she found the time to visit some of her favourite places by the seaside.

As the impressive sight of Little Challham's castle came into view, Belinda said, 'Would you ever think of moving anywhere outside Kent?'

'What's the rest of the world got that our village hasn't?' said Harry. 'How about you?'

The hesitation was longer than he would have liked; the knot was back in his stomach. Harry held his breath as he drove up to the castle. He was usually keen to admire the glorious views. This time, however, he was intent on trying to see if Marcus's car was already on the driveway.

All Harry needed was a bit more time with Belinda, the chance to form a plan of action to keep her busy for the next few days.

The sinking feeling of despair when they drew closer and Marcus's black Mercedes was parked right next to the main door was like a slap to the face.

There had been time on the thirty-minute drive back when Harry could have mapped out their enquiries. They were still a couple of minutes away from getting out of the car and finding Marcus. He couldn't find the words. When had murders ever left him speechless?

'Harry,' said Belinda. 'You're gripping that steering wheel very tightly. Your knuckles are white.'

'Sorry, Belinda. I was miles away.'

'Unlike my brother, who *is* supposed to be miles away.'

Harry pulled up at the other side of the entrance and sat with the engine idling.

'Aren't you coming in?' said Belinda, one hand on the seatbelt, a puzzled expression on her face. 'You always come in these days. There's bound to be biscuits or snacks of some sort.'

'Not today, thanks,' he said, plastering a meaningless smile on his face.

'You have to come in. He's been to Morocco. Who knows what goodies he's brought back?'

'From Morocco? I can only guess.'

She paused, seemingly reluctant to end the conversation there. 'Please come in and say hello, if nothing else. I'm sure he'd love to see you.'

Harry pushed out his top lip as he considered what to do. The last thing he wanted was to pretend to be enthusiastic at meeting Belinda's ex-boyfriend. On the upside, perhaps Ivan had aged really badly or put on several stone.

'I can see you're about to give in,' said Belinda. 'And besides, if my brother has got himself in another of his daft, crazy business deals, I could do with all the support I can get.'

He pressed the button to switch the engine off. 'Just ten minutes then.'

Harry's discomfort was instantly forgotten when Belinda gave him a smile that illuminated her whole face.

'Come on, H,' she said. 'You only had a half in the pub. Have a beer, at least.'

She nigh on skipped to the front door, then waited for Harry to join her. He took a deep breath and propelled himself through the doors. It was one of the few times that they hadn't gone into the castle via the kitchen door at the side. He could only put it down to Belinda's keenness – or trepidation – to see her brother.

He followed her along the main hallway, past the morning room, library and opulent dining room, out to the rear of the castle to where Marcus was usually to be found after 5 p.m. – the patio.

'Keep up, H!' she said when they reached the double doors leading to the place where they had sat together on many occasions, their conversation easy and fluid. Today, it was destined not to be so casual, what with Harry being very much on edge.

Harry and Belinda stepped onto the patio, the sheer beauty of the view not wasted on Harry, despite how he was feeling. He shifted his attention to the seating area. At first, he thought that his eyes might be playing a trick on him: there was only one person there, waving a bottle of beer at them.

'My two favourite people,' Marcus called at them. 'I've plenty of cold beers over here, come and join me.'

He pushed his sunglasses to the top of his head and then reached across to the silver ice bucket. With one hand, he grabbed two bottles of Peroni by their necks and with the other, a bottle opener. Once the lids were off, he passed them across and said, 'Here's to a wonderful surprise.'

With trepidation, Harry clinked his bottle against his friends' and hoped he didn't let himself down by hating Ivan on sight.

Belinda took a drink and turned her attention to Harry. 'You're going to love this.'

Now Harry's expression really must have given him away.

'How brilliant,' said Marcus, blue eyes twinkling. 'He really had no idea.'

'Had no idea about what?' said Harry.

'The present Marcus has for you,' said Belinda.

'For me?' said Harry, holding the cold bottle up to his forehead. Today was starting to become too much for him.

'Come on,' said Belinda, pushing her chair back. 'Bring your beer. We're only going to step back inside for a moment.'

Still none the wiser as to why the pair of them were so pleased with themselves, Harry did as he was told. Perhaps Marcus had had Ivan embalmed. That would be a turn-up for the books.

'Over here,' said Marcus, 'behind the settee.'

I hope it's not another corpse, thought Harry as he humoured them and stepped to the other side of the sofa.

Everyone looked down at the floor.

It certainly wasn't a dead body, so that was something. It appeared to be a carpet. Harry knew for a fact that he didn't look as pleased as Belinda and Marcus about the big reveal.

'He's speechless!' said Marcus, all dimples and floppy hair.

'He can't even remember telling me he wanted one,' said Belinda, equally as enthused by her floor having carpet.

'Er, when did I tell you what?' said Harry, checking the alcohol content on his beer bottle.

'Well,' said Belinda, 'you know that Marcus has been in Morocco?'

'Yes,' said Harry, now wondering if it was special souk cigarettes of the illegal kind that had affected their brains. It was alarming but would make more sense.

'You once told me that since you'd arrived in Little Challham, one thing you wanted more than anything was a Berber,' said Belinda. 'We recall you admiring the one in the study on a particularly miserable day when we got back from walking Horatio.'

'And it was absolutely not a problem for me to slip away into Casablanca and get you the finest rug in the land,' said Marcus. 'Don't you go thanking me, though. It was all B's idea.'

Harry's lips moved; no words came out.

The merriment on both of their faces meant that he would carry the truth to his grave. The object of his desires hadn't been the Penshurst Berber rug, but Marcus's Barbour jacket.

To make matters worse, Harry was fairly certain he had an allergy to wool.

TWENTY-FOUR

Harry left Belinda with his new gift and drove home. Usually, he would take solace in knowing he was picking her up later to pay Ben Davies another visit. Today, as well as being relieved that Ivan hadn't shown up, his head was full of whether he should bring up the envelope in his kitchen addressed to his ex-girlfriend. He was in little doubt Belinda had seen it and he had spectacularly failed to give her an explanation. Yet still she had bought him an expensive rug, one he now had to pretend to be in raptures over.

The envelope contained nothing more than a set of keys that Hazel had given him a couple of months after they had got together. They had frequently stayed at one another's houses; they had even tentatively spoken of buying a home together. That was until he had rushed in, led by his heart, and asked her to marry him. He couldn't blunder from one relationship to another, especially not with someone he hadn't known for very long. Every sensible part of his being told him that much.

He reached the bottom of the driveway and paused to check for traffic. The sight of Dawn Jones's Ford Fiesta hurtling around the green jolted him from his self-pity. How could he have forgotten Belinda's message that he was supposed to teach young Alicia everything there was to know about being a detective? He'd obviously spare the nine-year-old the parts about getting divorced due to too much time spent at work, never seeing the children once they'd left home and copious amounts of alcohol. So, not *everything* about being a detective.

Hurriedly putting together something a child wouldn't find lame or boring was not something Harry was a dab hand at. He could have asked Belinda's advice but as he had completely forgotten about it, it was too late for that.

By the time he reached the parking area at the back of the Gatehouse, Dawn and Alicia were out of the car and their dog Colonel was sniffing around the cypress trees he was so fond of.

Mother and daughter waved and the Great Dane barked and ran towards him.

'Harry,' shouted Alicia. 'I'm so excited about this.' To demonstrate, she jumped up and down. 'I've worn my camouflage outfit, so I've gone commando.'

Even her mother laughed at that one. 'Alicia, I think you mean you're dressed as a commando.'

'What's the difference?' she asked.

'Let's not worry about it,' said Dawn. 'I'm sure Harry has a lot of fun things planned for the next hour or so?'

'Hour? An hour, that's not a problem,' said Harry. 'I need to grab a couple of things from indoors.'

'I'll be back to pick her up before it gets too late,' said Dawn. 'We might as well make the most of the last few days of the school holidays.'

Harry left them in the garden saying their goodbyes while he rooted through cupboards and drawers, throwing random items into a carrier bag.

Ready at last, Harry came back outside to find Alicia standing by his car door.

'Are we going in the car, Harry?'

'Do you want to go in the car?'

'Yes!'

'That's lucky, because we're driving there.'

'Where are we going?' she asked as they got into his Audi.

'Detective skills can be developed anywhere at all, so do you have a favourite place?'

'Oooh!' Her face lit up as she grinned from ear to ear. 'We once went to EuroDisney and that was amazing.'

'I was thinking of somewhere we could get to, solve a crime and be back within sixty minutes.'

Alicia examined her watch. The lilac wristband was adorned with rainbows and unicorns. *She believes in mythical creatures, this won't be so hard*, thought Harry.

'I suppose that the nature reserve is the best idea,' she said.

'That's perfect.'

The journey only gave Harry so much time to put some ideas together. The kit lying on the back seat in an Aldi's bag wasn't very inspiring either.

'What part of detective work interests you the most?' he said as they pulled into the nature reserve car park.

'What's the thing called where you act sneaky and no one knows you're doing it?' said Alicia.

'Working for a tabloid newspaper and tapping celebrities' phones?'

She screwed up her forehead in concentration. 'No, it's surveying things.'

'Surveillance work,' said Harry, reversing into a parking space.

'That's it. Did you do much of that?'

'Sometimes,' said Harry. It was a tiny fib. By sometimes, he meant never.

'What's in the kit, Harry?'

'Evidence bags, and er... suchlike.' By evidence bags, he meant sandwich bags.

'Wow. Is there a magnifying glass?'

'Yep.'

'This is going to be great.'

They got out of the car, Harry grabbed the bag and they walked towards the footpath.

Once they were a hundred feet or so along the pathway, Harry said, 'How about we go looking in the trees over there?' He pointed to the left-hand side where the undergrowth was at its most dense.

'OK,' said Alicia, running off.

'Don't go too far,' he called, fearful he wouldn't be able to keep up.

'It's all right, I know the place pretty well,' Alicia called as she raced around the nearest hazel tree, briefly out of sight and then back again.

'OK,' said Harry, already feeling worn out, 'the art of surveillance is all about sitting still and keeping quiet.'

He picked a spot set back from the pathway. They could sit and observe anyone walking by without being seen.

'Here,' he said, pointing to a patch of dry, clear ground where they were shielded from view by bushes and shrubs. 'We can wait here and see who comes by.'

Alicia sat down cross-legged with an ease that Harry envied. His own descent was less elegant and what it lacked in speed, it made up for in grunting noises.

'Are you pretending to be a boar, Harry? Only I don't think we have any of those in Little Challham.'

'Let's see what's in the kit, shall we?' Harry pulled out the sandwich bags. 'These are for any evidence that we may find.' He rummaged in the plastic shopping bag and passed her a pair of latex gloves. 'This is so we don't contaminate the evidence.'

'They're a bit big.' Alicia held up her hands. The top of her fingers came to approximately where the knuckles should have been.

They heard someone walking along the path, their feet landing on dry twigs and scuffing stones and leaves announcing their approach.

Harry put a finger to his lips, took a pair of binoculars from the bag and handed them to Alicia. She held them up to her eyes and peered in the direction of whoever was approaching.

While she was busy, Harry took out his phone to make sure that Belinda wasn't trying to contact him. There was no reason that she should be, but it didn't stop him checking his phone. It also gave him a chance to see what the time was. All this had only taken twenty minutes. Perhaps another ten and they could head back.

Out of curiosity, Harry parted the leaves blocking his view to see who Alicia was watching.

The unmistakable pimply face of Greg Davies, son and heir of the Challham Valley Winery, came into view. He was dressed in a black-and-white checked shirt and black jeans and glanced behind him every three or four steps.

'Well, well,' murmured Harry.

Alicia immediately lowered the binoculars and whispered, 'Shush.'

Harry put out his hands in a placatory manner and shrugged. Satisfied, Alicia went back to spying.

Greg went past where Harry and Alicia were sitting and carried on walking about another twenty-five feet or so. He took his mobile phone out of his pocket and tapped away on the screen.

'I've done it,' said Greg to himself. 'She's going to be so impressed with this.'

With that, he put his phone away and walked towards the car park, a bit of a spring in his heels.

'That was fun,' said Alicia. 'Can we go hunting for the evidence now?'

'Exactly what I was thinking,' said Harry, pleased to get his circulation going again.

They packed up their belongings and walked back onto the path and then away from the car park. Alicia was content stopping every now and again and focusing the binoculars on birds in the trees, a squirrel and sometimes things she thought were there but weren't.

'It's probably your imagination,' said Harry, when she thought she saw a goat.

'I can see something shiny this time,' she said, standing on tiptoes and looking into the undergrowth.

Harry checked the time again. They had walked almost to the other side of the nature reserve where it backed onto some houses, their roofs and chimney stacks visible in the distance above the trees.

'We should head back now,' he said.

'But I haven't got to use the magnifying glass.'

'Perhaps another time?' said Harry, inflection almost matching the nine-year-old's for wailing.

She ran forward through the bushes.

'Alicia, we really need to—'

Harry stopped a couple of feet behind her. 'Oh, you were right. It was something shiny.'

'Can I keep the money?'

He looked from the discarded empty wine bottle next to the four pound coins on the ground to the pleading face of the child and said, 'We're supposed to hand money in to the police station but as they're mostly shut and they don't take lost property any more, I'm going with yes.'

'Hooray! This is the best surveying ever.'

TWENTY-FIVE

Belinda couldn't pretend that Harry's rapid departure had been anything but odd. He'd left with a promise to return later to pick up the rug and take her to visit Ben Davies at his vineyard. They knew his home address, so if that failed, they had planned to go there next, but from what his son Greg had told them, they were much more likely to find him at work than at home.

As Belinda took herself up to her room to get ready, she wondered whether she should be concerned that Harry had been acting so out of character. It certainly wasn't death or murder that made him uncomfortable, and she knew it wasn't the rug. Perhaps he was somewhat overwhelmed by their generosity. Marcus did have a tendency to pay over the odds for everything he purchased. She had once watched him barter with a street vendor in Istanbul so disastrously he'd paid more for a novelty T-shirt than the man had initially asked.

By the time she had showered, dried her hair and dressed in a short-sleeved grey silk blouse and emerald green three-quarter-length trousers, she decided that rather than second guess the problem, she would simply ask Harry. It was that easy.

Once she had made sure that Horatio was as happy as a young Labrador masquerading as a velociraptor could be, she scribbled a note to tell Marcus she was going out, texted Harry that she was on her way and left via the front door.

Belinda was all but at the bottom of the driveway by the time she saw Harry's Audi. He waved at her and leaned over to push the door open.

'You look great,' he said, face reddening to match his hair.

'Thank you,' she said, getting in and then clipping her seatbelt in place. 'Are you sure you're OK to drive?'

'Yes, I only had a half in the pub and a bottle of beer at yours.' He glanced over at her as they reached the far side of the green. 'I don't really fancy another drink today. To be honest, I think the cod from lunchtime is swimming about in my stomach. I'll watch you savour the wine.'

They chatted away, Belinda trying to decide whether to ask Harry what was wrong. He seemed in a much better mood, so she steered clear of the subject.

By the time they drove through the Challham Valley estate gates, Belinda had convinced herself that she had mistaken a time of reflection as sullenness and Harry's understated reaction towards the Berber rug as merely being overcome. There was nothing wrong with Harry Powell – it was all in her head.

'Belinda,' he said, 'you may have noticed I've not been myself in the last day or so.'

'Er, can't say as I have,' she lied.

'The thing is, I don't know where I'm going.'

'Over there,' she said, pointing to the space they'd parked in yesterday.

'No, I know where to park. I mean, in general.' He put the car in neutral and turned to face her. 'I've been a bit lost since I left the police, and well – if I'm being totally upfront, and laying my cards on the table...'

'Yes,' she said, staring right into his eyes.

'I'm thinking of taking things in another direction.'

'Go on.'

'I love... I love the idea of jacking in the Doggie Delight round and getting myself an entirely new job.' He grinned.

'Oh.' Her mouth was left in a perfect O shape as he put the car in drive and moved into a space next to a blue Honda Civic. Its lights flashed on and its owner approached holding a key fob.

'It's Steve Parry,' said Harry, oblivious to Belinda's goldfish impression. 'We never did get the chance to speak to him about his brother's diner. Still, there's no connection between Steve and John Farthing that we're aware of, so he's out of the running for murdering him in his own armchair.'

'Maybe now's a good time to ask him why he took Kulvinder's ticket to our wine tasting?' said Belinda.

Without waiting for a reply, Harry jumped out of the car and shouted, 'Hello, Steve.'

Steve Parry – late twenties, arms like tree trunks, thick mop of brown wavy hair – was rarely seen without his wife, Kulvinder. They were Little Challham's answer to the prom king and queen. At least, they used to be.

'Hi, Harry,' he said, looking a little startled. 'Hi, Belinda.'

'Steve,' said Belinda. 'I've seen you twice in one weekend, but no Kulvinder. Is she OK?'

'Yeah, yeah, she's completely wonderful,' he said, speaking extremely quickly. 'How about you two? Are you all right? The whole village is still talking about what happened on Saturday. And then old John Farthing? I didn't know him very well, but still, it's a shock.'

'Yes, we're pretty upset by it all,' said Harry. 'And so, like your good self, we've come out for a drink to steady our nerves.'

Steve's face paled. 'I haven't been drinking, but do me a favour, when you see Kulvinder, don't mention that I was here. Please. If you don't mind.'

'She doesn't know you're here?' said Harry.

'Just, don't mention it,' said Steve, clutching his car keys. 'I've been out to book us a nice table in Upper Wallop for lunch tomorrow and I fancied dropping in here on my way back.'

'Upper Wallop?' said Belinda. 'At the Horseshoes? I remember you recommending it to us a while ago. I'd like to give it a try some time.'

'Tell you what,' said Harry, 'how about we go tomorrow too? We'll no doubt see you there, Steve.'

'I possibly got the last table,' said Steve, 'so maybe not. Anyway, don't let me keep you. Bye.'

He got into his car, and drove out and away without even a wave or glance in their direction.

'Was it me, or was he acting odd?' said Harry.

'Yes, he was. Are we moving him up the suspect list for Sadie's murder?' said Belinda.

'He came to the wine tasting on Saturday in Kulvinder's place and now he's out without her.' Harry watched the dust left by Steve's car.

'And he seemed very cagey about what he's been doing. Kulvinder doesn't strike me as the sort to ban him from going out for a drink.'

'Perhaps he is the killer,' mused Harry. 'He's acting out of character.'

'Or maybe he's cheating on his wife and we've caught him out? Although they've not been back from honeymoon that long and seem to be madly in love,' said Belinda.

They started walking towards the tasting room, side by side, both in perfect step.

'There does seem to be something up with him,' said Harry. 'You can find out tomorrow.'

'Why me?' she said.

'You're friends with Kulvinder and you're bound to be more attuned to these things.'

'And you're something else,' she said, her tone reflecting the incredulity on her face. 'Why do I have to ask?'

'We arranged to meet them,' said Harry, holding the door of the tasting room open for Belinda, 'so you might as well take the opportunity to find out what's up.'

'Your generosity knows no bounds,' said Belinda.

The tasting room was a lot busier than it had been on Sunday lunchtime. Most of the tables were occupied, both inside and on the balcony.

They opted for a high table and two stools towards the back of the bar area, the height advantage meaning they still got to enjoy the scenery.

'I guess we have to go to the bar to order,' said Harry, as someone from the next table got up to buy a round of drinks.

'Allow me,' said Belinda. 'I'll see if Ben's here while I'm at it.'

Belinda stood and waited at the bar, both the servers already dealing with other customers. To the side was a door marked 'Private' with an entry keypad. Belinda and Harry had been at the other end of the bar on their previous visit, and she had missed this room. For a couple of seconds, she thought about knocking on the door to see who opened it.

Her hesitation paid off: the door was flung open and a very exhausted-looking Lucy Field, Ben's PA, stepped out into the narrow space behind the bar. Before the door slammed closed behind her, Ben's voice carried across the gap. 'I've had quite enough of this, Lucy.'

Lucy stopped short when she saw Belinda. It was as if she'd been caught with her hand in the till.

'Good evening, Belinda,' said Lucy, taking an elastic band from around her wrist and trying to secure her hair with it. 'Are you waiting to be served?'

'Good evening, Lucy. Yes, I am. A small Pinot Grigio, a tonic water, one for yourself and one for Ben too.'

The harried young woman cast her eyes at the closed door, started to shake her head and then followed it with a smile. 'That's so kind of you. I'll also have a tonic and I'll check with Ben what he'd like.'

'Come and join Harry and me, if you have time,' said Belinda as her drinks were handed over and the bill settled. 'We'd very much appreciate speaking to Ben again.' Then she had another thought. 'I'm sorry we missed Steve Parry earlier on. We saw him drive off.'

Lucy blinked several times, hesitated and said, 'Steve? Sorry, who?'

'Steve Parry,' said Belinda. 'He was one of the few people at Saturday's tasting who didn't leave in an ambulance. You can't have missed him. Late twenties, brown hair, arms the size of a heavyweight boxer's.'

'Oh, right, right,' said Lucy, executing a mock slap to her forehead. 'I really am all over the place. It's quite unlike me to be this forgetful.'

'He definitely was here, then?' said Belinda. 'I didn't catch a glimpse of someone I thought was him and do that face blur thing?'

'He was here,' said Lucy, 'now, he's not.'

'I know. I saw him drive away.' She gave the young woman the start of a smile, and then thought better of it. 'Whenever Ben's free, I could really do with talking to him.'

Aware that Lucy's stare was probably boring into the back of her skull, she walked back to their table.

'I saw that, but I couldn't hear either of you,' Harry said. 'Lucy's face was a picture. What did you say to make her look so worried?'

'Nothing really. Ben's back there in an office we didn't notice yesterday.' She leaned closer to Harry and told him what she'd overheard. 'I mentioned seeing Steve drive away. Even getting her to confirm he was in here seemed to make her jumpy.'

'Something's going on,' said Harry. 'You don't think Steve was here to see Lucy, do you?'

Belinda considered his question. 'People do have affairs, so I wouldn't rule it out.'

'Another relationship brought to an abrupt end,' said Harry.

'I can't see why else Lucy would be so reluctant to admit Steve was in here. Since when did client confidentiality extend to a man having a drink?'

'Lucy's coming over, you can ask her.'

Harry nodded at Lucy as she walked over to their table.

'Hello, Harry,' she said. 'And thank you again for the drink.' She clinked her glass of tonic water against Belinda's wine glass before setting it down.

'It's busy in here this evening,' said Harry.

'Yes, I'm due a break,' said Lucy, a scowl on her face. 'In fact, I should really have gone home a couple of hours ago.'

'Ben not joining you?' said Harry. 'I think Belinda mentioned we could really do with speaking to him again.'

She shook her head, tendrils of hair jogging about with the movement. 'He said he's very sorry, but far too busy at the moment. He works so very hard. Now, *he* should have gone home hours ago. It's his young lad, Greg, I worry about. Poor kid.'

'Sadie's death doesn't seem to have affected your business,' said Harry, gesturing at the busy bar.

'It's doing OK,' said Lucy. She fiddled with the cuffs on her blouse, forcing them down over her knuckles. 'I have to level with you, most people didn't like Sadie. She fell out with people – staff, customers and suppliers – when she ran the Fish by the Sea in Dover. That's not to mention the amount of wine producers she upset by writing scathing reviews of their wine, meaning local hotels, restaurants and bars all refused to stock it. There's more than one angry vineyard owner who was scuppered because of her.'

She took her glass with both hands and picked it up, taking a meagre sip. 'We've had confirmation from the police that the red wine was poisoned so we've had to pull the remainder of the batch as a precaution.'

'Ben's out of pocket too, then,' said Belinda.

'Ben doesn't care about the money!' said Lucy, with a sudden flash of anger. 'A woman died, a woman he knew. A renowned wine buff, who, although she might not have been liked, was still admired.'

'Can I ask,' said Belinda, 'was there anything going on between Ben and Sadie?'

'Hell, no,' said Lucy. 'Where on earth did you get that from?'

Harry picked his glass up, swirled it round, ice cubes clinking. 'This will sound rather ignorant to you, Lucy, but I don't think I fully appreciated quite how much *power* Sadie had.'

If nodding enthusiastically were an Olympic sport, Lucy would have been on the rostrum with a gold medal around her neck. 'She did have lots of power. Some would say perhaps a little too much.'

'Who might say such a thing?' said Belinda. 'Hypothetically...'

Lucy beckoned them closer. 'Hypothetically speaking—'

'Lucy,' said Ben. 'You've put in quite enough hours for today. Why don't you call it a night?'

His appearance at Lucy's elbow took them all by surprise, so much so that Harry began to splutter on his drink. A slap on the back from Ben soon sorted the problem.

'Don't keel over as well, Harry,' said Ben. 'I don't think Little Challham can take any more from you two. If I understand correctly, you managed to find another dead body this morning. That's quite some going.'

He placed a hand on Lucy's shoulder and gave it a squeeze. Belinda saw Lucy flinch and the muscles in her jaw tighten.

'Oh, that's terrible,' said Lucy, 'but Ben's right, I really should get home. Things haven't got back to normal since my mum was taken ill.'

'Thanks, Lucy,' said Ben. 'Have a good evening and if you need to take tomorrow off, I can cope without you.'

He turned his attention to Belinda and Harry; Lucy was all but pushed out of the way.

She made her way around the table back to the bar. The forlorn looks she threw Ben's way made Belinda feel a mixture of pity and sadness. It was as clear as day that Lucy adored Ben, and he didn't seem to requite those feelings.

'Did the police question you about John's death?' said Belinda.

Ben shrugged. 'Death? Murder? It had to be murder, right? If not, why would the police take the time to visit me? It was detectives from Major Crime. That's your old mob, isn't it, Harry?'

'It is, but sometimes these things are done for precautions,' he said.

'It had to be poisoning, surely?' said Ben. 'From what I've been told, he was surrounded by empty bottles, he died in his armchair, and the rest of the home brew crew were round at his house the night before.'

'Someone could have gone round there after they left,' said Harry.

'There's only two of them left – Daisy the postwoman and Richard Duke,' said Ben. 'I take it you've heard of conspiracy to murder?'

Harry bristled. 'Of course I have. I've worked on more than one conspiracy, you know.'

'Your theory is that Daisy and Richard killed John and Sadie?' said Belinda. 'I could speculate that this is all about the secret recipe to the wine they've been concocting. Although I'd be the first to admit that I don't think that's very likely.'

'In fact,' said Harry, 'it's possible it's you.'

'Me?' said Ben, putting his hands out in a defensive pose. 'I'm quaking in my boots. I have a vineyard, award-winning wines, contracts with some of the county's leading eateries, the tasting room, restaurant, and they have what? A few demi-johns full of wine that would melt your fillings. Be realistic. I wouldn't bump the competition off even if it was actual competition, but these amateurs?'

'I have to agree that they probably aren't a threat to your income,' said Harry.

'My point entirely,' said Ben. 'Even if I wanted to harm Sadie – and I didn't – I had no reason at all to kill John Farthing.'

'Why didn't you mention that you used to work for Sadie?' said Belinda, changing tack, a move she'd learned from Harry.

Ben didn't miss a beat. 'What's there to say? I told you I knew her, that I used to work for her is neither here nor there.'

'Or that when you left, you and she had a row?' said Belinda, enjoying herself now.

Ben let out a long sigh. 'OK, you've got me. We fell out because she didn't like the fact that I was going off on my own. That was years ago, and if I'd wanted to kill her, I would hardly have played the long game for the last ten years or so.'

'That's a fair point,' said Harry.

'No, it's not,' said Belinda.

'Are you sure?' said Harry.

'Yes,' she said. 'He didn't own a vineyard with so much at stake back then.'

'I take your point, Belinda,' Ben said, turning his attention solely to her, 'except that I didn't need Sadie. I didn't need her at all. If anything, she needed me. You see, over time, she had been so obnoxious to so many people, most of them didn't want her tasting their wines or coming along to their restaurants on opening nights and putting the kibosh on the entire event.' Ben spoke plainly with no apparent malice in his voice. 'I was about the only one who would entertain her. Me and the Little Challham home brew group, as it turned out.'

'What was that?' said Harry. 'What about the home brew group?'

Ben turned his eyes on Harry. 'They asked her to come along one night and review their latest batch of wine. Boy, did she go to town. She threatened to make it her personal mission to let every pub and restaurant in the county know how bad it was. I'm surprised that you didn't know.'

'We've been working our way through the home brew group,' said Harry.

'And so has someone else,' said Ben. 'Listen, if you want my advice, speak to Richard Duke and Daisy Thornton. They'll tell you all about Sadie and how she ridiculed everything they stood for. Anyway, I have to be off. See you later.'

With that, Ben was gone, leaving Belinda and Harry to exchange glances.

'That's a turn-up for the books,' said Harry. 'Ben seems pretty het up considering he's not involved.'

'Yes, I thought that,' said Belinda. 'But we still don't have anything that could be construed as evidence against him.'

'Are you saying you don't believe him?' said Harry, scanning the room to see which way Ben had gone.

'I'm not entirely sure, H. Ben was keen to stop Lucy from telling us something just then, sending her home so suddenly.'

'He also seems to want us to find out about the shame Sadie brought to John, Richard and Daisy's door,' said Harry. 'We're ruling out everyone else who's not a member of the home brew group, those who are still breathing anyway. Daisy is probably still at the police station. If Ben won't give us the full details, we'll go straight to the source.'

'Agreed,' said Belinda.

'Then we go to the police,' said Harry.

Belinda kept her answer to herself.

TWENTY-SIX

Harry wouldn't hear of Belinda walking home, and he declined a nightcap. He had phoned the Horseshoes and managed to book them a table for lunch the next day without any issue. It was another indication that Steve's attitude had been off.

'Steve is definitely up to something,' said Belinda. She had kicked her shoes off in the footwell and was stretching out, arms as far above her head as the car roof would allow.

'Yes, I have to agree with you,' said Harry. 'I recall him and Kulvinder telling us about a wonderful meal they'd had there, and today, he seemed reluctant to say more than a couple of words about it.'

'Other than it was probably full. We definitely need to talk to him again about Sadie.'

Harry felt the weight of Belinda's stare as he drove them towards Little Challham.

'What?' he said. 'You're staring.'

'I'm tired,' she said, 'but I feel restless. How about we go and see Richard tonight? He's bound to be home and even if the police did go to see him after his hospital stay, he might let his guard down if we drop by unexpectedly.'

'It's getting late,' said Harry, checking the time on the dashboard. 'He's probably in bed. Dreaming of profiteroles.'

'You're being mean again.'

'Sorry.'

She sat upright. 'Come on. Let's go and see him. What's the alternative? You drop me off, pick up your rug and go home?'

'Oh, yeah, fair point. You let me know which road is his when we get closer.'

'It's not far from the nature reserve,' said Belinda. 'His house is one of the original stone cottages and very sought after. The houses themselves are two up, two down but the gardens are amazing. The plots go back several acres. He frequently gets people offering him all kinds of money, but he refuses to sell.'

'If he's got so much space, why do they use John Farthing's house for brewing and storage?'

'A fine point,' she said, stifling a yawn. 'We'll ask him when we get there. Along with, "Did you kill Sadie and John?"'

'Subtle, very subtle.'

Harry drove towards the nature reserve, seeing very few cars on the road. It was getting on for 10 p.m. and he wasn't entirely sure that Richard was going to be overjoyed at them turning up so late, especially if he had a penchant for murdering people. It was still better than facing the rest of the night at home on his own with only an itchy rug for company.

'How well do you know Richard?' asked Harry.

'Not that well,' Belinda said. 'It's only been recently I've had much to do with him, and that's solely due to his contacts in the food business. I know he can't be all that bad because he's got two dogs.'

'Two dogs? Where does he buy their food from?'

'It's this second cottage on the left,' said Belinda. Once he'd pulled over, she put a hand out to stop him from getting out. 'Please don't start by saying you can fit him into your Doggie Delight food round. I don't think it'll go down all that well.'

'Don't be daft,' said Harry. 'I'll at least give him a chance to put the kettle on.'

They walked into the garden via the unlatched gate, a large expanse of lawn in between them and the whitewashed cottage. The path took them to the large black front door via an arbour, with honeysuckle and passion flowers climbing through the trellis. The rest of the garden was littered with shrubs and evergreen bushes, but little in the way of colour or flowers.

'The light's on in that downstairs window there,' said Harry. 'With luck, he's still up.'

Belinda lifted the metal door knocker and let it fall.

'That'll certainly wake the dead,' said Harry, 'or the rest of the street.'

They stood on the doorstep listening out for someone coming to the door, or at least stirring in some way.

'I thought you said he had dogs?' said Harry.

'He does: two lurchers.'

'Lurchers?' said Harry. 'If dogs really do look like their owners, this'll be interesting. I've never seen morbidly obese lurchers before.'

'We're not likely to see them now,' said Belinda. 'I suppose there's a chance that the police arrested him.'

'No, they didn't,' said Harry.

He carried on staring at the door knocker, fully aware from the sound of her shoes that Belinda had edged round to face him.

'How do you know that?' she said, tone chilly.

'I, er, spoke to one of my old team earlier and asked if they'd made any arrests other than Daisy,' he said. 'Besides, it would have been on the news.'

From the corner of his eye, he could see that her arms were crossed and he thought he heard a tut.

'I'll take a look round the back,' he said, stepping onto the grass, still averting his eyes.

'Mind the dogs don't bite you,' she said as he walked in the direction of the back garden. 'Oh, hang on. They'd be barking even if Richard's gone out. Perhaps he's taken them out for a walk.'

'Good,' said Harry into the darkness. 'At least something's going my way. I'm not entirely sure the scars have completely healed from the last time a dog bit me on the—'

'Harry,' called Belinda, from the other side of the back garden.

'How did you get over there so quickly?' he said, straining to see so much as a silhouette. 'What's that light?'

'It's my mobile,' said Belinda. 'I've turned the torch on. Why don't you put yours on and that way you won't... Ouch. Are you OK? What did you trip on?'

'I think I've found the rockery,' said Harry. 'I'll get my phone. If there's a rockery, there's likely to be a pond. I don't want to end up in it.'

He took his phone out, hit the torch button and then the entire area where he was standing lit up, dazzling his eyes.

'I've found the floodlights,' called Belinda.

'So you have.' He sighed and, shielding his eyes, made his way to where her voice was coming from.

'I'm in the shed,' she said. 'Come and see what I've found.'

When Harry's sight had returned after having his retinas scorched, he saw that Belinda was standing in the doorway of a large timber building, more log cabin than shed. She had found the internal light as well as the external one and the sight was on the disturbing side.

'He likes to hunt rabbits, then,' said Harry, superfluous words considering there were half a dozen carcasses suspended from the ceiling and on the worktop.

'Wherever he's gone, he's left that behind,' said Belinda, pointing to the large knife lying next to one of the rabbits, splatters of blood on the gutting blade.

'I don't think these have been here that long,' said Harry. 'They definitely haven't started to smell too much.'

'That must be where he is right now, then,' said Belinda. 'Out hunting rabbits.'

'He does have a touch of Elmer Fudd about him, come to think of it.'

'Should we wait?' said Belinda. 'He could be ages and we are on his land. He may not be too pleased to see us.'

'Let's come back in the morning,' said Harry. 'Come on. We'll leave everything as we found it.'

Ready this time, the torch already on, Harry stepped outside to wait for Belinda to turn the lights back off.

Something moving in the shadows caught his attention. For a moment, he thought it was a fox. It crept along the side of the border, its shape and size making it obvious it was far too large. The collar was a bit of a giveaway too.

'Here you go, it's all right,' he said, crouching down.

The lurcher eventually came over to where Harry was squatting down and after a whimper or two – from the dog, not Harry – she allowed him to read the tag on her collar.

'Hey, who do we have here?' said Belinda, bending down next to the dog and rubbing the fur on her head.

'This is Raven,' said Harry. 'Take a look at this postcode. Does this seem about right for this address?'

Belinda peered at the silver disc on the dog's collar. 'Yes, that's definitely local, but let me check. A lurcher wandering around in Richard's back garden is pretty conclusive, though. It must be his dog.'

As he waited for Belinda to tap the postcode in, Harry stood up to stop the cramp in his legs and to see if peering into the inky darkness would help at all. The only natural light was coming from the cloud-covered moon, and was mostly ineffectual.

'Yes,' said Belinda, 'it's this address or a very nearby neighbour.'

A noise carried through the night.

'Was that a dog barking?' said Belinda.

Raven stood up, gazed into the distance and gave a single bark in return. She then raced straight off into the gloom and was swallowed up by the night.

'We should try and find her,' said Harry. 'You said that Richard owns two dogs. It's weird that one's come back here and there's another one barking nearby. You also said this property backs onto the nature reserve?'

'Yes,' said Belinda. 'The area at the back of Richard's land is pretty much open ground. Perfect for hunting rabbits with lurchers.'

They set off, heading further into the blackness, every hundred metres or so calling out 'Richard' or 'Raven'. The light from their phones was a help, although it only assisted them to a point. A couple of times Belinda tripped, Harry catching her on the third occasion.

She smiled at him as he supported her, giving her time to get her breath back and test her ankle for damage.

'Thanks for stopping me from falling,' she said.

'Sorry I missed you the first two times,' he said. 'I hope those shoes weren't expensive.'

'It doesn't matter, I... Is that a light over there?' she said, craning to see over his shoulder.

Harry looked behind him to where a light of some kind lay on the ground, illuminating a nearby clump of brambles.

It was hard to make out where the light was coming from, but it appeared to be a torch dropped beside a mound of earth. A lurcher walked into the arc of light and sniffed at something close by. The dog gave a whimper and licked at whatever was wrapped around the torch. A second dog barked as Harry and Belinda got closer.

The second dog sat beside the mound, unmoving and loyal to the end. Raven continued to lick at what Harry could now clearly see was Richard Duke's hand.

He lay motionless on the ground, his head pushed down inside a rabbit burrow with a rock the size of a football keeping it firmly in the hole.

TWENTY-SEVEN

'Why does this keep happening to us?' said Harry. 'If everyone can just stop dying for five minutes.'

'Harry,' said Belinda, 'I don't think this is the time to get cross with the man. In case there's any chance he's still alive, I think we should at least try to get him out.'

Harry kneeled down beside Richard's motionless body. He tried to find a pulse on his neck. Unfortunately – thanks to the many chins and Richard's cranium being encased in a rabbit hole – he failed to find one.

'I can't find any sign of life, he's quite cold, and rigor mortis seems to have started,' said Harry. 'This is weird. There are some pound coins next to his head and an empty wine bottle a couple of feet away.' He glanced up at Belinda, who was trying to comfort the dogs.

For the second time that night, Harry was blinded by lights being shone in his face, only this time, his hearing was assaulted as well as his vision.

'Police. Stay where you are,' hollered a voice through a loud-hailer, a touch too close to Harry's ears to be good for him.

Instinctively, both Harry and Belinda put their hands in the air, blinking rapidly at whoever was shouting at them.

'You two *again*,' said PC Green, this time without the use of his ear-shattering megaphone. 'Give me a break!'

'It's not what it looks like,' said Harry still with his hands in the air, now on both knees, inches from a corpse with its head pushed beneath the ground.

'It looks very much like his head is in a rabbit hole with a rock on top,' said PC Green.

'Well, in that case, it is what it looks like,' said Harry.

'Only it's nothing to do with us,' said Belinda, lowering her hands.

'You're standing over a dead body and it's nothing to do with you?' said PC Green.

'Aha,' said Harry. 'How do you know he's dead?'

'Good point,' said PC Green. He beckoned two of his colleagues over and told them to get Richard's head out of the hole. 'In the meantime, you two, come and sit in the car, please.'

'Are we being arrested?' said Belinda.

'There'll be plenty of time for that, if need be,' said PC Green. 'I'd like you away from the area somewhere I can speak to you in private.'

Out of the direct light, Harry saw that there were three police cars in the distance and PC Green was leading them to the unmarked car on the left-hand side.

'How come we didn't hear you drive up?' said Harry.

'They're electric cars,' the officer said. 'Very quiet and cheap to run. All about the money and it scores big with the public if we care about the environment.'

'Why are you still on duty?' said Belinda as they reached the car and he opened the rear doors for them to get in.

'I was about to go off duty,' PC Green said, with a quick check of his watch and an ill-disguised sigh, 'when the call came in that someone was creeping around the back of Richard Duke's property and turning the lights on. The neighbours had seen him go out with his lurchers and knew it wasn't him. They were suspicious, so they called us.'

He got into the front seat and turned to speak to them both. 'Care to tell me what made you come out here tonight?'

'I'll level with you,' said Harry, hoping that honesty would do the trick. They had met with the clearly keen officer on enough occasions to be upfront. 'We wanted to look a bit further into Sadie Oppenshaw's death. It happened in Belinda's home and at an event that she organised.'

'It was a shock, a horrible shock, and I must say, for a brief time, we suspected Richard might have had something to do with it,' said Belinda. 'He did get carted off to hospital and then Sadie was poisoned.'

'True,' said PC Green, looking to make sure his colleagues were attending to the body and all was well before his attention returned to Harry and Belinda. 'That still doesn't explain why you were here tonight.'

'Richard exchanged a few words with Sadie at Saturday's tasting before he went off in an ambulance,' said Belinda. 'We wanted to ask him about the row, especially after we found John's body. Our suspicions fell on the beer and wine home brew group, particularly Richard. We spoke to Ben Davies earlier and he told us that Sadie also had a row with the home brew group. Now that two of them are dead, that only leaves Daisy as a suspect, surely. What if this is her covering her tracks by taking them all out?'

Belinda sat back in the car seat, an expectant expression all over her face. It was one that Harry knew and recognised. It was very much her 'don't mess with me' face. At that moment, he couldn't have adored her more.

'The only problem with that,' said PC Green, 'is that Daisy is still in custody at the police station.'

'Oh,' said Belinda.

'Blimey,' said Harry. 'So rather than the home brew group killing off their competition, someone's killing them off one by one.'

'Here's what'll happen,' said PC Green after a lengthier pause than Harry was expecting. 'I'll let the two of you go home while I finish up here and come and see you both tomorrow. How about that?'

Harry opened his mouth and Belinda put her hand on his knee. 'That sounds more than fair, officer.'

'I think you can call me Vince,' he said. 'We're several cadavers past formality.'

'How do you think Richard died?' said Harry.

'There's probably not very much oxygen in a rabbit hole,' said Vince. 'My guess is he suffocated.'

'We know that,' said Belinda, her voice thick with annoyance. 'But why did he stuff his head in the hole in the first place and who put the rock on top?'

'It's something that a post-mortem should shed some light on,' said Vince. 'It could be that the same poison is in all three of the victims' systems. It would suggest it's the same person, only they chose a different way to kill him. Perhaps they were hanging around watching to make sure he drank the wine.'

'There was an empty wine bottle next to him,' said Harry. 'It's strange that he wandered out here in the night with his two dogs and a bottle of wine. If it wasn't for the earth being pushed in around his head and a boulder on top, it might have looked like an accident.'

'Perhaps whoever did it, panicked,' said Vince, shifting in his seat. 'It could be that the poison didn't take effect quickly enough and in his drunken state, he went outside and was lured down on the ground by the coins. Depending on the poison and what it did to his mind, he may have been hallucinating or in a stupor.'

Belinda shivered. 'It's a barbaric way to kill someone. I only hope he was too far out of it to know what was happening to him.'

'There is one other thing,' said Harry, 'the dogs. What's going to happen to them?'

'Er, the local kennels, I suppose,' said Vince. 'I was more concerned with the dead guy than with his pets. I think it'll be best if we call someone out to take care of them. We're not entirely sure where Mr Duke's wife is at the moment. The neighbour who called the police told us she left earlier today and there's been no sign of her since. She works away a lot, apparently, she's some sort of mentor for small businesses and they book her for days at a time. We'll track her down as soon as we can.'

'I can look after the dogs for a day or two,' said Harry, running a hand over his stubble. 'I could do with the company and I really don't fancy the idea of them going to kennels, not after they've sat by their owner's body for who knows how long.'

He felt the briefest of squeezes from Belinda's hand on his knee.

'Sounds sensible,' said PC Green after a minute's thought. 'I'll have to clear it with my guv'nor in case she classes it as interfering with witnesses.'

Harry put his head back against the headrest. 'Why doesn't that surprise me?'

TWENTY-EIGHT

Belinda woke on Tuesday morning with a start. Her mind had refused to stop racing when she had eventually got to bed. It had taken her hours to fall asleep and even then, she had slept fitfully. Her mind refused to let her rest; in the end she got up before her alarm, roused by the notions in her head, all vying for attention.

Naturally, the murders were the most pressing of all, seeping into her dreams. She was keen to get out and do something. She was also more than mildly interested to see if Kulvinder turned up in the restaurant – Steve was definitely hiding something – and she had more than a passing interest in finding out how Harry had got on hosting two lurchers overnight.

With Horatio walked, and anything that needed her immediate attention completed, Belinda finally got ready for their lunch.

She took outfit after outfit from her closet until she settled on a cotton V-necked knee-length shirt dress. Harry had once commented on the cheerfulness of the multi-coloured polka dots against the ivory fabric. It was something that had taken her by surprise at the time and had made it one of her favourite dresses. She tied the belt, pinned her hair to keep it off her shoulders and rummaged in the closet for her red wedge sandals.

Why did she have butterflies? This was utterly ridiculous. She was a grown woman, not a teenager, and Harry had not asked her out. Her brother had put Harry up to this to thank her for a rug that he had seemed less than thrilled about in the first place. And they had chosen the restaurant because they had seen Steve Parry coming out of the Challham Valley estate and not trusted what he had said.

That's right, this was all about the murders. First Sadie, then John Farthing and then Richard Duke. The only thing that connected them – other than being killed in Little Challham – was wine.

Belinda realised that Harry would be at the castle any moment. She grabbed her bag and went downstairs to meet him, the thought of the common denominator running through her brain.

As she reached the bottom of the stairs, her brother's voice drifted along the hallway and she heard Harry laugh. If she wasn't mistaken, Marcus was talking about her. 'Good to see the old girl so happy,' was all she picked out before she bowled into the room.

'Ah, sis,' said Marcus. 'I was just saying to H that you've been as happy as anything lately. It's wonderful to see. Something's bringing out the best in you.'

'Hi, Belinda,' said Harry. His eyes widened. 'You look gorgeous in that dress.'

'Oh, thanks,' she said, switching her bag from one hand to the other. 'I've had it ages but I thought I'd go for one last shot at short sleeves and sandals before September gets its own way with the weather.'

All three of them stood looking at one another, not entirely natural smiles on their faces.

'Well,' said Harry. 'We'd better go in case they give our table away.'

'Oh, yes. You crazy kids have fun and don't do anything I wouldn't do,' said Marcus, rocking backwards and forwards.

'Such as training dogs to spot parking spaces,' said Belinda.

'Or selling tea cosies to the Moroccans,' said Harry.

'Fair enough,' said Marcus. 'That reminds me, have you got time for me to tell you about my latest idea?'

'No,' said Belinda and Harry in unison.

They left a slightly dispirited Marcus and walked out into the sunshine, grabbing for their sunglasses before walking to Harry's car.

'How did you get on last night with Raven and...' said Belinda.

'Rogue,' said Harry.

'Raven and Rogue?' said Belinda, giving him a quizzical look.

'From your expression, I gather you're not much of an X-Men fan?' said Harry.

'He named his lurchers after X-Men?'

'X-Women to be completely accurate.'

Smiling at Harry, she shook her head and got in the car.

'How are you going to broach the subject of Steve's suspicious behaviour yesterday at lunch?' said Harry.

'I thought you could start by asking him about his brother's diner,' said Belinda, with the start of a smile.

'Me?' Harry chuckled. 'Well played. At least there's no connection between him and the home brew group that we know of. It's still something we should completely rule out.'

'Good idea. You can cover that when you ask him about the diner.'

'It'll be my pleasure.'

Upper Wallop was a slightly larger version of Little Challham: it had three pubs, numerous restaurants of every international cuisine imaginable, an independent bookshop, several clothes shops, a hardware store that spanned six of the premises on the high street and a number of coffee shops and tea rooms. Belinda always loved spending a couple of hours there browsing the antique shops. However, it didn't have a castle and it didn't have Harry Powell.

They parked in one of the four car parks, at the midway point of the half-mile-long high street. The Horseshoes was positioned on a well-appointed spot on the corner, with a large south-facing garden and a welcoming façade. The restaurant itself was set back thirty feet or so from the edge of the pavement, giving ample space for four rectangular rattan tables and seats.

Kulvinder and Steve Parry sat at the table closest to the restaurant's entrance.

'Hello, both of you,' said Belinda. 'Lovely to see you. Kulvinder.'

They exchanged air kisses, while Harry and Steve waved awkwardly and nodded.

'You managed to get a table, then?' said Steve.

Harry made a point of glancing around at the other three empty tables and Belinda stepped towards the front door and surveyed the almost deserted interior. 'Perhaps they had a lot of cancellations,' said Belinda. 'It's that time of year.'

'I'll let them know we're here,' said Harry. 'Would you prefer to eat inside or outside?'

'Oh, outside, I think,' said Belinda. She made a show of considering each table in turn before deciding on the one closest to the Parrys.

'Long time, no see,' said Belinda to Kulvinder. 'We were supposed to catch up at some point over a glass of wine but Steve seems to be keeping you to himself.'

She noticed that Steve appeared to be a bit on the panicked side: he made a grab for his pint of lager and took a gulp.

'And you're drinking water while your husband is enjoying a beer,' she said. 'As you weren't able to make it to the wine tasting, I would have thought the least he could do is drive today.'

Kulvinder's flawless skin was glowing, and her hair was pulled back in a casual braid, accentuating her delicate features. 'I wasn't feeling all that well on Saturday, so Steve took my place. I didn't want the ticket to go to waste, although I was sorry not to get a chance to catch up. Another time, perhaps?'

About to answer her, Belinda was interrupted by Harry stepping back outside with a man whose face was so serious it was almost painful to observe him.

'This is Dan Windsor,' said Harry. 'He's the owner and has set some time aside to chat after the lunchtime rush.'

'Afternoon,' he said to Belinda. 'Pleasure to meet you. I'll send someone out to take your order.'

He held a menu out to Harry and gave another nod at Kulvinder and Steve. 'Everything OK over here?'

They murmured their approval about the empty plates in front of them.

Belinda ran her eye along the list and noted the absence of Challham Valley wines. She chose a glass of English rosé from another Kentish vineyard – it paid to keep tabs on *all* the wines available.

Dan went off to get their drinks, clearing Kulvinder and Steve's starter plates as he went.

The next few minutes passed pleasantly, the sun kept at bay by the large parasols between the tables. They placed their food order, chatted to one another and, most importantly, eavesdropped as much as they could.

Before too long, the waitress came back out with main courses for the Parrys and then immediately returned with Belinda and Harry's starters.

'Thank you,' said Harry. 'I was hoping we weren't going to have to wait too long. I didn't have any breakfast. My stomach thought that my throat's been cut.'

'I got the order in as soon as I could,' said the waitress. 'We've got a party of forty turning up any minute, so I didn't want your food held up.'

'Did you hear that, Kulvinder?' said Steve, at a greater volume than his remark really warranted. 'They've got a party of forty arriving soon. Almost full.'

Belinda ignored him, although she was still listening to almost every word the couple were saying.

'Belinda—' said Harry.

'Mm,' she answered, subtly moving her head to indicate Kulvinder and Steve. She sensed that Steve was building up to saying something. The way he was clattering his knife and fork and fiddling with the corner of his serviette were tell-tale clues.

'Would you excuse me?' said Kulvinder as she stood up from the table. 'Little girls' room.'

Sensing the opportunity to get Kulvinder alone, and find out if everything was all right between her and Steve, Belinda grabbed her handbag and said to Harry, 'Sorry, H. Give me a minute, would you?'

She followed Kulvinder to the ladies' toilets, working her way through the crowd of forty who had just arrived. They were milling around trying to find their seats, and generally getting in her way.

Fortunately, Belinda reached the toilets only a beat or two behind Kulvinder who had paused to look in the mirror, index fingers prodding at the corners of her eyes.

'You OK there, Kulvinder?'

She made a noise, a bit like a 'harrumph'.

'Anything you want to tell me?' said Belinda, standing guard at the door. 'Is it Steve?'

Kulvinder's eyes welled with tears. 'Of course it's Steve's.'

'I thought so!'

'I'm not surprised you guessed,' she said, opening her handbag and taking out a small battery-operated fan. 'I'm up and down to the loo all the time, I'm too hot and I'm either eating for England or I'm throwing up.'

Belinda stood motionless. 'Oh, you're pregnant.'

'Hang on,' said Kulvinder. 'You seem surprised. What did you think was going on?'

'Nothing, nothing. I was worried about you, that's all.'

'I really do have to go,' Kulvinder said, heading into a cubicle.

'I'll catch up with you later,' said Belinda, cross with herself at having totally misread the situation.

A little crestfallen, she walked back to her seat to find Harry and Steve chatting away.

'Steve here is only a rugby fan too,' said Harry. 'If we can get our hands on some tickets for Twickenham, we might make a day of it.'

'Great idea,' she said, retaking her seat and picking up her wine.

Steve drummed his fingers on the table and checked his watch. He looked relieved when Kulvinder reappeared. His body language that Belinda had taken for something more unpleasant, was probably no more than anxiety for her wellbeing.

Belinda was still desperate to ask what he had been doing at the Challham Valley estate and why it was such a secret.

The only thing stopping her blurting it out was how wrong she had been about the pregnancy. She should probably rethink the entire thing.

Suddenly, Dan Windsor appeared again, this time looking less worried. He had an enormous envelope, in the style of a lottery winner who had just been presented with an oversized cheque.

Belinda stared, Kulvinder stared, Harry looked round to see what they were staring at and Steve jumped up from his seat.

'Kulvinder,' he said, joy dancing across his face, 'my beautiful, beautiful wife, and mother of our unborn child—'

'You're kidding me!' said Harry. 'Well, I'll be. That was the last thing I was expecting. You had no idea either, did you, Belinda?'

'Not now, Harry,' said Belinda.

'To celebrate this wonderful news,' said Steve, flapping his hand at Dan who stood holding the envelope aloft, 'I've bought you a gift.'

'How lovely,' said Harry.

'I know how fond you are of a glass of wine,' said Steve. 'Unfortunately, for many months to come, alcohol won't be an indulgence we can partake in. This is my last pint until you're able to drink again.'

Really? thought Belinda.

'Really?' said Harry.

'So we can make it a truly special occasion,' said Steve, 'I've got us – you – this...'

He stretched out his hand to the enormous envelope. Dan passed it over and moved back to the doorway.

'What I've got here,' said Steve, 'is the lease of forty vines – one for each month we've known each other – for the next three years. I did the deal yesterday at the Challham Valley estate, and even though they don't usually have enough staff on a bank holiday, they did it for us! They couldn't be more thrilled that we're expecting a baby.'

'I don't know what to say,' said Kulvinder. 'This is so thoughtful.'

Belinda felt a tiny bit jealous that someone wasn't presenting her with such a great present, but now wasn't the time to wallow.

'But do you actually get any wine from it?' said Harry.

All of them gave him daggers.

'Naturally,' said Steve. 'It's forty-eight bottles every year, plus we get invited to the leaseholder weekends... Only when the time is right, obviously.'

He gave Kulvinder another adoring smile.

Belinda had been so wrong about Steve, it was alarming. How could she have been so distracted that she actually thought he was up to something unpalatable?

TWENTY-NINE

Soon after Steve presented Kulvinder with the magnificent gift, absolutely perfect for a wine lover, Harry tried to imagine what sort of present Belinda would appreciate. How could he get her to react with the same pure unbridled joy that Kulvinder had displayed?

As ever with Belinda, it was impossible to know. But at least Harry had managed to rid himself of the sinking feeling he'd had when Marcus had told him that Ivan was about to arrive. He would have to accept his fate and accept that things were unlikely to develop between him and Belinda. How could Harry ever hope to compete with someone who had played such a huge part in Belinda's life, especially as they seemed to have unfinished business? Why would someone like Belinda show any interest in a retired police officer selling dog food for a living when she hadn't severed all ties with South Africa's anti-poaching wildlife and animal protector? Ivan was bound to be a cross between Crocodile Dundee and Tarzan.

Kulvinder and Steve stayed and chatted for a few more minutes, Harry deftly working into the conversation whether Steve had ever been interested in home brew.

'Home brew?' said Steve. 'It's never entered my head. We're not big drinkers anyway, and we both work long hours. The forty-eight bottles we're due will end up vintage by the time we get through them. Why do you ask?'

'No particular reason,' said Harry. 'There seems to be a few people in the village who've taken to brewing their own. Have you ever been interested in the food and drink business?'

'If this is about my brother's diner that Sadie slammed and put out of business, it's all in the past,' said Steve. He spoke with little passion and gave no indication that Harry had opened an old wound.

'But she was the reason your brother had to sell up?' said Belinda.

'Oh, yes,' said Steve, reaching for his wallet to settle their bill. 'He took the money and set up his own firm as a landscape gardener. He couldn't be happier. It's hard work but he loves it and works outdoors, in the fresh air, and doesn't have to deal with the same stress. He's got contracts and customers all over the place. I've never seen him so happy, when I do see him. He's usually always working.'

Kulvinder stood up, followed by her husband. After a brief goodbye, they walked back out onto the pavement towards the high street.

'Nothing Steve said there gave us much to think it's either him or his brother working their way through the home brew group,' said Harry.

'And we know it's not Daisy as she was in a police cell,' said Belinda.

'It's frustrating but perhaps Dan might be of some help... or it's back to the drawing board.'

'Whiteboard, surely?' she said.

Harry asked Dan for the bill, rejecting Belinda's offer to contribute, and thanked her again for the Berber rug. He gave it his best shot at reassuring her that he loved it.

He sat and watched Belinda savour the rest of her wine while they waited for Dan, considering what would be his perfect gift. He would have preferred some Kent hops leased to him for five years of top-quality beer, but he had most things he wanted in life, so why push his luck?

When Dan came back outside with the bill and the credit card machine, he pulled over a chair from the next table and said, 'What exactly was it you two wanted to know?'

He had an intelligent, if understated face. His hazel eyes were alert and Harry doubted that much escaped him.

'It's a bit sensitive, to be honest,' said Harry.

'You know that Sadie Oppenshaw was murdered?' said Belinda.

'Clearly not that sensitive,' said Harry, adding a generous tip via the card reader.

'Yes, I did hear,' said Dan. He gave a short laugh. 'At a wine tasting, I hear. Some might say poetic justice, but I have to hand it to Sadie, she might have given my restaurant a total slating – food, staff, décor, service, wine, and she went to town on the wine – but do you know what?'

'You hated her enough to kill her?' said Belinda.

Dan looked completely startled. 'What?'

Harry made a mental note that it was not a good idea for Belinda to drink a large glass of wine at lunchtime in the sunshine, and then ask questions of potential murder suspects.

'I think what Belinda means is did you have an axe to grind?' said Harry.

'No.' Dan shook his head. 'To begin with, naturally, I was angry, upset and thought about closing the place down. The locals kept coming but when I asked them if they enjoyed it, they were perhaps more than honest. We retrained the staff and hired a new chef, switched the wines and beers, and the change was amazing.'

The restaurant manager took a long look at his premises. 'I owe her a favour. If it wasn't for Sadie, I wouldn't have revamped the menu and got to grips with the staff problems.' He stood up, putting the chair back. 'Thanks to you both for giving us a try today. I really need to get inside.'

They took their dismissal as what it was and walked out of the restaurant's seating area and onto the pavement.

Neither of them fancied a stroll around the shops and the market town was getting busier, so they decided to make tracks and go home.

It didn't go unnoticed by Harry that Belinda was extremely quiet on the way back. He wondered if he had upset her, but she seemed deep in contemplation.

'Will I see you tomorrow?' he said as he drove along the castle driveway.

'I expect so,' she said. 'We have three murders to solve.'

He pulled up at the side of the castle. 'Are you sure you're OK? If you don't mind me saying, you look tired.'

'I don't mind you saying.' She gave the start of a smile. 'I should take Horatio out for a nice long walk. He's been a bit neglected by me these last few days, the poor little mite.'

Harry gave her words more consideration than they deserved. He was stalling. 'I know what you mean. I've got to take the X-Ladies out for a stroll too. Hopefully their superpowers haven't kicked in or I'll be going home to them doing the wall of death around the dining room and I'll never get my rental deposit back.'

She laughed and said, 'It's OK, I know the landlady and I've heard she can be quite reasonable when it comes to witness protection programmes of the canine kind.'

Harry watched her go to the door where she had to fend off an assault by Horatio. He greeted her as only dogs could get away with: the pure unbridled dance of joy, the world's waggliest tail and a headbutt to the thigh. Perfection.

In typical Marcus fashion, he had misled Harry completely. Harry had tried to clear this up and now understood that he'd mentioned

Ivan only as part of the ruse to surprise him with the rug. When he pressed Marcus on the details of Belinda's ex's whereabouts, he got the usual daftness that accompanied everything Marcus did. The only concrete fact he was able to ascertain was that Ivan wouldn't be arriving in Little Challham imminently. It had calmed Harry's feelings for now, although he had a deep fear that sooner or later, he would turn up.

The rest of Harry's afternoon was mapped out. Once he got home, he'd take the dogs out, deliver a few orders and then provided the dogs were OK, he'd leave them while he went over to the depot to collect the rest of the week's deliveries. It felt unfulfilling, to say the least.

He sat in his car at the end of the castle's driveway, with no clear recollection of having driven down it, and wondered where he was going with all this. He had worked hard for thirty years as a policeman, and had taken retirement hard to begin with, easing into his new job, and then Belinda had come along.

The engine cut out as he put it into park, right in the centre of the open gates. He ran his hands across his face, fingertips rubbing into his eye sockets.

Should he go back and speak to her? Tell her how he really felt about her? Should he speak to her or do the decent thing and stand aside in case Ivan actually did turn up?

With an indecisive sigh, Harry opened his eyes and saw Daisy Thornton making her way to the delicatessen across the green.

'Not in custody now, then, Daisy,' said Harry to himself. His mind made up, he headed for home to drop the car off before he went to speak to her.

The Boxed Larder was only a short stroll from the Gatehouse. Harry walked across the green, saw that the blind was down and the door was displaying the 'Closed' sign.

Only too aware that he might be walking in on a couple in a state of undress, he made his way along the short side alley. The delivery yard was at the back and was where he had previously seen Daisy go when her postal round seemingly called for special customer care.

He heard scuffling in the back yard and cautiously peeked around the corner, hoping that the young couple weren't up to something that would be burned into his mind's eye for all eternity.

It was so much worse than what he had feared.

THIRTY

It took Harry longer than it should have done to figure out what he was looking at. Even then, he couldn't be sure that he wasn't having a hallucinogenic flashback, tripping thanks to a poisoned risotto. His brain tried to remind him he hadn't been poisoned in the first place, and that what he was watching was worryingly real.

Daisy Thornton was in Martin Box's back yard, wearing her Royal Mail shirt and shorts, standing in a children's paddling pool, crying silent tears, solemnly treading grapes.

She was sideways on to him and seemed to be marching on the spot, bashing her feet down to the bottom of the plastic paddling pool, one after the other, with the most concerning type of anger – measured anger.

When it got to the point that he felt like watching had propelled him to weird voyeur status, Harry gave a cough and stepped into the yard.

Daisy screamed, lost her footing and fell straight into the mushy pulp of several thousand grapes.

She stared up at him, tears rolling down her cheeks and straight into the fruity mess. 'I've hit my elbow.'

Unsure of the etiquette for helping a young woman out of a

paddling pool of stamped-on grapes, Harry said, 'Blimey. Bet that smarts.'

'It does,' she said, wiping her face with grape-stained fingers. 'Ow, ow. Now I've gone and rubbed it in my eyes.'

Reluctant as he was to use his favourite hanky, Harry knew he had no choice but to offer it to the distraught woman as she lay propping herself up on one arm. Daisy's long messy hair added to the budget mermaid look, if mermaids had taken to frolicking around in frogspawn. It wasn't Harry's area of expertise. Daisy's Royal Mail uniform was soaked in grape juice, although he was strangely relieved that she had at least taken her boots off.

Harry held out a hand to help her up, steadying himself in case she pulled him headfirst into the gloop.

Once Daisy was steady on her feet and dabbing her eyes with the handkerchief, Harry said, 'I know it's not really any of my business, but any chance you'd like to explain what you're doing?'

'Martin was supposed to help me,' she said, tears not relenting. 'I'm desperate, I didn't know what else to do.'

'OK... Why are you doing it at all? I know you're in a wine home brew group—'

Daisy started to sob.

Harry held out his hands, palms towards her. 'Sorry, sorry. You *were* in a wine home brew group and now it's more of a solo enterprise—'

Daisy made a wailing sound.

'Wrong choice of words,' he said. 'Forgive me, please. And why don't you at least get out of the paddling pool?'

She gingerly stepped over the ledge and onto the concrete floor.

'Thanks, Harry,' she said. 'I don't know what to do. It's all gone very wrong, you know? I started to panic.'

'Where's Martin?' said Harry, aware that he had wandered into the unsecured back yard of a man whose girlfriend was on the periphery of a murder investigation. Harry didn't fancy a surprise knock to the back of the head by either a jealous boyfriend or the murderer trying to literally kill off the competition to help the love of his life.

'He's at home with his mum,' said Daisy. 'I've told you I have a cat, so he can't stay at my place. This is the next best thing.'

Harry was a man of the world but even this set-up was a bit much for him. 'You mean, you and him...' He pointed to the grapes.

'No! We meet here when the place is closed or we— Hang on, we don't do that in here,' she said, looking mightily unhappy with Harry's train of thought. 'Is there something wrong with you?'

'Wrong with me?' he said. 'You're the one writhing around in a bowl of squashed grapes.'

'It's not a bowl, it's a paddling pool. Besides, I have to do this.' Daisy tried to brush the mess from her feet but didn't get very far. 'Look at the state of me. I don't know what I'm going to do.'

'My advice would be to hose it off, then get into the shower or perhaps a bath,' said Harry.

'Not that,' she said, avoiding making eye contact. 'I don't know what I'm going to do about *everything*.'

'What does Martin think you're doing here?' said Harry, more than a tad worried where this was going.

'I asked him to help me out with the home brew and he said he was busy, but that I should do whatever I needed to do. We don't usually make the wine like this, only I can't think straight.'

'I see,' said Harry, folding his arms and surveying the mess of the yard. He had never ventured inside it before, not having had any reason to. It was a thirty-five-by-thirty-five-foot space and other than the odd pallet or cage – and the paddling pool – was almost empty. 'What did he think you were going to get up to on your own?'

'Don't blame him,' she said, the threat of tears present once more. 'I've been so scared.'

'Of Martin?'

'Martin? Strewth, no. Not him.'

Her face was pale, and she was shaking. It was barely perceptible, yet Harry noticed her shoulders tensing inside her grape-stained shirt.

'Do you want me to call Martin?' he asked.

She shook her head. 'I don't think so.'

'What are you scared of?'

For the first time since he'd helped her up, Daisy looked straight at him. 'Whoever killed John and Richard is going to come for me.'

Her eyes were bloodshot, and she looked petrified. She hugged herself, her arms skinny and birdlike in her short-sleeved shirt.

'What makes you think that?'

Daisy gave a shrug. 'Don't know, but they're dead so it follows I'll be next.'

Harry stepped forward, thinking he should comfort her, but unwilling to touch her and stain his own clothing. He wanted to be a better person but also to avoid a boil wash.

'I think that's very unlikely,' he said. There probably was every chance she was next, but he hoped to avoid hysterics. 'If you're worried, we should speak to the police.'

'They're not going to be interested,' she said. 'They arrested me and didn't have enough to keep me, so they sent me away. All they said was that I wasn't to go anywhere.'

'When were you released?' said Harry.

'Only a few hours ago. They didn't interview me for all that long considering how long they kept me. By the time they took my clothes, went over a bunch of legal stuff and I had to wait for a solicitor, I'd already been there for what felt like an eternity. About the only evidence they had was that someone said they saw me at John Farthing's house a second time, on my own. This was much later, after Richard and I had already gone for the evening.'

Harry put his hands on her shoulders; she looked up at him. 'Where were you?'

'I was at home. Richard's wife dropped me off a bit after 10 p.m. and once I'd run myself a bath, I called Martin. Sometimes, the phone is the only intimacy we can manage. My alibis were the phone records.'

'How long was the phone call?'

Daisy had turned away from him, so her features were more difficult to make out. 'Three hours and fifty-six minutes.'

'Three hours and fifty-six minutes?' said Harry. 'That's some sort of intimacy.'

'See why the police had to let me go?' she said. 'Whoever said they'd seen me go back, said it was around midnight.'

Harry had no reason to doubt her. Donald Faraday must have been mistaken. He was, after all, basing his identification on someone's walk. Daisy couldn't have murdered Richard either if she was under the watchful eye of the police custody staff at the time.

'I think you should get cleaned up,' said Harry. 'The best thing is for you to come over to my house, and we'll get this mess sorted out before every insect in the county descends on us. Then we'll give PC Green a call and let him know where you are in case he thinks you've gone AWOL.'

She looked forlorn, yet somewhat relieved. 'OK, thanks, Harry. Can I ring my neighbour and ask her to look after my cat?'

He nodded. 'No problem.'

They stepped away from the yard and made their way back along the alley. Harry said, 'Any particular reason the paddling pool is shaped like an octopus?'

'They were out of sharks.'

THIRTY-ONE

Belinda brewed herself a coffee and calmed the over-excited Horatio while she drank it. She mulled over how she was going to spend the rest of her day. It wasn't as if she hadn't had a very full and busy life before Harry came along and the good folk of Little Challham took to murdering each other in alarming numbers. It was just that time seemed to stretch longer without her friend to talk to: an hour felt longer than sixty minutes, a day elongated beyond twenty-four of those tedious hours.

She shook herself out of her negative state of mind, traded her dress for cut-off jeans and a navy blue T-shirt, grabbed Horatio's lead and took him out for a stroll across the estate.

The views were as spectacular as ever, her dog overjoyed at each scent. The fresh air was invigorating as always.

Careful not to over-exert the young Labrador in the heat, Belinda took them on a route close to the barn where the wine tasting had taken place. It had only been three days ago, and yet felt as if it could have been much longer.

Belinda strode across the grass, trying to picture where vines might be planted, and how successful this enterprise could be. Perhaps she should leave it to the Ben Davieses of this world. It would, after all, involve her hiring an estate manager, a vineyard manager, a wine consultant, not to mention sales, delivery, cellar hands, an admin team. The list was endless.

Try as she might to concentrate on where she was going to find so many staff, her mind kept returning to the three murders in as many days. Wine connected them all, but was that the reason they were all killed? Could the home brew be that much of a vintage?

Daisy was the only one left alive in the group. She had a motive for killing Sadie if she had ridiculed their efforts. But why would Daisy bump off her own teammates?

She needed to speak to Harry. Things were probably not all as they seemed with Daisy, but thankfully the police had her locked up, so she and Harry had time to think. Their local postwoman was either the killer, or likely to be the next victim.

Belinda's feet took her back to the side kitchen door, her dog running ahead to reach his water bowl. Mind made up, she took her mobile phone out of her pocket. It was time to talk suspects and motives.

Her phone buzzed into life and Harry's name appeared on the screen.

With a smile in her voice, she said, 'Hi, H, I was just about to call you. Everything all right?'

There was the briefest of hesitations and he said, 'Hi, Belinda. I'm OK but I'm after a favour.'

'Go on.'

'Are you in a position to lend me some women's clothes?'

'Pardon?'

'Women's clothes. You know, a skirt, blouse, trousers...' There was muffled talking as if he had put his hand over the receiver. 'Shorts, apparently.'

'Harry, I don't want to judge, but I'd prefer it if you told me the ladies' attire is for you and not Raven and Rogue. That's too weird.'

He chuckled down the line. 'No, no. They're for Daisy. She fell over in the paddling pool.'

'When did you get a paddling pool?'

'I didn't, she did. She slipped on the grapes and now her uniform is covered in pips and all sorts.'

'Harry,' she said, a touch of urgency to her voice, 'am I on speakerphone?'

'No.'

'Great. I don't want her to hear this, but I was going to call you about her. There's something not right. She's either the killer or next to be killed. Whatever happens, be careful.'

The line went quiet. Belinda's heart was in her mouth.

'Harry, where are you?'

'I'm here. I was letting her know where I keep the towels.'

'She's at your place? Don't turn your back on her. I'll be right there.'

'Belinda, wait—' Harry lowered his voice and Belinda could hear a door close. 'Listen, we know she didn't kill Richard because she was under arrest when he died, so we've nothing to worry about on that front. But once you're here, we'll call PC Green. He promised to speak to us today anyway.'

'I'll be as quick as I can.'

'Make sure you walk down – you had wine at lunch... oh, and bring shorts and flip-flops.'

With that, he hung up.

THIRTY-TWO

It crossed Belinda's mind more than once, as she raced around finding some suitable attire, that Harry's life might actually be in danger. If not from Daisy herself, there was the chance that someone was about to creep into the Gatehouse and finish their home brew cull.

Belinda knew she shouldn't drive, although what were the actual chances of getting stopped by the police in her own driveway? Harry was practically next door to the entrance, but so was the green, teeming with young children who might run out in front of her. No, no, she would walk. Or jog.

She considered abandoning the clothes for Daisy and grabbing one of the gardeners for a lift. She had passed one on her way back inside from walking Horatio but in the amount of time she would waste finding him again and driving round to the front of the castle, she would probably be at Harry's anyway.

No, she'd grab a selection of garments that an off-duty postwoman/murder suspect might wear and get on with it.

Arriving at Harry's perspiring more than she cared to, slightly out of breath and very worried, was not how she wanted to make an entrance. But this was Harry, so she made haste. Once at the front door, she rapped the heavy black metal knocker as hard as she could.

'Blimey, Belinda,' said Harry when he opened it. 'I thought the bailiffs were here. No one knocks that loud, not even the police.'

'The police must have to knock loudly,' she said, trying to look over his shoulder. 'What about warrants and raids?'

'Largely, we kick the door in rather than— Oh, come in.'

She had grown tired of standing on tiptoe and besides, if she wanted to make sure Harry wasn't in any danger, standing on the doorstep wasn't going to cut the mustard. 'I've got a selection of things for her. Where is she?'

She stopped in the living room, hands on her hips, sunglasses skew-whiff.

'You're smiling,' she said. 'Why are you smiling?'

'It could have waited another half an hour or so, but I'm touched you're here so quickly.'

'Where is she and what's happened to Raven and Rogue?' said Belinda. From Harry's casual manner, it was evident that they hadn't come to any harm. Not so far, anyway.

'They're all in the garden. Come and have a look at how great they're all getting along.'

Belinda walked across the short hallway to the kitchen, where the window gave a full view of the garden, as well as of the two lurchers and Daisy. The young woman's hair was wet as if she had only just got out of the shower, and she was dressed in one of Harry's shirts. It seemed to be from his old work wardrobe – standard collar, a row of white buttons up the front and long sleeves which Daisy had had to roll up.

'She's made herself at home, then,' said Belinda.

'It was either that or wrap herself in a towel. I wasn't expecting you to be that quick.'

They both watched Daisy, who was sitting in one of the garden chairs, her legs stretched out in front of her in the sun, her top half and the snoozing dogs in the shade.

'I was worried about you,' said Belinda. 'That's why I was so quick.'

She wasn't looking at Harry but knew from the noise that he was scratching at his stubble. 'I apologise if you thought it was an emergency. I didn't give you any reason to worry about me. Besides, the police let her go because she was on the phone at the time Donald Faraday said he saw her at John's house. He must have got it wrong. Not to mention she was under arrest at the time of Richard's death. All I asked was, could you pop along with some clothes for Daisy.'

'That's the sort of thing you'd have said if she'd had a knife to your throat or was about to water-board you with poisoned wine.' Belinda spun around to face him. 'Please don't laugh at me. I was really worried.'

'I'm sorry. I tell you what, how about we have a code? If one of us is in danger, about to get hurt, we get the name of a drink into the conversation. Merlot or Cabernet Sauvignon.'

'Spitfire or IPA?' she said, not able to stay angry with him for longer than it took to down a swift half.

'Besides,' he said, 'I've got the X-Girls out there to take care of me.' He nodded at the relaxed scene through the window, all three of his house guests dozing in the warmth of the late afternoon.

'You're forgetting,' she said, eyebrows raised, 'the superheroes were with Richard Duke when someone stuffed his head in a rabbit hole and weighed it down with a boulder.'

'I've been thinking about that,' said Harry, folding his arms across his chest. 'Unless Richard was heavily drugged or completely out of it as the poison took effect, the only one who could have got away with that is Mrs Duke.'

'Mrs Duke was conveniently out of town,' said Belinda. 'Any idea if she's surfaced anywhere yet?'

'Not a clue, but speaking of clues, I've called PC Green and he's going to be here any minute. He wants to speak to both of us again and I need to let him know that Daisy is going to be staying with me for a few days.'

It was fortunate for Belinda's sang-froid that Harry couldn't see her expression. Her eyes were riveted by Daisy's very long and shapely legs.

THIRTY-THREE

In an effort to avoid PC Green's blushes, Belinda insisted that Daisy go and put on some of the clothes she had brought along. She packed her off upstairs, before rejoining Vince and Harry outside.

'Vince,' said Harry, 'you did say it was OK to call you Vince?' The officer, who had shed his jacket, nodded. 'I really think that Daisy is terrified. She was treading grapes in a paddling pool this afternoon.'

'I'm sorry, she was what?' said Vince.

'That's exactly how I sounded,' said Belinda, taking a sip of her lemonade.

'Other than blind panic, I haven't got to the bottom of why yet,' said Harry. 'I thought it best to wait until you got here. She told me she was on the phone at the time Donald Faraday said he saw her go back to John's house.'

Vince bit his lower lip, considered his words. 'It turns out that Mr Faraday is about to have one of his two cataracts removed next week. He was basing the entire identification on a walk and long blond hair.'

'That's embarrassing,' said Harry, eyes wide.

'I know,' said Vince. 'What a waste of time, and it gets us no closer to who's killing the home brew group.'

'Something we do want to ask before Daisy comes back,' said Harry, 'is what's happened to Richard's wife?'

'Yes,' said Belinda, edging forward on her seat, 'is she a suspect? We thought it had to be someone who knew the dogs or they might have attacked the killer.'

All three pairs of eyes turned towards the lurchers whose snores almost drowned out the conversation.

'We're still trying to find Imogen Duke,' said Vince. 'Her mobile phone has been off and she wasn't at the hotel she was booked in to. We can't rule her out until we speak to her. One thing we did find in one of the flower beds was an empty bag of dog treats. Someone possibly lured the dogs away from Richard as he crawled around on the ground. Mrs Duke would certainly know what goodies the dogs liked.'

'Donald Faraday – cataracts aside – said he saw a woman walking back towards John Farthing's house,' said Belinda. 'He might have mistaken Daisy for Richard's wife.'

'Imogen would definitely have known where John lived. That Sunday evening, she dropped her husband and Daisy off and picked them up again,' said Harry. 'On Monday morning, we found him dead.'

Vince gave this some thought while he sipped his drink. 'It's a possibility. We know that Mrs Duke is a brunette, but we also know the street lighting in Sellindge Close is virtually non-existent and Donald's eyesight is questionable. Until we find her, the last person we can be certain she spoke to, other than Richard, was Daisy.'

As if on cue, Daisy trotted out into the garden, holding a glass of lemonade. The pink linen shorts and white shirt she had taken the liberty of tying at the waist suited her, Belinda silently and grudgingly admitted. Daisy stopped in her tracks on seeing the police officer at the garden table.

'Hi, Daisy,' said Vince. 'Don't worry, I'm only here to make sure you're doing as well as you can be, and that Harry here is looking out for you. He told me on the phone that you were going to stay for a while.'

'I don't want to go home,' she said. 'I feel safer with him than I do by myself.'

'Would you come and answer some questions?' Vince said. 'Because this is a murder investigation, it's best to come see you in person and check on a couple of things.'

'More questions? Oh, I suppose so.' She huffed but took a seat opposite him.

'Why were you wearing your uniform today when you haven't been at work?' asked Vince.

She shrugged and said, 'You took my other uniform when I was at the police station and I wanted things to feel normal.' She looked down at her glass and swirled the ice cubes around. 'I also thought I had less chance of getting killed if I stood out in a Royal Mail uniform.'

Belinda doubted that made sense but kept the thought to herself.

'And why were you stamping on grapes in a paddling pool?' said Vince.

'I was panicking,' she said. 'In the last few days, three people have been murdered in this village, and two of them were friends of mine. Then, I get arrested.'

Daisy had been rubbing the ends of her fingertips together; now she stopped distracting herself and met Vince's gaze. 'We'd promised Frank at the Dog and Duck that we'd supply his wine, so I was trying to make some. With the others gone, I didn't want to let anyone down so I bought up all the grapes I could get my hands on and got cracking. I know how crazy, not to mention unhygienic, that sounds. I would never have let anyone drink any of it.'

'Under the circumstances,' said Belinda, 'I think that Frank would understand. I definitely won't hold you to the beer order for the New Inn.'

Daisy looked at her. 'Please don't cancel the order. We were working really hard to supply the local pubs. All the stuff we've been giving away has gone down well. We just weren't in a position to start selling it until the licences had come through. Besides, I'm going to need the money. I've just spent a fortune on grapes and an octopus-shaped paddling pool.'

'Where's the beer kept?' said Vince. 'It's not at John's, Richard's or your place. We searched them all.'

'It's at the new premises we started renting a month or so ago,' she said, turning her attention to Rogue who'd meandered over for some fussing.

'What!' said Vince. 'You never thought to tell us about this?'

'You didn't ask,' she said, scratching behind the dog's ears.

'I think I did.' Vince sat back, steely look on his face. 'Even so, you didn't consider mentioning it at any point.'

'Hang on,' said Belinda. 'Never mind that. Why were you squashing grapes at the back of the delicatessen if you have premises?'

'The wine-making kit isn't in the lock-up, and besides, I don't have the key.' Daisy watched Rogue as she walked away back to the shadier part of the garden.

'I think you should tell us exactly where it is and I'll get a search team to get over there right now,' said PC Green, clearly trying to keep calm, but not doing a very good job of it. 'Once they're ready, we can meet them there. Any idea where the key is?'

She shrugged. 'Either at John's or Richard's, I suppose.'

Vince took a couple of long, slow breaths and said, 'If we can't find it, we'll get in somehow. What's the address?'

'It's Unit 3B, Honeypot House, Honeypot Lane, Lower Wallop.' She pushed her feet under her chair and leaned forward on her knees. 'You will help me, won't you? I think someone's going to kill me.'

'You can stay here for as long as you need to,' said Harry, his smile crinkling the corners of his eyes. He looked over at Vince. 'Providing that's acceptable to you.'

'Or she could stay with me,' said Belinda. 'Let's be honest, I have more room than Harry and I could do with the company.'

'I'm happy to stay here,' said Daisy, a little too quickly.

'Look, I've let my boss know that Daisy is here, so if that changes, you'll have to let us know.' Vince pulled his grave expression again. 'Don't do anything without telling me first. I can't be clearer than that.'

Suitably chastised, Belinda knew that she would have to work on Harry before he agreed that the young woman with the very shapely legs should move up to the castle. In the meantime, she needed to speak to Harry on his own.

Vince had to make a couple of phone calls and Daisy was busy sunning herself, so as soon as Harry glanced her way, Belinda inclined her head towards the house and mouthed, 'Kitchen' at him.

With more subtlety than she would have given him credit for, Harry started to gather the empty glasses and lemonade jug. Seizing her chance, she jumped up and walked to the back door, holding it open for him.

Once they were both inside, she closed the door and said, 'We need to talk about this without Daisy hearing.'

'I don't think she's the killer,' said Harry, putting the glasses in the sink. 'I know that Donald Farthing *said* he saw her go back to John's house. Even leaving aside Vince's revelation of his star witness's deteriorating eyesight, Donald based her identity on her walk. That's a stretch too far, and besides, her mobile phone and boyfriend would say otherwise. It couldn't have been Daisy. And don't forget, she can't have killed Richard.'

Belinda arched an eyebrow at him. 'Boyfriends and girlfriends lie all the time, you know that. Is there any way that she could have left her mobile at home with the call connected and gone to John's house?'

Harry considered this for a second or two. 'It's possible, I suppose, but would she have had the strength to hold John down and pour alcohol down his throat? Vince hasn't been too forthcoming with the post-mortem results as yet. If we're saying that he was poisoned, we don't know whether it was a build-up or one hit. Don't forget that whoever it was would have needed a fair bit of strength to have kept Richard's head in the ground for a time too.'

Belinda checked through the window to make sure that the other two were still outside. 'That makes it sound as if you don't think a woman would physically be able to murder someone.'

'I suppose that if Richard had been tricked into putting his head in the hole after being poisoned, it might not have taken a huge amount of muscle to move the boulder. That would have held him in place. It's possible it was a woman.'

'I have the strength to murder anyone I choose, thank you very much,' said Belinda, gathering herself up to her full height. 'So why can't it be Daisy?'

'Everything's pointing towards someone destroying the competition, which includes Daisy.' Harry paused and looked at Belinda. 'If we're ruling Daisy out, she could be the next victim. How much safer will she be with you? How much safer will you be with *her*?'

'Well... much safer. I have locks on the doors and Marcus is there and some of the staff live in. That's why.'

That was a terrible lie, but she couldn't tell him the truth about why she wanted Daisy to move out.

THIRTY-FOUR

Vince's face was full of fury. He looked as if he might explode with rage.

'Is something wrong, Vince?' said Belinda as she loitered in the kitchen doorway. Daisy stood to the side perfecting her picture-of-innocence look, twirling the ends of her hair around her fingers.

'The lock-up contains alcohol,' he said.

'Yes, we know,' said Belinda. 'Casks of it, apparently.'

'Then that's a problem for a search team,' said Vince.

'Oh, I see,' said Harry.

Belinda looked from serving to retired officer and back again. 'Are the search teams all Temperance Society members?'

'No, I think Vince has just been told by his DCI that the place is a bonded warehouse,' said Harry, going back to washing up the glasses in the sink. 'That's quite the pretty pickle, then.'

'Bonded warehouse?' said Belinda. 'So the police can't get in?'

'No,' said Vince, his tone flat. 'We can't. No one can without the proper authority. It's to do with the movement of goods that are subject to excise. We have to go through the proper government channels to carry out a legal search and make sure anything we seize as a result of it is legitimate. There's no way around it.'

Harry said, 'That really will hold you up. In fact, it'll be as straightforward as getting into a customs house that stores alcohol.'

'I'll be off now,' said Vince. He pointed his finger at Daisy and said, 'I suggest you don't go anywhere near the lock-up.'

'She doesn't have the key,' said Belinda.

'I don't have the key,' said Daisy.

Vince nodded at Harry, got into his unmarked Ford Mondeo and drove away.

'What should we do now?' said Belinda, not relishing the idea of an afternoon of sitting around.

'We could go to the lock-up,' said Daisy, still twisting her hair around her index finger.

'You don't have a key,' said Harry. 'I was standing right here when we all confirmed this.'

'Daisy?' said Belinda.

'John always took care of the legal side of things,' said Daisy, a sly smile transforming her features. 'It was either twenty-four-hour security guards, something we couldn't afford, or CCTV, codes and alarms. We went for the cameras and alarms.'

'Are you telling me that you have the codes to get in?' said Belinda, warming to Daisy more than she had imagined.

'Yep,' said Daisy.

'Now, hang on,' said Harry. 'We told Vince—'

'He'll get over it,' said Belinda. 'Besides, we only need to have a look around. This may be our only chance to find something that the police might overlook without Daisy's help. Think about it: Daisy can't let the police in and it might take ages for Vince to get the proper authority to get inside.'

Harry wiped his hands on the tea towel. 'It's not a good idea. I'm telling you, we shouldn't be doing this.'

'Can I say something?' Daisy glanced at Belinda and then held Harry's gaze. 'I know that Belinda is extremely upset about Sadie Oppenshaw's death because it happened on her property, at an event she organised. Imagine how I feel having had two of my friends killed.'

'I—'

'Let her speak, H,' said Belinda, reaching over to take the sodden tea towel from Harry to stop him wrapping it round and round his knuckles.

'We were really starting to get somewhere in the last couple of weeks,' said Daisy, with a pride that hadn't previously shown itself. 'We'd been using John's shed for the stuff we were giving away, but the lock-up meant over a thousand pints a week, not to mention wine. And what's more, we could undercut the likes of Challham Valley.'

'Think about it, Harry,' said Belinda, standing beside Daisy. 'What if we find something at the lock-up that gives us an idea how or – as importantly – who poisoned the wine and killed three people? Not to mention, we might stop the killer from murdering someone else.'

'Then we go straight to the police with whatever we find?' said Harry.

'Agreed,' said Belinda and Daisy.

'Shall I get my whiteboards back out?' said Harry.

'No,' said Belinda and Daisy.

Once Harry had put the dogs inside the house and got his car keys, the three of them got into his Audi and headed for Honeypot House.

The route took them past the outskirts of Lower Wallop, along a dual carriageway and the back of a superstore. They drove into the industrial estate, past a veterinary practice, a tyre fitter, an electrical and plumbing wholesalers and a specialist engraver's and trophy suppliers.

The entire site consisted of twenty or so units, most of them positioned at the far end of the estate. It was encased by a tall fence of spiked metal posts – the only entrance was the gate they had driven through.

'It's the one on the other side of the engraver's,' said Daisy, moving to lean forwards between the two front seats.

Belinda was grappling to get her seat belt off and get to the lock-up before the car was fully at a stop.

'Belinda, wait,' said Harry. 'We don't know what we might find. If there's something important, we're going to have to let the police know.'

'We can worry about that if we need to.'

Belinda and Daisy were out of the car, heading towards the main door, Harry trailing behind.

It took them a surprisingly short amount of time to get inside the premises. There were several doors with security locks and keypads, including one that required Daisy to use her thumbprint. Once inside, Belinda and Harry marvelled at the size of the place. It was around a thousand square feet and held various-sized pieces of stainless steel beer-making equipment.

'You own all of this, Daisy?' said Harry, taking in the fermenters along the far side of the lock-up, cables and pipes leading from them to the rest of the gear.

She hooked her thumbs into the pockets of her shorts. 'John paid for it all. He bought the mash tun, the hot liquor tank, the kettle over there.' She nodded towards the three biggest vessels. 'And all of the rest of the equipment you see in here, and the big chiller at the back. We need somewhere that can be kept at a constant twelve degrees Celsius and it all costs. A lot.' Daisy walked in a small circle. 'I suppose that whoever inherits it from him owns it now.'

'How much did you invest?' said Harry. 'If you don't mind me asking.'

'I only gave my time, so I'm not going to be entitled to anything at all.' She said it without a trace of bitterness.

'What exactly are we looking for?' said Belinda.

'Some sort of clue that will help us find out who killed John and Richard,' said Harry. 'But I couldn't begin to tell you what that is.'

Belinda noticed Harry checking his watch.

'We shouldn't be in here for longer than we have to be,' he added.

'No one else will be able to get in,' said Daisy. 'I'm the only one alive who knows the code or who has a thumb with a pulse, so we're quite alone.'

The hairs on the back of Belinda's neck stood on end.

'Let's get on with it, anyway,' said Harry. 'I'll check the chiller.'

His footsteps resounded as he strode towards the rear of the industrial unit.

'Don't worry,' said Daisy. 'He can't get locked in – there's a large safety handle on the inside.'

'Phew,' said Belinda, not sure where to start on the impossible task of searching for the unknown.

Belinda found herself in the small office. There was only one desk, a chair and a table with a stack of papers on it. Nothing seemed out of place. They related to bills, invoices, licences for brewing and one that was pending to allow them to sell alcohol. Nothing jumped out at her.

'That's strange,' said Daisy, her voice carrying into the office.

'What's strange?' said Belinda.

'Some of the smaller pieces of equipment look like they've been moved,' said Daisy.

Belinda went to join her where she was examining a metal shelf that ran along the wall outside the office.

'Anything missing?' said Belinda, surprisingly relieved to hear Harry's footsteps approaching.

'Nothing out of place that I can see out there,' said Harry. 'What have you two found?'

They watched Daisy as she checked each piece of equipment on the shelf. She wrinkled her nose up at a used coffee mug that had been discarded, leaving its contents to grow its own fur coat.

'Either no one's been in here for days,' said Harry, 'or the cup was left some time ago and not washed up.'

'A habit of John's,' said Daisy. 'He was always leaving them here or in the office. I can't see that anything's been taken. Only that it looks as though it's been moved.'

'When were you last in here?' said Belinda.

'I was here on Friday with John and Richard,' she said. 'None of us stayed long and we all left together. We were going to discuss how to tackle the beer orders when we got together on Sunday night at John's. We sorted out how we were going to take it in turns here and get in someone else to cover for us when Richard or I had to be at work.'

Daisy's shoulders dropped and she traced her fingers up and down the shelf. 'We knew that we could easily make around twelve hundred pints of real ale a week. We had pubs and festivals agreeing to take our stock too. I guess that's all over now.'

'Wait a moment,' said Harry. 'You said you've got CCTV.'

Daisy's head jerked up. 'How stupid of me! Of course we've got CCTV. Let's have a look.'

She went to a large metal door set back in the wall. She punched in another code and the catch released.

Inside was a screen around the size of a large computer monitor and a series of buttons for the controls. Daisy pressed one of them and said, 'John and Richard struggled with this system a fair bit, especially John. He was forever trying to reset it and failing miserably.'

Belinda kept one eye on what Daisy was doing and the other on Harry, who was mesmerised by the screen. At least, that's what she hoped was taking all his attention.

'Here,' said Daisy after ten seconds or so. 'I have to leave it on record – it's one of the HMRC conditions that we don't switch it off – but I can run back over the last few days to see if anyone comes or goes. If I do it at super-fast speed, it won't take long. It'll be less tedious than trying to work out if anyone came in, and besides, they're not unique door codes so it won't tell us who it was.'

The footage blurred backwards at incredible speed, showing a totally uneventful view of the main door earlier that day. The same was true of Monday, then Sunday and then on Saturday, three figures approached the front door.

With trembling fingers, Daisy hesitated to pause the footage.

'Daisy,' said Harry. 'We need to see who that was.'

'I think I know,' said Belinda.

'I don't think I want to know,' said Daisy.

Harry had operated enough CCTV systems in his policing career to take over. He paused it and pressed play.

At thirteen minutes past eleven on Saturday morning, hours before the Challham Valley vineyard wine tasting had taken place at the castle, John Farthing, Richard Duke and Ben Davies had walked through the security door of the lock-up.

'They went behind my back,' said Daisy. 'Now two of them have been murdered. I told you I was next.'

THIRTY-FIVE

It was getting dark by the time the three of them left the industrial estate. Daisy had stopped convulsing long enough to get them back out through the security doors and safely into the back of the Audi.

Harry told Belinda that he would drop her off first before heading home. They would speak to her first thing to discuss where they should head from here.

'I don't think that we'll get a lot of sense out of Daisy tonight,' said Harry. She had crawled across the back seat and was staring out of the window into the gloom of the early evening.

'Are you sure that you don't want me to stay too, make sure she's OK, or even bring her to stay at mine?' said Belinda.

He couldn't decide whether Belinda was genuinely trying to help, or being a touch jealous. She had nothing to be worried about. Besides, it didn't seem like Daisy was capable of coherent speech, let alone anything that Belinda could fret over.

'I think she'll fall asleep immediately once we're back and I won't hear a peep out of her until the morning. First thing tomorrow, as soon as she's feeling up to it, we'll call Vince and let him know what we've found on the CCTV. I know he's going to go into orbit, but we'll deal with that in the morning.' As he spoke, the castle came into view in the distance. Only a few of the lights were illuminated, giving it a half-lived-in appearance, as if some of it was closed for business.

'You're quite right about how Vince is going to react,' said Belinda. 'But CCTV of Ben Davies being at the lock-up doesn't make him guilty of three murders. All the police can do is speak to him about it and he'll say he was there on a business trip.'

'Sadly, you're right,' said Harry. 'There's not enough to arrest him, let alone charge him with anything.'

Belinda insisted that he drop her at the bottom of the driveway and wouldn't take no for an answer. Worried that her vociferous arguing would upset Daisy, he let her out where she asked and headed back around the green to the Gatehouse.

Raven and Rogue were mildly interested in their return home, as only someone else's dogs can manage. They both welcomed the dog biscuits that Harry gave them as Daisy murmured, 'Night, Harry,' and headed for the stairs.

'Are you sure you're doing OK?' he asked her. 'Do you need anything?'

'No,' she said, waving away his concern. 'Thanks for giving me somewhere safe to stay.'

Harry let the dogs out into his garden, the security light coming on as they bounded across his lawn. He made a promise to take them for a long walk in the morning. Lurchers needed a fair amount of exercise, something that concerned Harry all the while he was looking after them. It also seemed a strange choice of dog for someone of Richard Duke's girth, but he put it down to their rabbit-hunting skills.

Once Raven and Rogue had done what they needed to, Harry called them inside and considered relaxing for an hour in front of the TV.

He could hear a curious sound coming from upstairs. Even the lurchers looked to the ceiling. His first thought propelled him into action – Daisy was being attacked in her sleep. But as he started towards the kitchen door, he realised that the noise was a deep and rhythmic one, not one of someone being beaten to a pulp. She was snoring. Yet it was snoring like no other.

He was on the ground floor, at the furthest point from the spare bedroom, and it was still bothering him.

Rogue whined and put her head down, Raven walked round and round in a circle. Harry opened the fridge and checked what was left. He fancied a snack. He also fancied getting some sleep. That didn't seem likely.

Until they solved the murders and it was safe for Daisy to go home – if she wasn't murdered in the meantime – Harry had no chance of getting a restful night's slumber.

'She either needs to be killed or move out,' he muttered to himself. He opened the cupboard to get a mug out as his mobile phone started to ring.

He picked it up and said, 'Belinda, hi. Is everything all right?'

'Yes, completely fine,' she said. 'Listen, Harry, I've been thinking. We should—'

'Oh, I understand,' he said, phone in one hand, amusing novelty mug in the other. 'What drink are you enjoying right now?'

'What drink am I—? No, it's all perfection itself here, other than Marcus and not one, but two of his crazy business ideas. Thanks for the concern but I'm not being held captive. Quite the opposite. I was thinking about what we saw on the brewery's CCTV tonight.'

'The brewery? Yes, I suppose they are a brewery. We said we'd speak about this in the morning and call Vince Green. Remember?'

'But that's my point,' Belinda trilled down the line. 'We saw Ben on their CCTV going to Richard, John and Daisy's premises. Daisy looked so genuinely shocked when we watched it that I think we can rule her out – again. The other two were up to something with Ben that they didn't let her in on.'

Harry looked up to the ceiling, where the wheezing and snorts seemed to be getting louder.

'Can you see a plan forming here?' said Belinda.

'Tennis ball in the pyjamas?'

'What are you on about?'

'Sorry,' said Harry. 'What's your idea?'

'It's simple and yet genius. We go to the Challham Valley estate and find evidence that Ben's behind the murders. Once we get that, we tell our new best friend Vince Green what we've found, Ben gets arrested, the police have the correct paperwork to search the brewery and the CCTV corroborates us.'

Harry put the mug back down and considered his options.

'What was that noise?' said Belinda.

'Er, noise?' said Harry, with another glance at the ceiling.

'It sounded like you were moving about.'

'I put a cup down,' he said, walking to the table and sitting down. 'Daisy's gone to bed, so I was about to make myself a coffee.'

'Coffee? You'll never sleep then. Tell you what – you come and pick me up in twenty minutes and we'll pay a late-night visit to the vineyard. That way, we may catch Ben doing something he shouldn't be. You said yourself that the CCTV probably wouldn't even get him arrested, let alone charged. If we get something more concrete, we'll be doing the overstretched, overworked, underpaid police a favour.'

He stared up at the ceiling again.

'Someone was trying to kill off the competition,' said Belinda. 'The answers must be in Challham Valley Winery. We should go tonight before we speak to Vince and the police start questioning Ben. Before he has a chance to destroy the evidence.'

'Really? Now?' he said, feeling his resolve crumble. She had a fair point.

'You can sleep when you're dead,' she said and hung up.

'That's about the only chance I'd have of getting any kip,' he said, before patting the dogs on the head and getting ready to go out once more.

THIRTY-SIX

'Hello, again,' said Harry as Belinda got back into his car.

He had driven up to the castle to meet her and she'd jumped into the passenger seat, sleep-deprived but alert.

'There's no time like the present,' she said. 'I got home and thought that we should go and see what we can uncover about Ben now. To be honest, I'm surprised that you were so easy to persuade. I would have thought that you'd have been more reluctant to leave Daisy.' She would never admit that she was mightily relieved he had agreed to come along.

'I've got to level with you, I don't think that she's in any imme-diate danger. The killer seems to be poisoning or drugging the victims, so as long as she doesn't get out of bed and polish off a bottle of wine, she'll be fine.' Harry knew that he had locked up the house and there were two dogs on the prowl. To be fair, they were two dogs that had apparently failed to stop their own owner's murder, but perhaps they would pick up crime prevention as they went. Not everyone was a fast learner.

'If you're prepared to leave her, I'm sure she's as safe as houses,' said Belinda. She settled back against the seat and looked out at the bright stars stappling the night's sky.

'When we get there,' said Harry, turning into the road that led to the vineyard's entrance, 'what are we going to say if we see Ben?'

'Say to him?' said Belinda. 'We're not going to say anything to him. We're going to make sure he's left the building and break in.'

'We're what?' He pulled over and sat looking at her, his mouth hanging open. 'I can't break into a vineyard.'

Belinda scoffed at him.

'Your attitude isn't helping,' he said. 'I definitely can't break into a vineyard and a brewery on the same day. It's a – it's a crime wave.'

'Would it make you feel any better if we waited until after midnight, and then it would be a different day?'

'No!' he said. After a couple of seconds, he added, 'Possibly, actually, it would.'

'Come on then, H, let's go and see what Ben's been up to.'

When they reached the road that ran alongside the vineyard, Harry pulled the car into an access road for one of the nearby fields.

'We can sit here, wait until the lights go off in the tasting room and watch who comes and goes,' said Harry. 'It's close enough to see any vehicles, although we may need the binoculars to read the number plates.' He opened the glove compartment and removed the binoculars that he and Alicia had used on their trip to the nature reserve.

'Seriously?' said Belinda. 'You're driving around with these? Are you trying to be a cliché amateur detective?'

'There's nothing amateur about my detective skills,' he said, sounding slightly hurt. 'This is from my grab-bag when I took Alicia on her surveillance training the other day.'

For the first time since they had left the castle, Belinda turned to face him and said, 'I'm sorry, I'd forgotten you were going to do that and I'm sorry for ridiculing you too. I know how seriously you take these things. How did it go?'

Harry scratched at his stubble and said, 'Not too bad considering that I'd put it together under time pressure. We went out to the nature reserve and she managed to find some pound coins.'

'Pound coins?' said Belinda. 'Like the ones we found in the rabbit hole along with Richard's very dead cranium?'

'Strewth, I hadn't thought that the two were connected,' he said. 'There's been so much going on that I didn't even link something so seemingly innocent as finding money on the ground. Or the empty wine bottle alongside the coins.' He covered his face with his hands. 'I'm losing the plot, Belinda.'

She put her hand on his arm and shook it. 'Come on, Harry. Give yourself a break. When did we last get a chance to catch up properly without worrying that Vince or Daisy would overhear us?'

Harry sat up straighter, hands back on the steering wheel. 'You're right. First Sadie's death, then John's, then Richard's, Daisy thrashing around in a children's paddling pool, Alicia finding pound coins in the nature reserve and then I saw Greg Davies wandering along—'

'Hang on. You saw Greg Davies where?'

'He was in the nature reserve... Oh. I told you I'm losing the plot.'

Now wasn't the time to get angry.

'When did you see him and where was he?'

'Me and Alicia went late on bank holiday Monday afternoon. We started off sitting off the pathway, you know, carrying out surveillance. She's a really lovely kid. She told me a joke about—'

'Harry.'

'Sorry. We were only about a hundred feet or so away from the car park. It's a public area, frequently busy. I didn't think much of seeing someone out for a stroll, even if he was paying more attention to his phone than the flora and fauna.'

Belinda had let go of his arm and was now kneading the sides of her head. 'A very nerdy young man who struck us as being very into his sci-fi books and little else was ambling along and you didn't think to tell me?'

'He had his face in his phone! For all I know, he was probably reading a book while he traipsed along.' Harry gave a little laugh.

'Perhaps he was texting or talking to someone. Did he say anything?'

Harry had the good grace to look embarrassed. 'Now you mention it, he said something like, "I've done it. She'll be impressed with this."'

Belinda knew that it had merely slipped Harry's mind, but this was not like him. 'Do you think he could have dropped the coins and the empty bottle?'

'I don't know.' He chewed his lower lip. 'Alicia only really found them because she was larking around with the binoculars and was off the path. I've no way of knowing whether Greg had come from that bit of the woods or not.'

'What bit of the woods?'

'We found them towards the rear of the nature reserve where it backs onto houses.'

'Houses like Richard Duke's? He could have been watching Richard, or even swapping a bottle of Richard's wine for a poisoned one.'

'Oh, my giddy aunt,' said Harry. 'I hadn't given it a second thought since Monday. We need to tell the police.'

'Not now,' said Belinda. 'The building's gone dark and there's a car just leaving. We get into the vineyard, see what we can find out and *then* we call the police.'

THIRTY-SEVEN

Belinda and Harry crept along the side of the road, ready to get out of view of any passing traffic. The car they had seen leave the Challham Valley estate had driven off in the opposite direction. They had further luck when they discovered a break in the hedges along the perimeter.

By this time, it was after midnight and the faint moonlight wasn't making their journey across the uneven ground any easier.

'I'm going to have to use my torch,' said Harry. 'One of us is in danger of breaking an ankle otherwise.'

'Fair enough,' said Belinda, feeling her way around the trees in the orchard. 'I don't fancy kicking over a beehive either.'

Apart from the sound of foxes and owls, very little stirred as they stole their way towards the main buildings.

As they got to the edge of the car park, emergency lighting in the tasting room giving out a faint eerie glow, Harry said, 'How are we going to get in if it's locked up?'

'I was hoping that they'd left a window open or the keys in the door.'

'Seriously? A set-up like this. I doubt that very much.'

'We don't have time to look everywhere, but I think that our best chance of finding anything is in the tasting room. It's where Ben's office is.'

It didn't take them long to make their way around the base of the building, trying windows and doors, but to no avail.

'This is hopeless,' said Harry, running an eye over what parts of the upper floor he could make out in the dark.

Belinda felt a crushing sense of disappointment. They had come this far, and she was sure there was something here that would help them solve the murders, if only they could get inside.

'There's no way of getting in without actually causing damage,' said Belinda.

'I'm not doing that. We'll get caught and I don't fancy getting arrested.'

She loved that he wouldn't consider smashing a pane of glass, even to solve three murders. His principles were part of his charm.

'Why are you smiling at me?' said Harry. 'I can't make out much, but I can see your teeth.'

'Come on,' she said. 'Perhaps we'll have more luck at the tour booking office.'

'I think you're barking up the wrong tree with young Greg,' said Harry, but fell in step beside her, shining his torch on the ground.

'We'll find out in a moment, won't we?' said Belinda, hoping that their luck had turned a corner.

The small one-storey building was dark, apart from a soft glow from the emergency exit lights.

'I didn't notice the staff room right at the back of the booking office when we were here on Sunday,' said Belinda, face pressed up against the window. 'I can only see it now because the interior door's been left open. I can see straight through.'

Harry joined her gazing through the window, heels of both hands up to the glass and his face close to the pane.

'There's something on the table there in the back that doesn't seem to be quite right to me,' he said.

'What? You mean there next to the coffee percolator?'

'Is that what it is?' said Harry. 'That's very fancy. We're probably talking Harvey Nichols, at the very least, John Lewis—'

'Harry, is there any chance you can stop going on about the coffee machine and tell me that you've brought the binoculars with you?'

'What, these?' he said with a grin and handed them to her.

'You are such a superstar.'

He preened. Even in the poor light, she could see it.

Belinda tried to focus on the table. With what little light there was glaring against the glass, the distance across the booking office to the staff room, plus the coffee machine obscuring her view, she was struggling.

She lowered the binoculars. 'I can't be certain, but it looks sort of hairy.'

'Hairy? Hairy like what?'

'Well, like hair.'

'Good grief! Do you think it's a head?' Harry reached for the binoculars. 'No, it's a bit small and flat for a head. Phew, that's a relief. Unless they've scalped someone.'

'Harry!' said Belinda. 'It's a wig. I think it's a blond wig.'

'Why would there be a blond wig in the staff room? Greg or Ben have access to the booking office, plus all the other staff who work here. This doesn't really narrow it down.'

'It's more likely to be either Greg who works here in the booking office, or Ben who'd have the keys to every part of the winery,' said Belinda.

'Or someone panicked and left it here by accident,' said Harry.

'Donald said he saw a woman walking to John Faraday's house the night he was murdered,' said Belinda. 'Perhaps a long blond wig made him think it was a woman, and then he convinced himself it was definitely Daisy.'

'Right,' said Belinda. 'Now we call the police.' She took her phone out of her pocket.

Harry put a hand over hers. 'Think about it for a moment: we're trespassing on someone's land, we're peering through a window at a wig, and we're going to call the police and say, "The wig did it." Sorry, but we need more.'

'Do you have any further suggestions?' said Belinda, back to that crushing despair that they were getting nowhere.

They both looked forlornly through the window.

'We didn't try the door to see if it's unlocked,' said Belinda.

Harry tried the handle. It didn't budge.

'That's that, then,' he said.

'If we can't take the evidence with us,' said Belinda, mobile phone still in her hand, 'the least I can do is to take some pictures.'

She lined up several shots of the wig, zooming in as much as her mobile phone would allow.

'Belinda—' said Harry.

'I'm taking one more shot. I want to make sure that these are good enough to show Vince.'

'Belinda—'

'I'm almost done.'

'Belinda, someone's coming. I can hear a vehicle.'

Panicked, Belinda allowed Harry to grab her hand and lead her away into the trees.

They stood behind the cover of the branches as a small white van with 'Security Guarded' emblazoned on the side of it drove across the car park and towards the booking office.

The van stopped short of the building and a man in a hi-vis jacket got out. He gave a cursory check in all directions, a complete slow circle with his torch – more for show than anything else, thought Belinda – and ambled towards the door. He stood on the veranda where only a minute before, Belinda and Harry had been. He peered through the window and tried the door. Satisfied, he made a call and said, 'Alpha Delta, one six. Hello, Barry, it's Stan. No. There's no one here. It must have been a false alarm.'

With that, he was back in his van and away again.

Harry let out a long, slow breath. 'That's enough for one night. Come on, let's go.'

For once, Belinda agreed with him.

THIRTY-EIGHT

Harry hardly slept all night. From the moment he had got home, to the moment he got out of bed the next day, he was fully aware that Daisy was alive and well from the amount of noise she was generating. He attempted to sleep with a pillow over his ears but that made breathing more of a problem. He failed to stop his mind from working through the murders and what he and Belinda needed to do.

The sun was coming up and not only had Harry got no further with working out who the killer was, he was exhausted.

He sat on the edge of the bed, knowing that he had a long day ahead of him. Murders aside, the dogs needed a decent walk, he needed to get some work done and there was hardly any food in the house. Apart from dog food. Happily, he had that in spades.

Weary but determined to get through the day without nodding off, he forced himself to get up and showered.

The noise got worse as he opened the bedroom door and went towards the bathroom.

After a shower of some ten minutes in duration, Harry emerged from the bathroom as refreshed as he was going to be. With his dressing gown on and rubbing his hair with a towel, he opened the door to see Daisy leaning against the spare room door frame.

Although he was reluctant to allow his eyes to travel away from her face – she was in the hallway in her borrowed nightwear for starters – her expression was one hundred per cent annoyed.

'The sound of the shower pump is *so* loud,' she said. 'I've been awake ever since you turned the taps on. It's a tad on the inconsiderate side.'

Momentarily he was speechless. He opened his mouth to say something that he would probably later regret. Then a thought struck him.

'Daisy, the last thing I want to do is stop you sleeping,' he said. 'I've an idea that will help. Get yourself dressed and you can go and stay with Belinda. She offered, and besides, why wouldn't you want to stay over in a castle?'

He walked away, frisking his reddish-grey hair with the towel and whistling the theme tune to *The Dukes of Hazzard*. It must have been the combination of Daisy, Duke and shorts.

'Belinda,' said Harry, all but throwing Daisy's meagre possessions across the threshold of the castle front door. 'Thank you so much for this. I know this is the best place for her. I've got so much to do, what with walking Rogue and Raven, sorting out the supplies for work and well... stuff.'

His friend picked up the beach bag she had only taken to Harry's the day before, turned a slightly intrigued look from Harry to Daisy and said, 'Always happy to help you both out. Why don't you come in?'

They stepped into the hallway, Belinda moving aside to allow the two of them in.

'Wow,' said Daisy, who was wearing another of Belinda's blouses, this time a lemon-coloured cotton one tied at the waist, and the same shorts from the day before. 'I've only ever dropped the post off. I've never actually been across the threshold. This is seriously impressive. The high ceilings, the wooden floor, the staircase. You're really fine with me staying?'

'For a day or two,' said Belinda. 'I'm sure we'll have worked out who the killer is long before then.'

'Or killers,' said Daisy, her attention drawn to the magnificent staircase.

'Why do you say that?' said Belinda.

'For example,' said Daisy, 'all this time, you've been convinced it's not me because I have an alibi. It could be me and Martin doing it together.'

'What would your motive be?' said Harry, now not so sure he should have brought someone on bail for murder to his friend's home.

Daisy opened her arms and said, 'Perhaps I was desperate to come to the castle.'

'Then you should have taken a guided tour,' said Belinda, her face showing she wasn't in the mood for time-wasting.

Daisy grinned and said, 'Any chance of a coffee?'

'Come on,' said Belinda. 'Leave your bag there and I'll get someone to take it up to your room.'

They walked to the garden kitchen, a room favoured by Belinda and somewhere Harry always felt remarkably comfortable. Belinda set about making them coffee.

'Thanks again for this, Belinda,' Harry said. She smiled at him as she got cups from the cupboard and milk from the fridge.

'Oh, yeah, thanks so much,' said Daisy, busy texting.

'We have to let Vince know that Daisy's here,' said Belinda.

'I've already sent him a message,' said Harry. 'He's bound to want to come and see us.'

Once Belinda had placed the cups on the table, she said, 'Harry and I discovered something last night, Daisy.'

Daisy sat at the table, long blond hair draped over her shoulders. 'Last night? What happened last night?'

Harry and Belinda exchanged looks. Daisy's earlier comments about there being two killers had put him on edge. This was Belinda's call: they were now in her home so any information his friend wanted to impart was fine by him. At the end of the conversation, if there was any chance that Belinda might be in danger, the suspected murderess wasn't staying.

'We went to the Challham Valley estate after you were asleep,' said Belinda.

'I didn't hear you,' said Daisy, look of surprise crossing her face.

'I'm not surprised,' said Harry. When their curious expressions turned to him, he added, 'After the day you'd had, you were dead to the world.'

'Anyway,' said Belinda, picking her phone up from the kitchen table, 'I need to show you this.'

Both Harry and Belinda watched Daisy for any sign of pretence or faked surprise as the photos on the phone were shown to her one at a time.

'We took these last night, at the tour booking office at Challham Valley,' said Harry. 'This first one here is definitely a blond wig, not dissimilar to your hair.' He felt the need to point at her head, in case she wasn't aware where her hair was located.

'It's a wig,' said Daisy, mouth open and eyes large.

'I take it you're talking about the one in the photo and not your own,' said Harry, earning him an intense stare from Belinda.

Daisy tugged at her own locks. 'Is there something wrong with you? Naturally it's my hair. It's what this wig, here, is plonked in front of that's the shocker.'

She gave a bewildered shake of her head and blew the air from her cheeks.

Completely flummoxed, Harry stared intently at the phone screen. 'What? The coffee maker? I thought that was top end.'

'No,' said Daisy. 'How could I have been so stupid? That's how they did it! Don't you see now?'

'Hello, you three,' said Marcus from the doorway. 'Sorry to interrupt you, sis. I have a couple of business ideas I'd like to run by you. Would now be a good time?'

'No,' said Belinda. 'It really wouldn't.'

He gave one of his most alluring smiles to Daisy who crossed her legs and moved to lean one of her arms on the top of the chair. 'Oh, hi,' she said, smiling back. 'I'm Daisy. I'm your postwoman.'

'Well, I'll be,' said Marcus. 'Unusual uniform, by the way. I don't believe we've had the pleasure.'

'And you won't have the pleasure now, Marcus,' said Belinda.

'Don't worry about me,' he said. 'I'm not in a hurry.'

He took a seat and said, 'One of my business ideas – listen closely if you've money to invest, Daisy – is moustache guards! Think about it. If you've facial furniture, and let's be honest, many people do these days – men mostly, I think. I can never be too sure who I'm offending these days. I'm saying men, but it could as easily be women, or in fact, it could be they. To be honest, as long as they've got a few quid, I couldn't care less. I've designed a handy lid to put on your pint glass so the froth doesn't soak your top lip's coiffure. It's like an umbrella for your face.'

'Marcus,' snapped Belinda. 'We were in the middle of something here. Do you mind?'

'No, carry on.'

'What were you saying, Daisy?' said Harry, feeling as though he was probably the sanest and calmest in the room.

'The photo,' she said, 'show me again.' She enlarged it. 'I've been very stupid, so stupid.'

Her eyes, now wide and unblinking, darted from Belinda to Harry.

'You don't know what this is, do you?' She pointed at the photo.

'De'Longhi?' said Harry.

'No.' Daisy shook her head. 'It's a table top still.'

'What?' said Harry.

'What does it do?' said Belinda.

'Oh, that's clever,' said Marcus. 'Is that how they made the alcohol?'

'Sorry, sorry,' said Belinda, holding her hands up in surrender.

'Will one of you tell me what a table top still is and what it's been used for?'

'We've got one similar to this at the lock-up,' said Daisy, jabbing at the phone screen.

'And it's used for what, exactly?' said Belinda.

'Making alcohol,' said Marcus. 'We used to use a much less sophisticated version at boarding school. Happy memories. Or lack of them, now I come to think about it.'

'It's like making your own hooch,' said Daisy. 'The alcohol levels would be very high. For example, say you start with a base alcohol, such as unhopped beer or cider. By passing it through the still you burn off the alcohol as it has a lower evaporation point than water.'

'With you so far,' said Harry.

'So, the alcohol and some fluid vapour are caught in the chimney system and redirected into another vessel,' said Daisy, her audience enthralled. 'That will increase the ABV – that's alcohol by volume to you – of the end product. If you use cider, it becomes calvados brandy, and beer becomes whiskey. If the beer contains rye in the base mix it become bourbon. The more times you pass liquid through the still, the smoother it gets. Jameson's whiskey, for example, is stilled three times, and is very smooth as a result.'

'Alcohol itself has no smell or taste,' said Harry. 'It's why police officers have to state in evidence that someone smelt of intoxicating liquor and not alcohol. Sadie wouldn't have been able to taste anything but the wine. If someone had upped the alcohol content, or even added something else to the wine, she'd have had no way of knowing.'

'But Richard Duke didn't die instantly,' said Belinda. 'We know that because he left the house and went outside with his dogs and ended up putting his head in a rabbit hole. Someone finished him off by holding him there.'

'Perhaps the percentage of alcohol wasn't high enough to finish him off,' said Harry. 'Think about it – Sadie was very small in comparison. She died quickly. John died in his armchair, so we don't know how long that would have taken.'

'Whoever was doing it didn't always get the dosage right,' said Belinda.

'I say,' said Marcus, 'this is all incredibly exciting.'

'People have died, Marcus,' said Belinda. 'It's not exciting at all.'

'Sorry, sis.' He got up and planted a kiss on the top of her head. 'Listen, I've got to be off. I'm meeting a fellow in the village to talk to him about beard glitter.'

'Did you say "beard glitter"?' said Harry.

'Yes, I did,' said Marcus, moving closer to Harry and staring at his chin. 'I'd say it's rather like a beard-jazzle and you could be my new model. The face of the beard-jazzle.'

'No, you're all right, mate,' said Harry, with a slow shake of his head.

'Is your brother usually like that?' said Daisy, watching him leave the kitchen and go off in the direction of the garden.

'It's a long story, but yes,' said Belinda. 'How difficult is it to get a table top still?'

'It's not.' Daisy settled back in her chair, playing with the ends of her hair. 'You could get one online or from a home brew shop or suppliers. We didn't really have any use for ours as our licence was only ever for wine, cider and beer. We'd have needed a different licence for anything over thirty-one per cent and never had the time to make spirits anyway.'

'If yours is still at the lock-up and they're that easy to buy, anyone could have bought it,' said Belinda.

'But it does narrow it down to any of the staff at Challham Valley vineyard who had access to the one in the office,' said Harry. His expression hardened. 'Our prime suspects have to be Ben and Greg.'

'Ben was at the lock-up with John and Richard,' said Belinda.

'But both the wig and the still were in the staff room at the booking office where Greg works,' said Harry.

'And you saw Greg at the nature reserve where you found some pound coins on the way to Richard Duke's house hours before he was murdered,' said Belinda.

'This is all getting a bit much for me, you know?' said Daisy. 'I'm a postal delivery person who wanted to make a bit of real ale and some wine to supplement my income. Now I'm on bail for murder talking to you two about suspects.'

The last few days did appear to have taken a toll on her. Her skin looked a bit blotchy and she had dark rings under her eyes.

'We have a swimming pool if you'd like to go for a swim. Clear your head?' said Belinda.

At this news, Daisy's face lit up.

'Come with me and I'll find you a suitable costume.' Belinda led the way upstairs to find her guest something else to wear.

Harry refilled his coffee while they were gone, and marvelled at the generosity of his friend. As soon as this was over, he was going to tell her what was going on. He knew he could rely on her support. She might even think more of him. Wouldn't that be a bonus?

THIRTY-NINE

With Daisy out of the way, merrily swimming up and down in the pool, Belinda took the opportunity to speak to Harry alone.

'Why were you so keen to bring Daisy over here?' she asked as they took Horatio for a stroll around the castle grounds. The Labrador was running off and sniffing in all of his favourite spots.

'No particular reason,' said Harry. 'I think that she could probably have done with having another woman around, especially as she seems to like your clothes so much.'

Belinda considered this for a moment. She chose to ignore the red tinge to his cheeks, which was not brought on by physical exertion as they were currently moving downhill at a fairly gentle pace.

Whatever the reason, Belinda was glad that Daisy wasn't at Harry's home, not that she had any right to tell him what to do. The envelope addressed to Harry's ex-girlfriend coupled with Belinda's inner turmoil at seeing Ivan on her brother's video message, were surely bad omens. It would wait for another time. Once the killer had been caught, they could sit down and have a frank conversation about where they were in life. For now, they had to catch a murderer.

'The only way the police are going to take us seriously is if we find a way to flush the killer out,' said Belinda, stopping to give a shrill whistle at Horatio who was digging frantically at a mole hill. 'If it's Ben or Greg or even Ben *and* Greg, it's either because Ben really was rattled about Sadie and the power she had over the local wine trade, or misguided loyalty from Greg over the threat to his dad's empire.'

'Both of them have access to the tour booking office where the wig and still were kept, but then so do the rest of the staff,' said Harry.

'I can't see a member of staff being prepared to murder three people, all because of potential terrible reviews and some tough competition for their employer,' said Belinda. 'It's so revolting, I can't think who would do such a despicable thing.'

'The easiest way to find out who it is, would be to lure them somewhere by pretending we have a vital piece of evidence, get them to confess and we've got them bang to rights,' said Harry.

'Not a phrase I've ever used, but, yes, that's about it. Except how do we do it?'

'We're going to need some help,' said Harry. 'Any ideas?'

Belinda turned to him with a grin from ear to ear. 'As it happens, I do.'

By late afternoon, everything was in place. Harry was pacing nervously in the drawing room. More than once, Belinda saw him turn towards her where she sat in the armchair, head back, trying to enjoy a camomile tea.

Daisy was out on the patio, listening to Marcus's plan for world domination of beard and moustache accessories, and Horatio snoozed by the open patio door.

'I think it's time, Harry,' she said.

He looked very nervous, something that she would ordinarily have found funny, but there was a lot at stake.

'OK.' He smiled and straightened his jacket. She appreciated the effort he had made. He had gone home to make sure the lurchers were suitably refreshed and returned dressed in a pair of black trousers that she suspected were from his previous life as a detective inspector, a cream shirt and a casual black jacket.

Belinda herself had opted for a black-and-white-print midi dress. The square neck and simple straps gave her room to move, something she needed to do after spending a considerable time talking the plan through and making phone calls.

'Let's go ensnare a killer,' she said.

They took Belinda's Land Rover to the Challham Valley Winery tasting room.

'Ready?' said Belinda as she turned off the engine and looked over at him.

Wordlessly, he undid his seat belt, cracked open the passenger door and nodded.

She was worried about Harry. Was this really the sort of thing she should be getting him mixed up in? She was anxious that he was doing it for the wrong reasons.

'Harry.' She placed her hand on his arm, stopping him from getting out of the car. 'As long as you're sure.'

'Wouldn't be anywhere else right now,' he said, giving her hand a reassuring pat.

They walked from the car park to the entrance of the tasting room. They had timed their visit for when the tour booking office was closed up for the day, giving them one less thing to contend with.

Once in the lift, Belinda said, 'If luck is really on our side, Greg will be in the bar.'

'Fingers crossed,' said Harry. 'As long as she's definitely here as well.'

The doors opened to reveal a half dozen customers occupying four of the tables. Three men of about thirty years of age sat at one table by the window, a man in his mid-sixties sat at another, a woman in her fifties sat at one of the high tables near the bar and the final person was a woman who sat with her back to the lift, at a table in the middle of the bar area.

Her dress was red silk, her bare arms tanned and toned. Her brunette hair was mid-length and was pulled back with a crystal hair barrette.

Belinda pointed to the woman. 'That's her.'

'Really?' said Harry. 'It can't be.'

'Come on.' Belinda walked towards her, with a quick wave at those assembled behind the bar. As she had expected, Ben Davies was on the other side of the counter chatting through the stock with the ever-exhausted Lucy Field. Belinda was relieved to see Greg also in the bar at the far end by the kitchen door, head down, tapping away on his mobile.

Ben and Lucy looked up. Both smiled and waved, although they paused when Belinda and Harry approached the woman sitting with a mineral water in front of her.

'Hello,' said Belinda, stopping at the table. 'I'm Belinda. We spoke on the phone. This is Harry.'

The woman looked up and smiled at them, a sad, lost air to her movements. It looked as though she'd been crying and had hastily reapplied her make-up. Her eyebrows were dark, her mouth wide and her lips full, balanced out by elegant cheekbones.

'Please, take a seat,' she said. 'Harry, I have to thank you for looking after my dogs,' she went on, turning her attention to him. 'You don't know what it means to know they've been well cared for.'

'Er, er, hello,' he said.

'Harry, this is Imogen Duke,' said Belinda, a little guilty she had surprised him with this, but also a touch amused at his reaction. To be totally fair, Imogen Duke hadn't been what she was expecting either. She resembled a modern-day Lauren Bacall, so his reaction wasn't completely out of proportion.

'I'm Imogen,' said Imogen. 'I understand that you found... Richard.'

They paused in a loaded silence as she stuck out her chin and tried not to cry.

'Sorry,' she said. 'We were the best of friends, we really were. I can't believe what's happened. It's like a bad nightmare that I think I'm going to wake up from, except I don't.'

'The last thing we want to do is upset you further,' said Belinda, kicking at Harry's foot under the table to stop him gawping, 'but is there anyone in the bar, or behind the bar, that you recognise? I wouldn't ask you if it wasn't important.'

Taking her time, as the truly heartbroken do when every movement hurts, Imogen turned to look at each of the customers in turn and then everyone behind the bar.

'Before you answer,' said Belinda, 'could I ask that you stand up and take a closer look over at the bar?'

Clearly slightly puzzled, Imogen got to her feet and, blinking away tears, did as Belinda asked.

'No,' she said when she sat back down. 'I'm very sorry, but no, I don't know any of them.'

'Thank you, anyway,' said Belinda. 'How about Harry walks you back to your car? I need a minute here.'

Neither Imogen nor Harry appeared entirely convinced they understood what had happened, but they obliged and left the bar via the lift.

Ben was staring after them, Lucy was polishing glasses and Greg gave the impression he hadn't so much as glanced up from his phone.

Belinda got up from the table and walked to the bar. She stood directly in front of the vineyard owner. 'Hello, Ben. Quiet in here today.'

'Can I get you something?' said Lucy. 'Glass of wine? Something to eat?'

'Who was that?' said Ben, pointing towards the lift doors.

'That was Imogen Duke,' she said. 'Terribly sad, isn't it? She's understandably beside herself with grief. I only popped over in case she hadn't paid her bill.'

'No, it's all settled,' said Lucy, 'but thanks for checking.'

'Do you think she killed him?' said Ben.

'I don't think so,' said Belinda. 'She doesn't strike me as the type, and anyway, she's unlikely to have murdered John and Sadie. No motive that I can see and very little in the way of opportunity. No, there's something we're missing. Luckily, for us, we've had a bit of a breakthrough.' She leaned further over the bar towards Ben, her voice loud enough for Greg to hear too. 'The police want to come back and search the barn again first thing in the morning. They've had some sort of forensic result come back, and, well... But please keep this to yourself. Harry would go absolutely into orbit if he knew I was telling you.' Belinda glanced over her shoulder. 'Can't be too careful. Anyway, fingers crossed that this will be over soon. Take care.'

With that she walked away. Her hand was shaking as she tried to summon the lift, forcing herself not to repeatedly jab at the button.

Then she was inside the empty lift, doors about to close when she caught a glimpse of Ben grabbing Greg's phone from him and pressing his index finger into the lad's chest.

Belinda reached the ground floor and walked to the car park as fast as she could without actually running. She gave the impression of taking it all in her stride, but right at that moment, her strides would have been more akin to leaps.

There was no sign of Imogen in the car park, only Harry standing next to her Land Rover.

'Did she get away all right?' said Belinda.

'Yes, she's as fine as she can be.' Harry stood between her and the driver's door. 'More importantly, are you?'

With a nod and a forced smile, she said, 'It was a bit nerve-racking. Now it's over, I feel as though it was a bit of a buzz.'

'Let's not get too carried away,' he said. 'We've still got to get through tonight.' He stepped out of her way so that she could get to the door.

'By the way,' he said, 'any reason you didn't tell me what Imogen looked like before we met her?'

She shrugged. 'Would it have made any difference if you'd have known she was so attractive?'

'I suppose not,' said Harry. 'But I had a picture in my head of what Richard Duke's wife was going to look like. I haven't seen such an unlikely pairing since... Roger and Jessica Rabbit.'

FORTY

Belinda had to hand it to Harry: for a man who had privately admitted that he had never once in his police career carried out surveillance work, he sounded very calm and settled in the dark of the night, his silhouette illuminated by only the faint glow of the emergency lighting.

They had hidden away in the barn on the Penshurst land some hours ago, before it had started to get dark. Belinda had insisted that they couldn't go on a stakeout without recliner chairs.

'No one says "stakeout," and no one goes on surveillance with a chaise longue,' Harry told her for the tenth time.

'Then why are we here in the former venue of a disastrous wine tasting and somewhat more successful murder, almost in the horizontal position?'

'Because we needed to get into the barn without being seen, and your idea of backing a van up to the doors and having your gardeners unload furniture was the best way to do it.'

'Thank you.'

'You're welcome.'

They were silent for a short while until Belinda's phone lit up, almost dazzling in the darkness. 'It's Marcus,' she said. 'He's texted to say that he and Daisy are getting on like a house on fire and she's thinking of going into business with him.'

'Anything about what they're actually supposed to be doing?'

'Er... let's see. Oh, yes. They're both in their positions. The night vision glasses are superb. He's just seen two foxes that looked as if they were— Never mind about that. He can see the area leading up to the back of the barn and Daisy is at the castle keeping watch on the front. I'd say we've got it covered.'

'As long as we really can trust Daisy,' said Harry.

'Bit late for that now,' said Belinda.

The silence returned for the briefest of time until Harry's stomach started to growl.

'That's very loud,' said Belinda. 'Any chance you can stop it doing that?'

'Not unless you've brought some food with you?'

'No. All we've got is that flask of coffee that Daisy made for us. It's probably getting cold by now.'

'You arranged for armchairs, but not—'

Belinda's phone lit up once more. 'It's Marcus again. He can't get hold of Daisy but thinks he can see someone walking through the woods heading this way.'

'Game on, then,' said Harry, easing himself out of the chair. 'I'll stand next to the door out of sight. Once they're inside, I'll be able to grab them as they come in.'

She nodded and then realised that he probably couldn't see her from where he was. Butterflies were colliding in her stomach as she got up from her own chair and felt her way round to her position, where one of the vineyard's advertising boards could serve as her hiding place.

They stood poised, waiting.

For what seemed like an eternity, nothing moved or stirred. And then they heard it, the unmistakable sound of someone forcing a panel on the other side of the barn.

Of course whoever it was would come back the same way they had first forced their way inside. Since the police had released the place, all Belinda had had time to do was instruct the estate manager to put a temporary fix in place. The noise was becoming louder and more frantic. Whoever it was, meant business.

Holding her breath, Belinda watched as the light from a torch shone in slivers through the gaps in the wooden slats, the flashes jerking and frantic as a gloved hand broke through. Then a second hand holding the torch. More wriggling and inching along as a balaclava-covered head appeared. The sight of the face hidden from view made it hit home that this was a killer who would go to any lengths to avoid being identified.

The hands crept forward, pulling the rest of the intruder's body behind it, scraping along the wooden floor. The second their torso was through the gap, Harry sprung the width of the barn to grab hold of an arm and Belinda reached beside her to the light switch.

'You scared me – let go,' shouted the person Harry had grasped.

Belinda looked on in disbelief. It was neither Ben nor Greg. That much was clear.

Unable to trust her ears, the only way to be sure was to see the intruder's face.

'It's not what you think—' they started, but the words were lost as the barn door was shoved open and Marcus tumbled inside, complete with someone held in a headlock.

'Look who I've got!' he said. 'Saw him sneaking away again. Thought the toe-rag had seen me so I grabbed hold of him and got him over here.'

Marcus's face was red and sweaty and he was slightly out of breath, although he looked like he was having the time of his life.

'I'm going to tell my dad,' said Greg Davies from somewhere around Marcus's left armpit.

'Oh, you will, will you, you little scally.' Marcus tweaked the lad's pimply nose.

'Let him go, Marcus,' said Belinda. 'He's not the killer.'

'No?' said Marcus.

'No, he's not,' said Ben Davies, appearing in the barn doorway. 'Let go of my son.'

He appeared bigger and taller than normal. Perhaps it was the threat to his offspring, or maybe murder did that.

'It's her you want,' said Ben, pointing across the barn towards the woman Harry was still struggling to keep hold of.

She ripped the balaclava from her face with the arm Harry wasn't holding and shouted, 'What are you *doing* here?'

'Lucy!' said Belinda. 'Lucy!'

'Hello,' said Marcus. 'We haven't had the pleasure.'

'Not now, Marcus,' said Belinda.

'I followed you here,' said Ben.

'You knew it was her?' said Harry.

'I had my suspicions, but didn't want to admit it,' said Ben. 'At first, I excused her behaviour because her mum's been so poorly. Now, I don't know.' He shook his head.

'And what's your son doing here?' said Belinda.

Marcus released his grip on Greg.

'I only did it to impress her,' he said, his hands trembling as he wiped them over his face.

'Lucy?' said Marcus.

'No! This girl I know,' said Greg. 'Me and Jenga have been friends for a while, and we got talking online. I was writing my own computer game. She loves dragons and elves and all that. It's like Pokémon, but with mystical creatures. You see, I was tracking the rejuvenating snake through the forest over there and—'

'That's enough, lad,' said Harry. 'You're embarrassing yourself. We'd all have more respect if you were coughing to murder. No one would go to such sad lengths to avoid prison. I believe you.'

'That leaves you, Lucy,' said Belinda. 'You were the one breaking back into the barn. Care to show us what's in the bag?'

Lucy made an attempt to push the small black bag she wore across her chest out of the way, but Belinda was too quick. She unzipped it and pulled out a lighter, a box of matches and a bottle of barbecue lighter fluid.

'Oh, right,' Lucy said, 'and I'm supposed to simply confess, am I? Don't be stupid. You've got me breaking into a barn with my shopping. That all you got?'

Belinda stepped up close to her, dwarfing the other woman. 'You came to my barn and planted that bottle of wine, not caring if it was Sadie you killed or Sadie, me and Harry.'

'Prove it.'

'Stan, if you would,' called Belinda.

A man stepped out of the shadows. He had a mass of white hair and had seen so many summers without the wisdom of sunscreen that his face looked like a saddlebag.

With a hugely dramatic flourish, he held aloft a small black plastic bag and pulled out a blond wig.

'It's a head!' said Marcus. 'Get him.'

'For goodness' sake,' said Belinda. 'Stay where you are. He's on our side. It's the wig Lucy wore to fool John Farthing's neighbours into thinking Daisy had gone back to the house. Stan got it for me from the tour office. It'll have her DNA in it.'

'Stan works for me,' said Ben.

'And he also works for me,' said Belinda. 'He's worked for my family for years. Well, when he's not playing golf on the Costa Del Sol, anyway.'

'Can we get back to the murders?' said Harry. 'And perhaps leave employment rights to another time?'

'He's right,' said Ben. 'Lucy, poisoning Sadie was bad enough, but John and Richard? What's the matter with you?'

'She's in love with you, Dad,' said Greg. 'Anyone can see that.'

'What?' said Ben, his face the very picture of confusion. 'I had no idea.'

'Really,' said Lucy, her knees giving way under her. 'All the hours I worked, all the extra weekends I cancelled to come to the vineyard and make sure things were perfect, and you didn't even notice.'

'I – I don't know what to say,' said Ben, trying to shrink back into the shadows, at least having the decency to look down at his feet. 'I was so wrapped up with work, I had time for nothing else.'

'I noticed that.' Greg, now unrestrained by Marcus, moved over to Ben. His father put an arm around him and pulled him closer.

'How could I not recognise a murderer amongst us? Right there on my own team.' Ben glared at her. 'Why did you kill Sadie?'

Lucy's face was painful to look at. She had been destroyed and she knew it. 'You hated Sadie when you left the Fish by the Sea. You told me that you'd been angry and more determined than ever to get even with her.'

'Yes, but by being successful, not by killing her off,' said Ben. 'I didn't hate her, I hated what she'd said at the time. Don't you see the difference?'

'Why John and Richard?' said Belinda. 'Why kill them?'

The young woman turned her attention to Belinda, her eyes wide and her face suddenly impassive, which was no mean feat considering how unhinged she seemed to be.

'I heard the three of them plotting to start their own brewery. Beer! What do I know about beer? They wouldn't have needed me, would they? Ben wouldn't have needed me. When that pork monster Duke collapsed, I thought it had saved me a job, but no, he was fine.'

'So, you took him poisoned wine and watched him drink it?' said Belinda.

'You sat and watched him drink it?' said Ben. 'What sort of a monster are you?'

'I didn't want to be on my own,' said Lucy, a tremor to her voice. 'I thought that after sitting with John, watching him drink the poisoned wine and how quickly it took him, it would be the same for Richard. I'm truly sorry I got it wrong.'

'There's something so very wrong with you,' said Ben, his arms shielding his son.

'When I realised Richard was going to suffer, I tempted him

with the two things that I knew would work,' said Lucy, her voice pleading. 'Money and wine. I lured him to the hole with the coins and a bottle of wine and I tried to make it quick.'

'The only problem with that,' said Harry, 'is that I know you took pound coins with you because I found some in the nature reserve, so don't make out it was spur of the moment. This was something you thought through. They're bound to have your fingerprints on them.'

Lucy all but collapsed as Harry held her arm.

With that, the sound of the predictably late arrival of the police drowned out anything else she might have attempted to say.

PC Vince Green parked the marked car on the grass outside the barn and got out. Belinda noted that he was back in uniform and had his sergeant with him. She had a serious face, with eyebrows to match, and her uniform had clearly been measured with someone else in mind.

The two officers hurried inside the barn to be met with a sea of expectant faces.

'Care to tell us what this is all about?' said the stony-faced sergeant. 'We've had a call from someone who thought matters were getting a little out of hand.'

'Sorry,' said Daisy, her head peeking around the door, 'my nerve went. I'm so sorry. I called the police and told them that the murderer was here in the barn and that you were all in danger.'

'Officer,' said Belinda, 'I think you'll find that Lucy here broke in with her firestarter kit to burn down my barn and any potential forensic evidence that might have been in here.'

'What potential forensic evidence?' said Vince.

'Of all the stupid—' Lucy tried to break free from Harry's grasp, only causing him to grip her arm tighter.

'I possibly led her to believe that there was something significant to be found in here,' said Belinda. 'Harry and I watched her prise the side off the barn and crawl in with lighter fluid and matches some minutes ago. I'd say that was pretty good evidence, wouldn't you?'

Vince, a slightly baffled look on his face, took out his handcuffs and said, 'Lucy Field, I'm arresting you on suspicion of the murders of Sadie Oppenshaw, John Farthing and Richard Duke...'

He took hold of her wrists and the others watched, fascinated, while he cautioned her and she started to sob.

'It's almost a shame, really,' said Belinda. 'I feel a bit sorry for her, don't you?'

'Nah,' said Harry.

'Any reply to the caution?' said Vince to Lucy.

She fixed Ben with a steely stare. 'I came from my own mother's funeral to put in a double shift at the vineyard, and he didn't even notice I was wearing black all day.'

Harry leaned across so only Belinda could hear. 'Now I feel some sympathy for her.'

FORTY-ONE

Lucy Field was in the back of the police car, Ben was comforting his son and Stan had been relieved of the wig he had been waving at anyone who was interested.

'My sergeant is making sure that there's room in the cells before we leave for the nearest police station,' said Vince. 'It's been a busy night. She's probably the only one under arrest for three murders, though, so we shouldn't have too much of a problem.'

'Was it definitely alcohol poisoning?' said Belinda, trying to take a peek through the police car window.

'We had the post-mortem results on Sadie come back on Monday,' said Vince. 'Being a bank holiday weekend, it took slightly longer to get toxicology results. Her alcohol levels were very high, but as she was at a wine tasting and of slight build, on its own, I'm not sure we'd have had all that much to go on.'

'Are you saying that Lucy might have got away with it?' said Harry. 'That's a worry.'

'Sadie was on medication for her allergies and what with the time delay on the results, it didn't help us rule anyone out,' said Vince. 'If what you've said is correct and Lucy really did go inside both John Farthing's and Richard Duke's houses and watch them drink poisoned wine, there's bound to be DNA evidence to put her there.'

Belinda looked towards the police car; Lucy was staring out the window straight at her. She felt an icy chill run the length of her spine. 'To think, she might have got away with murder.'

'John Farthing's alcohol level was off the charts,' said Vince.

'We think that Lucy was distilling alcohol through the table top still, the alcohol levels getting higher and higher,' said Belinda, showing Vince the photos on her phone. 'We took these at the booking office.'

'When were you at the booking office?' said Vince.

'Er... never mind about that now,' said Harry, 'but if you send some of your colleagues over there, I'm sure you'll find Lucy's fingerprints on it. I doubt she was wearing gloves when she was at work.'

'The amount of alcohol that John Farthing drank, he was probably dead before he'd finished the bottle,' said Vince with a sorry shake of his head.

'The same wasn't true of Richard Duke, though,' said Harry.

'Mrs Duke claims that her husband only drank in moderate doses,' said Vince, aware that Lucy was beginning to cause his sergeant problems in the back of the car. 'But even a small amount of alcohol that strong is still enough to cause kidney and brain damage.'

'The reason that he had his head down a hole was that he was disorientated,' said Belinda. 'He carried on as normal, but the high alcohol percentage affected what he was doing, hence he put his head in a hole. Bizarre.'

'Sorry, folks, but I have to go,' said Vince as a banging on the car window from his sergeant prompted him to turn his attention elsewhere.

'Vince seems like a decent sort,' said Marcus, who had been uncharacteristically quiet for the last couple of minutes. 'He looks as though he might be trying to grow a moustache. Do you think he'll be up for one of my moustache guards for when he's out having a pint?'

'After the last few days, Marcus,' said Harry, 'anything is possible.'

Harry wandered off outside to speak to Ben and his son, leaving Belinda and Marcus alone in the barn.

'I forgot to say, sis, with all the hullabaloo of the last couple of days,' said Marcus, putting an arm around his sister, 'Ivan had hoped to fly over and give you some news in person.'

At the mention of his name, she straightened her shoulders and felt the tension creep across her neck.

'He said to let you know that he's getting married,' he said in a soft voice. 'I'm sorry, but I think it's right that he doesn't pay us a visit under the circumstances. He was insistent he told you in person, but once we'd had a chance to talk it through, we agreed it was for the best. Of course, this was after I'd told old Harry that Ivan was going to drop by and surprise you and he's been absolutely fantastic about it.'

'Has he?' Was this why Harry had seemed a little distant at times?

'Yes, very understanding.' Marcus let go of her shoulder. 'Now, about Daisy. She's a belter, isn't she? I'm off to find her.'

Belinda watched Harry walk back towards her, the start of a smile on his face.

'What was that about?' he said, gesturing at Marcus as they ambled back towards the castle.

'He seems to be very smitten with Daisy,' said Belinda, 'although I don't think it's reciprocated.'

'At least you'd know that your mail would be on time.'

She laughed. Harry always managed to make her do that.

'Fancy a beer?' she said.

'As long as it's not one you made earlier,' said Harry.

FORTY-TWO

To Belinda, it felt like they were back on track: things returning to how they had been a few weeks ago. The two of them, side by side on the patio, making small talk, putting the world to rights. Belinda providing the snacks and Harry hoovering them up. Everything was comfortable once more – like their friendship.

The September evening had brought with it cooler weather and the hint that what remained of the summer should not be taken for granted. Darker nights were coming.

'Any idea how Daisy's getting on?' said Harry.

Belinda gave a soft laugh. 'Didn't you hear? It turned out that John Farthing left her his share of the brewery in his will and Imogen Duke has sold her Richard's share for a steal. She's gone into business with Ben Davies and handed her notice in at Royal Mail.'

'Well, at least things worked out for someone,' said Harry.

They sat within arm's reach of one another, drinking in the remains of a handsome sunset.

'I gave what you said some serious consideration,' said Harry.

'About what? I talk about a lot of things.' She winked at him, and savoured the red wine Harry had brought for them to share.

'What you said about me getting stuck and looking to make some changes to my life. You know, go where the challenges are.'

The smile froze on her face.

'For a start, I needed to put some things behind me.' Harry looked ahead across the grounds. 'I had a set of Hazel's house keys – my ex-girlfriend.'

'Yes, I – I remembered her name.'

'I thought it was about time I returned them to her. I posted the envelope the other day. It took some courage if I'm honest.' He turned to look at her but didn't catch her eye. 'It's about time.'

'I'm sorry things are still very difficult for you,' said Belinda. 'Let me know if there's anything I can do to help.'

Harry glanced at his watch. 'You've already done more for me than you could possibly know. I'm sorry but I can't stay too long this evening. In all the chaos of solving murders with you – again – I forgot to tell you that if all goes well, I could be moving on,' he said, crossing his fingers.

She blinked in rapid succession.

'Aren't you going to wish me luck?' he said, wine glass up to his lips, waiting for her answer.

'Without question,' she said. 'Good luck.'

Harry took a tentative sip of his drink. 'I think I picked a good bottle here. If the wine tasting taught me anything – other than try not to let the bodies stack up – it was to go to the supermarket when the deals are on.'

Despite the chasm of despair that had opened in front of her, Belinda still laughed.

'I have to hand it to you, H,' she said, 'it's not bad wine.'

She played with the stem of her glass, fingers clammier than they should be.

'So, where exactly are you heading off to?' she ventured. 'That's if your mind's made up.'

Harry made a meal of sniffing his wine, holding it up to the light and taking a healthy glug.

'Well, not far,' he said, coy smile creeping across his face. 'Not far at all. In fact, we drove fairly close to it the other day.'

Belinda sat up a tad straighter in her seat. This was good news, very good news. They would still be able to see each other. Wherever he moved to, she owned his rental property. Surely, he would feel obliged to see out his six-month lease before moving on. The thought of him not being on her doorstep filled her with dread.

She would cope with it. She just didn't want to.

'Once I've had my job interview in the morning, I'll be able to give you some indication,' he said.

'Job interview?' she said.

'Yes,' said Harry, putting his wine glass down. 'What else did you think I was talking about? After the conversation we had about people really doing the things that made them happy and what was important to them, I took your advice and did it.'

'You did?' she said. 'Good for you.'

A dim and distant recollection of the exchange they'd had as they'd flitted through the countryside came back to her. She had tried to be subtle about his job options. She knew that he wasn't entirely happy with the role he had found himself in after thirty years in the police. The details of their conversation were a touch on the hazy side, what with all the murders going on.

'The one thing I've always wanted to do,' said Harry, arms flung wide open. 'Work in a zoo!'

'A zoo,' repeated Belinda. 'You've always wanted to work in a zoo?'

She was less sure whether she was remembering this conversation or if this was wishful thinking. If Harry got the job, with the zoo only half an hour away, there was no reason why he should leave Little Challham.

'I'd better leave you to it,' said Harry. 'I should at least go home and gen up on the difference between a black rhino and a white rhino.'

'It's mostly to do with their lips.'

'I know, it was a joke,' said Harry.

There were a few seconds of silence between them. Belinda said, 'The job won't involve staying over, will it?'

'Staying over?'

'Living with the animals?' Why had she said that? It made her sound slightly crazy.

'Why would it involve me living there? I'm going for a job in security. What exactly happens in a zoo to warrant security, I'm not completely sure. Perhaps I'll have to break up the gorilla fights.'

Belinda laughed. 'I hope they give you back-up for that.'

With a chuckle, Harry picked up his glass and drank the rest of his wine. He looked over at her and said, 'If I get the job, do you fancy going out for a meal with me to celebrate?'

'I couldn't think of anything I'd rather do more.'

'You've no idea how much that means to me.'

In one movement, as if he was afraid that he'd change his mind, he put the glass on the table, stood up and leaned towards her.

'Thanks for the last few months,' he said. 'I've had the best time.'

He kissed her on the cheek and said, 'I'll call you tomorrow after my interview, if that's all right with you. Bye.'

From the safety of her spot on the patio, Belinda watched Harry walk away and whispered, 'You had me at Merlot.'

A LETTER FROM LISA

Dear reader,

Thank you so much for reading *Murder at the Castle* and finding out about Belinda and Harry's latest exploits. If you'd like to keep up to date with all my latest releases, just sign up at the following link. Your email address will never be shared and you can unsubscribe at any time.

www.bookouture.com/lisa-cutts

It's been wonderful to expand on Little Challham and the surrounding countryside and I hope you've enjoyed finding out more about the locals and their quirks. It's been great fun to have Belinda and Harry working together again to stop the killer in their tracks. Their army of allies – and enemies – is growing.

If you would be kind enough to leave a short review for this, the second in the Belinda Penshurst mysteries, I would be very grateful. It makes such a difference in helping readers to discover one of my books for the first time. Please get in touch on social media, especially if your travels take you to the hop farms or vineyards of Kent.

Thank you so much and thank you again for reading,
Lisa

facebook.com/lisa.cutts.505

twitter.com/LisaCuttsAuthor

instagram.com/lisa_cutts

ACKNOWLEDGEMENTS

Writing can be a fairly lonely business, made so much more fun by readers who have got in touch and the unfailing support of other writers. Crime Scene, I don't always have time to meet up, but thank you – you have done more for me than you'll ever know.

Once again, I'm so very grateful to the amazing Bookouture team, particularly Ruth Tross for her wonderful editing skills and enthusiasm for all things Belinda and Harry. The joy of writing the books has seeped into the editing process – a rare thing indeed. I owe a huge debt of gratitude to Alex Holmes and Martina Arzu in editorial, Kim Nash, Noelle Holten and Sarah Hardy for their unfailing hard work in publicity, Lisa Brewster for the cover, Alex Crow and Hannah Deuce in marketing, and Jon Appleton and Rachel Rowlands for copyediting and proofreading. I can't thank you enough.

Huge thank you to Jim Dempster, founder of Range Ales Brewery, a gunshot away from Hythe Ranges, Lympne. I owe a huge debt of gratitude to you for your help and insight into the process of brewing beer and how to make turbo cider – oh, and how to murder someone with alcohol. Major Crime will never find us.

I remain forever grateful to bloggers and reviewers everywhere who have supported me and my books, especially the new series. To name but a few for their invaluable help: Karen Marwood, Karen King, Donna Morfett and Danielle at The Reading Closet.